A Rogue
of My Own

JOHANNA
LINDSEY

A Rogue
of My Own

Pocket Books

New York   London   Toronto   Sydney

Pocket Books
A Division of Simon & Schuster, Inc.
1230 Avenue of the Americas
New York, NY 10020

This Pocket Books export edition June 2009

For information about special discounts for bulk purchases,
please contact Simon & Schuster Special Sales at
1-866-506-1949 or business@simonandschuster.com.

The Simon & Schuster Speakers Bureau can bring authors to your live event.
For more information or to book an event contact the Simon & Schuster Speakers
Bureau at 1-866-248-3049 or visit our website at www.simonspeakers.com.

Manufactured in the United States of America

10   9   8   7   6   5   4   3   2   1

ISBN 978-1-4391-5740-4

For Mom

A Rogue of My Own

Chapter One

Buckingham Palace. Rebecca Marshall still couldn't believe she was going to be living there. She'd known for a week, but the reality of it simply hadn't sunk in. But now here she was.

Becoming a maid of honor at Queen Victoria's court was the biggest surprise she'd ever had in all of her eighteen years. Her mother, Lilly, had been hoping for this elite position to be bestowed on her daughter, but Lilly hadn't told Rebecca that she'd called in a few favors to obtain it. She hadn't wanted Rebecca to be disappointed if it didn't come to pass.

Rebecca wouldn't have been disappointed. She'd never even considered being a maid of honor at the royal court. But she knew that it was something her mother had aspired to. Lilly often spoke of her lost chance to be a maid of honor, or even a lady of the bedchamber once she'd become a married woman. Her family had been staunch Tories like her husband. And with the Whigs in power, controlling all of the court appointments, Lilly had been unable to achieve her fondest wish and had finally given it up. After all, the Whig political party had retained power for a long time.

But now the Tories, more recently called Conservatives, were finally back in office, with Sir Robert Peel as the new prime minister. Out with the old, in with the new, as it were. With new appointments being made, Lilly had quickly petitioned party officials for an appointment for Rebecca. There was no guarantee that Rebecca would receive one as there weren't many appointments to be had. But the letter had arrived last week. And like an excitable young girl, Rebecca's mother had actually shouted for joy after reading it, she had been so thrilled. And her excitement had been contagious.

The last week had been a whirlwind. Mother and daughter had only just started planning for Rebecca's come-out in London during the next winter Season, which was still months away. They were still in the early stages of having her new wardrobe designed, with nothing created yet! So many extra seamstresses had to be hired, and decisions had to be made quickly. There were trips back and forth to the nearby town of Norford, sometimes two or three trips a day. And underlying it all was the excitement and Lilly's nonstop chatter about this being the most golden opportunity of Rebecca's life.

It was also going to be the biggest change in Rebecca's life since her father's passing. The Earl of Ryne had died when she was only eight. Lilly had never entertained the idea of remarrying. The earl's title had gone to a male relative of his, but the manor near Norford where Rebecca had grown up wasn't entailed. She'd spent her whole life there, hadn't even gone off for her schooling as had some of her closer friends. Lilly hadn't been willing to part with her, so she had arranged for Rebecca to have the best teachers right there at home.

Rebecca had loved that arrangement. It allowed her and her mother to spend a lot of time together. Both adept horse-women, they rode nearly every day when the weather was good. Rebecca was going to miss that. With both of them having so many friends in Norford, there was always someone stopping by to visit, or some social gathering to attend. Rebecca was going to miss that, too. But they wouldn't be so far apart. Norford was only a few hours' ride north of London. However, Lilly was determined to give Rebecca some time to get settled in and used to her position, before she visited. She didn't want to appear to be an overprotective mother, even if she was!

Actually, this appointment to the queen's court would be the second golden opportunity for Rebecca that mother and daughter had extensively discussed. The first had arisen five years ago when they were in complete agreement on their first choice for Rebecca's future husband. No need for a Seasonal launch if she could catch *his* eye, and he was a neighbor, too, Raphael Locke, the Duke of Norford's heir. So convenient! But the esteemed fellow had up and married someone else before Rebecca was old enough to put herself forward, and that had ended that.

Such a shame. She had been looking forward to being a part of that interesting family. Preston Locke, the duke, had five sisters, all married and living elsewhere now, but they often returned to Norford for visits. Lilly had told stories about the days when most of those ladies had still lived at home and how the Lockes had quite dominated the local society, and in fact some of the grander parties Rebecca had attended had been at Norford Hall when she was a child. She had almost got closer to that family when she became friends with the youngest daughter of the house, Amanda Locke. It was too bad they had lost touch with each other after Amanda was sent off to private school.

The duke hadn't entertained much after that because it was only him and his elderly mother in that big house. His wife had died years ago, and while every available lady in the neighborhood had probably tried to catch his eye over the years, he remained a widower. But Ophelia Locke did the entertaining there now, the woman who had captured Raphael's heart before Rebecca could!

Two lost opportunities in that illustrious family, a best friend and a husband. But this new opportunity was upon her. A maid of honor at Queen Victoria's court! Rebecca knew all the benefits. Holding the position was comparable to attending the most elite finishing school in the world. She'd be meeting the most important people in England and royalty from across the Continent. There was no reason to wait for a Season if you were part of a court with a queen who loved to entertain. If Rebecca was lucky, the queen might even have a hand in picking her future husband. Anything was possible.

Miraculously, Rebecca's wardrobe was finished in time for her departure for London and was much grander than it would have been for a mere Season. Lilly had spared no expense. And she accompanied Rebecca and her maid, Flora, to London.

It wasn't the first time Rebecca was seeing London. There had been a few shopping excursions over the years, a horse race Lilly just had to attend since the sire of her mare was racing that day, the wedding of an old friend Lilly had been invited to, and, of course, Rebecca had joined her on all of those trips. But this was the first time she was seeing Buckingham Palace. There had been no reason to visit it before when no monarchs had made it their home until now.

Alighting from the coach with her mother and Flora, Rebecca stood there in awe of the grand structure that *she* would be living in for months, possibly years. It was so much bigger than she had imagined! Even the marble arch of the ceremonial entrance was stories high! Palace guards were marching nearby in their brightly colored uniforms. Other people passed under the huge arch that Rebecca would be walking through.

Her feet wouldn't move. Nervousness nearly overwhelmed her. She already knew Lilly wasn't going to escort her inside, but she wasn't ready to say good-bye! She'd never had to say good-bye to her mother before, not like this.

Lilly took her hand and squeezed it. She understood. In that simple gesture, she gave Rebecca courage.

"Your father would have been so proud, had he lived to see this."

Rebecca glanced at her mother. It was a poignant moment. Lilly was so happy for her daughter, and yet she was no doubt recalling her own missed opportunities. It was in her expression, close to tears yet smiling.

"You two aren't going to cry, are you?" Flora asked in a complaining tone.

Lilly laughed. Rebecca managed a grin. Flora was good at relieving tension with her candor.

Unfortunately, Flora wouldn't be living in the palace with Rebecca. She would only stay long enough today to get Rebecca settled in. They both knew that Rebecca wasn't going to get a room to herself. There simply weren't enough rooms for all the members of the court, let alone for their servants. So Lilly had rented a flat for Flora nearby so she could come to the palace each day to maintain Rebecca's wardrobe and perform her usual duties.

Lilly had been entertaining the idea of buying a town house in London for Rebecca's first Season. But now that Rebecca's "Season" had begun under a completely different set of circumstances, Lilly was more hesitant about the idea. While some of the ladies at court owned homes in London where they spent their nights instead of sharing a room at the crowded palace, Lilly wanted Rebecca to experience every aspect of court, and the surest way to do that was to live there. If the Marshalls had a town house, Rebecca might be tempted to go home to it each night.

Lilly gathered Rebecca into her arms for a long hug. "I'll see you in a few weeks, darling. At least I will *try* to stay away that long."

"You don't have to—"

"Yes, I do," Lilly cut in. "This is *your* time, not mine. You're going to enjoy every minute of it. But you must write me every day. I want to hear about everything."

"I will."

"But most of all, Becky, enjoy yourself. Wonderful things are going to happen for you. I just know it."

Rebecca really wished she had more of her mother's enthusiasm, but her own excitement had waned now that their separation was imminent. This was her mother's dream. She wished Lilly could have had it instead of her.

But for Lilly's sake, she put on a bright smile, gave her mother one last hug, and hurried inside the palace.

Chapter Two

D'YOU THINK WE'LL EVER get there?" Flora whispered to Rebecca with a grin as they followed a liveried servant who was dressed more grandly than some noblemen down an incredibly long corridor.

The maid was joking, but the footman leading the way heard her and glanced back to reply, "Lady Rebecca's room is just around the next corner. It's actually closer to the main rooms than the accommodations some of the other ladies have been given. The queen remembered meeting the Earl of Ryne when she was a child and suggested the room herself. A good start for you, m'lady."

Flora beamed. Rebecca blushed. A footman shouldn't know things like that. Then again, this was the palace! The servants here probably knew more about the courtiers' private lives than anyone else did. Hadn't her mother warned her not to snub any of them?

"I never snub servants," Rebecca had reminded her mother.

"I know you don't, m'dear, this just wouldn't be a good time to start."

Just one of many silly things Lilly had said in the last week, due to her exhaustion in getting Rebecca ready for her new life at the palace. However, after a good night's sleep her mother had brought up the subject again.

"If the servants take a liking to you, they can be extremely helpful. Remember, working at the palace is their livelihood. Some of them may even deal in one sort of intrigue or another, just to keep above the rest. But the point is, they will have information that *you* will find useful, and if they like you, they won't mind sharing it."

With her mother's advice in mind, Rebecca smiled at the footman and said, "Thank you . . . ? "

"John Keets, m'lady."

"Thank you, John. It's good to know my father is well remembered."

He nodded. He was a personable fellow with sandy-brown hair, tall, young, his expression completely stoic until he spoke, when it became much more friendly. Flora was actually giving him an admiring glance. But then Flora cast admiring glances at most men. As she was a pretty young woman with black hair and brown eyes, she usually got more than her share of glances back.

The maid had worked for the Marshalls for the last six years. She was only a few years older than Rebecca, but she'd been taught by her own mother, who had also been a ladies' maid, how to excel in that profession, and the Marshall ladies had never had their coiffures done up so superbly prior to Flora's arrival.

John noticed Flora's glance and, in his own way, returned the compliment with one of his own. But they had finally reached the end of the corridor, a T. He turned right and opened the first door they came to.

"Your trunks will be delivered shortly," John said, ushering them into the small room. "And removed, as soon as they are unpacked. You will be sharing the room with Elizabeth Marly. Unfortunately, the queen isn't aware yet that Lady Elizabeth can be something of an instigator. You might not want to become too friendly with her."

He said no more. He'd said so much! What the devil did "something of an instigator" mean?

Flora must have been having the same thought because as soon as the door closed behind John, she said, "That sounds ominous."

It did, but Rebecca wasn't going to jump to conclusions. "It could mean she just starts things, they don't have to be bad things, maybe just things inappropriate for the palace?" At Flora's doubting look, she added, "Well, I can better judge once I meet her, and I'll have no choice about that, since we're sharing this room."

Flora snorted. "*This* room is much smaller than I imagined it would be. Why, it's barely the size of your dressing room at home!"

Rebecca grinned at the disdain that had crept into Flora's tone. Actually, the room was much bigger than her dressing room, just much smaller than her bedroom at home.

"I don't think we're meant to spend much time here. It's just a place to sleep and change clothes," Rebecca replied.

"And you'll be bumping elbows doing that."

That was true enough. There wasn't much clear floor space. A double bed that looked more like a wide cot, with two narrow bed tables on each side of it that held the only two lamps in the room, took up most of the space. There was no fireplace, only a brazier that probably wouldn't be needed for another month. A small tub was located behind a screen in one corner, along with a commode stand with a pitcher of water and several towels. There was a tiny, round table that might hold a tray of food, but only one narrow chair, and a single vanity table. The room's most prominent features, however, were the wardrobes, which lined two and a half walls! They even blocked the windows, which let in only a smidgen of light around the edges of the wardrobes on that wall.

Flora was staring at the wardrobes, too. "Imagine that, and a good thing, too. I assumed that you'd have a separate dressing room, even if you had to share it. I never imagined your room here *would* be a dressing room. And of course there would have to be this many wardrobes for two ladies, wouldn't there? Your fancy gowns will take up at least one wall of these. Half of them better be empty . . ."

The warning note ended with a task as Flora opened the nearest wardrobe and found it full. She moved down several feet before opening another and found it full, too. So Lady Elizabeth had claimed that wall, obviously. Flora moved to the wall with the blocked windows, but the first wardrobe she opened there was also full, and the next. She finally found one that was only half-full, and the last two were empty. She also checked the two wardrobe filling up half of a third wall. Only one of those was empty, too.

Flora started to laugh. "D'you get the feeling Lady Elizabeth wasn't expecting to share this room?"

"It would appear so," Rebecca agreed.

"Well, the lady has too many clothes, there's no doubt of that. But she's going to have to get rid of some of them, or end up with wrinkled gowns, because you're claiming half of these, Becky my girl, and I'm going to see to that right now."

Flora got to work moving dresses around. Rebecca helped

her. The room had no bureaus either, not that there was any space for them, but at least the bottom of each wardrobe had a large drawer where she could store clothes that didn't need to be hung up.

They hadn't had to stuff Elizabeth's clothes into her share of the wardrobes—too much. She'd actually been using one whole wardrobe for just two ball gowns, and another for what looked like an assortment of costumes.

"There now," Flora said, satisfied with the new arrangement. "We should be able to make do with just this one wall, so the lady can have the extra two wardrobes, but no more'n that. *You're* not getting wrinkled just because *she* brought too many clothes to court. And you know," Flora added, staring at the wall of empty wardrobes waiting to be filled with Rebecca's clothes, "there's no reason for you not to have a little light. These wardrobes aren't ideally situated. Why block both windows when it isn't necessary. They can be moved a little both ways so you can squeeze in there to open a window if necessary. I'll borrow a strong shoulder when your trunks arrive."

Flora did just that, getting at least half of one window unblocked. The two men who carried in the first of Rebecca's four trunks didn't mind helping at all, once Flora smiled at them, and a dirty sheer, white curtain that had probably been hidden for months or longer was revealed. Flora promised to get it cleaned tomorrow.

The maid left soon after that to get her own flat in order, chuckling on her way out the door, "My rooms are bigger than yours," which left Rebecca smiling.

Her humor didn't last though. She was overwhelmed by how alone she was going to be here at court.

She'd been tutored at home, so she'd never been separated

from her mother before. Not a day of her life had gone by without her mother being nearby. For that matter, Flora had been within shouting distance, too. But this court appointment was definitely a cutting of the apron strings, and it was happening much sooner than Rebecca had expected, and without her having a husband to rely on.

Yes, there would be endless opportunities to socialize and meet interesting people, and, yes, she'd probably meet her future husband here. But deep down, Rebecca would have preferred a normal come-out during a normal Season, with her mother by her side. She just hadn't been able to spoil her mother's elation by telling her that. Yet they weren't just mother and daughter. They were actually friends. She should have told her. . . .

Chapter Three

NOTHING WAS SCHEDULED FOR the remainder of the day, which was why Flora had left after unpacking the trunks. For Rebecca, it was time to relax, get settled in, and recover from an exhausting week. She had been assigned to the Duchess of Kent, Queen Victoria's mother, but the duchess wasn't even in residence today and wasn't expected back until tomorrow.

Rebecca stretched out on the bed. As she lay there, she thought about the queen. She was in residence, but Rebecca might never meet her. After all, not everyone who lived in the palace was introduced to the queen. Or she might meet her and they could become great friends. Anything was possible when you lived in the palace, Rebecca thought as she dozed off.

"What did you do?" a shrill voice asked. "Why did you move those wardrobes? I sleep late. You will, too. We don't need daylight waking us earlier than necessary."

What a rude awakening from her brief nap! Rebecca blinked her eyes open to see the young woman who had entered the room and apparently lit one of the lamps next to the bed before she started her tirade. Short and plump, she was pushing at the seams of her orange day dress. She had dark golden hair tightly coiffured except for a few ringlets about her cherub cheeks. Someone should tell her that orange was not her color, Rebecca thought. It made her look sallow. She might have been pretty if she didn't have such a snarling expression.

Green eyes were glaring at the wall where half of a window was exposed. The sun had set while Rebecca had napped. No light was currently coming from that direction.

Still half-asleep, Rebecca thoughtlessly replied, "That's what curtains are for."

"Curtains, no," the lady disagreed in the same sharp tone. "Thick drapes possibly, but we can't reach the bloody pulls for drapes, can we? If we had some, which we don't."

Rebecca was quickly waking up. The lady really was angry and not even trying to hide it. About something this trivial?

Rebecca sat up and frowned at the window that was causing such offense. This was not a good start if this was Lady Elizabeth, and she had no doubt that it was.

"I could tack a petticoat over the window before retiring and remove it after you awake in the morning?" she offered. "I'm sorry, but daylight has never woken me so I don't think of it as a nuisance. Lighting lamps in this room when daylight can stream in seems rather silly."

She probably shouldn't have added that, because the young woman turned away from the wardrobes and glared at her. "Then you've never slept in a room with windows that face the sunrise, have you?"

Rebecca flinched inwardly. "No, I can't say that I have, and you've definitely made your point. I will be sure to rectify the problem."

When Rebecca stood up, she towered over the shorter girl. Like her mother, she was rather tall at five feet nine inches. She took after her mother in most things, actually. Both of them were slim yet curved nicely where they ought to be. Both were blond, though she might have gotten the golden shade of her hair from her father, since Lilly was a much lighter ash blond. She had her mother's blue eyes, too, though Rebecca's were a darker shade of blue. But they both had high cheekbones, a patrician nose, and a gently curved, firm chin, all of which Rebecca was grateful for, since Lilly was considered quite a beautiful woman.

Rebecca smiled, making an effort at a new start. "Lady Elizabeth, I presume?"

"Yes, and you are—?"

The young woman's tone was still stiff and somewhat imperious. Rebecca found it hard to believe that Elizabeth hadn't been informed who her new roommate would be.

"Lady Rebecca Anne Victoria Marshall."

She almost blushed. She rarely mentioned her middle names when she met people. Her family and friends merely called her Becky, though her mother was known to call her Becky Anne when she was delivering a scolding. Rebecca was sure her parents simply hadn't been able to make up their minds about her name, which is why she'd ended up with so many. But she had no idea why she'd just given them all to her roommate. Possibly because she already suspected they were not going to be friends. Which was too bad. They were going to be sharing a bed, for goodness' sake. They needed at least to be cordial.

"Named after the queen, were you? How droll," Elizabeth remarked before she marched over to one of her wardrobes and yanked open the door.

Perversely, Rebecca was delighted that it was now her wardrobe and said, "No, actually, she wasn't the queen at the time nor even in a close running when I was born. You, however, share your name with many queens. Do you find that droll, too?"

Elizabeth glanced over her shoulder. "You shouldn't have touched my belongings. Don't do it again."

"You weren't here—"

"The arrangement was perfect as it was."

Rebecca choked back a laugh at that petulant reply. "No, I beg to differ, it wasn't even close to equal. It still isn't. We left you the extra two wardrobes."

Elizabeth apparently wasn't grateful for the boon. She didn't even acknowledge it and instead inquired, "We?"

"My maid and I."

"Your maid got a room here?" Elizabeth swung back around with a gasp. "How did you manage that?"

"I didn't, and, no, she didn't. We—"

"Ah, you have a town house," Elizabeth cut in. "My family doesn't have one, so my maid had to stay at home. But if you have a house in London, why don't you use it instead of crowding me in this small room?"

If Rebecca had had any doubts that Elizabeth resented her presence, they were now gone. The young woman couldn't have stated more clearly that she didn't like having a roommate. Rebecca could have been embarrassed by it. A girl with less mettle might have been. But she wasn't for a good reason, which John Keets, bless him, had given her.

"Even if this room hadn't been assigned to me, which makes it half mine, it was chosen for me at the queen's suggestion. I don't think I'd care to insult the queen by requesting a different room, but if you find the arrangement so deplorable, perhaps you should make that request for yourself."

Elizabeth's cheeks flushed with embarrassment. Had she really thought that she could cow Rebecca into leaving or apologizing for the situation, just because Elizabeth had moved in first?

"But as I was going to say before you interrupted," Rebecca continued, "no, my family doesn't own a London house, but we found a flat nearby for my maid, so she can come to the palace daily to attend to her usual duties."

"How nice for you," Elizabeth said in a pouting tone. "Not everyone can afford such frivolous luxuries. Where is your maid now?"

Rebecca was blushing a little and she didn't know why. Of course not all noble families were wealthy. That hers was wealthy was certainly no cause for embarrassment.

Fortunately, Elizabeth had moved over to the single vanity they would be sharing, so she didn't notice the blush. She pulled out the velvet-cushioned stool that had been shoved underneath the lace-edged table and sat down to check her coiffure.

To Elizabeth's back, Rebecca said, "There was no reason for Flora to stay, since there is nothing on my agenda today for which I would require her assistance."

"Not everything at the palace happens with a great deal of warning. You will need to adjust accordingly on occasion, if you intend to be well prepared for any happenstance."

That actually sounded like good advice, Rebecca realized,

she just couldn't imagine why the resentful girl would want to give her good advice.

"Perhaps you can make amends for the changes you made to my room—without permission—by having your maid do my hair. I've been using Lady Jane's maid, but she's rooming on the other side of the palace."

Rebecca should have known Elizabeth would have an ulterior motive for offering her advice.

"I doubt Flora will be agreeable to the extra work," Rebecca replied.

But Elizabeth didn't let it go at that. "What has she to say about it? She works for you, she does what you tell her."

"Actually, she works for my family. Maybe you would like to take this up with my mother?"

That brought a sour expression to Elizabeth's face. "Never mind, I'll manage as I usually do."

Rebecca shook her head. If Elizabeth had made a little effort to be friendly to her, Rebecca would have left the matter to Flora. She would even have slipped the maid some extra coins for her trouble.

Before she forgot about it and heard more strident complaints from her roommate in the morning, Rebecca dug out her thickest petticoat and squeezed between the wardrobes to tuck it over the old curtain.

"Did you bring a costume?" Elizabeth asked. "Drina has declared a masque for tonight."

"Drina?"

"The queen, of course."

Rebecca could be forgiven for her mistake because only members of the royal family called Queen Victoria by her childhood nickname. Surely she hadn't been put in a room with a member of the royal family and had unknowingly been treating one of them less than deferentially.

For the first time in her life she wished that her mother had raised her more traditionally instead of in the relaxed manner that she did. If her father hadn't died when she'd been so young, her upbringing would probably have been more in line with that of other young gentlewomen of her day.

Virtuous, innocent, yes, indeed, she was barely eighteen and had never been kissed. Adept at playing at least one instrument and singing—yes, she could sing, but she was simply all thumbs when it came to musical instruments and she'd tried four different ones before Lilly had thrown them all out. She should know a smattering of a foreign language or two, and she was indeed fluent in French. Dutiful, yes, she was a dutiful daughter and she could probably be a dutiful wife. At least, she would try. Too scatterbrained to be able to form an intelligent opinion, no, she was a complete failure there.

Lilly had confided, "We're just supposed to keep our intelligence, if we have any, mind you, to ourselves. And you've been warned, m'dear. If you have to pretend to be stupid, then you must do so. Unfortunately, it's what the average nobleman expects of his wife, but maybe you will be lucky enough to marry a man who is not average. Maybe your husband will enjoy having an intelligent conversation with you that doesn't revolve around servants and the household, which is all most husbands expect their wives to be knowledgeable about. But if you aren't that lucky, well, you're smart enough to be stupid!"

Of course, if Lilly had raised her in the strictly traditional manner, she would probably have fled in tears from Elizabeth's abrasiveness. But life with her mother had given her the tenacity to stand up for herself. Life with her mother had taught her that there was more to being a woman than what men expected. Life with Lilly hadn't ruined her, it had prepared her for anything—except insulting a member of the royal family.

All color drained from her face with that thought. "You are related to the queen?"

"Whatever gave you that idea?" Elizabeth said in a smug little tone.

Rebecca understood now that Elizabeth was merely making sure that Rebecca realized that she knew much more about the court than Rebecca did. The alarm she'd caused Rebecca had merely been an added bonus for her.

Relieved that she hadn't insulted royalty, but annoyed with Elizabeth, Rebecca said stiffly, "I wasn't informed about any masque."

"You weren't here to be informed, were you?"

That was true enough, but surely she wasn't expected to attend without being invited. Elizabeth apparently thought otherwise.

"It can be hoped you brought more than one costume with you, and items to improvise others. The queen enjoys all sorts of entertainments, but she truly loves costume balls, and even if she refers to such an event as a masque, you can be sure you need to attend in full costume. She is young, after all, not too many years older than you and I. Why wouldn't she be fond of the same things we are?"

Rebecca felt herself blush again. A costume, the one thing she and her mother had overlooked for her wardrobe. She didn't even have a domino mask for a half-costume.

Elizabeth guessed as much. "Well, that's a shame. Off to quite a bad start, aren't you?"

Was that a bit of relish Rebecca detected in Elizabeth's tone?

Probably, yet the girl continued, "I'd loan you one of mine"—
she paused for a long glance up and down Rebecca's tall, slim
frame—"but they obviously wouldn't fit."

"I will simply have to be excused—"

"Not unless you're ill, which you aren't. We're expected to
attend all of the entertainments, to fill out the court, especially
since the foreign dignitaries who are favored with invitations
need ladies to dance and converse with. It's all in the interest of
the monarchy putting on a good show."

Lilly had warned her about that. It's why court could be
considered the come-out to top all come-outs. She would meet
some of the most eligible bachelors in the world and, in return,
be part of the pomp and circumstance designed to impress
those same dignitaries. She would have to let her mother know.
Lilly could arrange to have some costumes sent to her by the
seamstresses at home, who already had her measurements, but
that still wouldn't take care of tonight. But *how* could this
count against her when she simply hadn't known?

"I believe I am feeling ill—"

"Be quiet and let me think," Elizabeth said. "The other ladies who might have extra costumes you could borrow are like
me, too short to accommodate your height. What did you do,
take after your father?"

"No, my mother."

Elizabeth wasn't listening. "Let me see if I have anything
that might be useful," she said, and went straight to one of her
wardrobes. After a moment of rummaging around in it, she
swung around holding a tricornered hat of the sort favored several centuries ago. She was even smiling. What an amazing difference it made to her face. It softened the edges and made her
look friendly!

"My last roommate left this behind. It's too bad she took the jacket and breeches with her that finished off the costume, but I'm sure we can find you a jacket, maybe even the breeches to go with it. Some of the footmen around here dress quite lavishly, in case you didn't notice."

Rebecca frowned doubtfully. "And my costume would be?"

"A musketeer, of course. I'm sure no one will notice you don't have a rapier to add the final touch. It's the old-fashioned hat that makes it, you see. And it's such a perfect costume for a woman. A man couldn't pull it off. Remove the hat and he wouldn't be in costume! But a woman—it's the one time we can wear breeches, you know! For us, it *is* a costume and a good one."

Elizabeth was right, actually. And she seemed so pleased with herself for finding this solution for Rebecca that Rebecca didn't have the heart to say she'd rather take her chances with the disapproval she might incur for not attending than show up in a silly-looking patched-together costume that could earn her disapproval of a different sort, for trying to masquerade as a man.

"You will want to put your hair up under the hat," Elizabeth added as she tossed it toward Rebecca. "It's too bad you sent your maid off for the day, isn't it?"

There, that was better. That catty remark and tone were more in line with what Rebecca expected from the other girl. She could be forgiven for mistrusting her roommate's sudden offer of help.

But Elizabeth didn't seem to expect an answer. She pulled a costume out of her wardrobe for herself, but didn't lay it down on the bed. She just draped it over her arm.

"I prefer to have my hair done first, which usually means I

must cart my clothes all over the palace so I can dress afterwards," she said with a sigh. On her way out the door, she added, "I will have a jacket sent to you."

She probably wouldn't do any such thing, Rebecca thought as she sat down on the bed, alone again. Elizabeth's mentioning the inconvenience of having to go to someone else's maid to have her hair done pretty much guaranteed it. She was sure Elizabeth wouldn't do her any favors. But then a jacket was delivered, and not five minutes later another footman handed her some breeches to go with it. Suddenly Rebecca felt quite bad for doubting Elizabeth Marly.

Chapter Four

REBECCA WAS RATHER PLEASED as she stood back from the vanity mirror to have a better look at her improvised costume. She wished the room had a longer mirror, but the oval one at least let her see some of her length.

Her height was going to help her pull this off. The breeches actually fit! That made her decide to go ahead and dress the part of a dashing cavalier. Had the jacket been less fancy, she might have claimed the role of a pirate instead, then she wouldn't have had to stuff her hair away. The hat, with its rakishly long feather, would probably have worked either way.

While she would rather have looked perfect for her first public appearance at court, the costume was obviously a costume. She turned around and glanced at her backside in the mirror and was assured that she could pass for a man until someone got a look at her face. Finished primping, she was beginning to feel excited. This was her first ball of any sort. She would have missed it altogether if not for Elizabeth's help. She owed the girl an apology for doubting her.

She hurried out of the room, then slowed down considerably as the long corridor stretched in front of her and she realized she had no idea where the ball was taking place. One of the main rooms, surely, and once she got to the end of the corridor, there would no doubt be servants she could ask.

"Got your days mixed up, old chap?" a male voice asked from behind her. "The costume ball is tomorrow night." The man turned his head and glanced at her briefly as he walked by.

Rebecca stopped in her tracks. Him? What was *he* doing here?

The man didn't stop to hear her reply, not that she could have replied because she was speechless. His long legs carried him far beyond her and soon he was out of sight. He hadn't looked at her closely enough to realize his mistake in assuming she was a chap. But she'd seen enough of his face to recognize him and be rendered dazzled and dumbstruck for the third time *he* had come into her view.

She thought of him as The Angel. He was too beautiful to be just an ordinary man. So tall and strapping, with long black hair that bounced about his shoulders with his long stride. She'd thought his eyes were a light gray, but then she'd never been so close to him before. At his brief glance just now, she saw that they were actually a lovely shade of pale blue.

The first time she'd ever seen him had been in the town of Norford, and she'd been so awestruck, she'd imagined an ethereal glow about him, thus he'd become The Angel in her mind. The notion had been reinforced the second time she saw him, when he'd been riding along the road to Norford Hall, a sunbeam peeking through the tree branches shining directly on him, like the light of heaven. She'd been awestruck that time, too. She might have thought she'd imagined the whole thing if she hadn't been with her mother the second time and Lilly had noticed her reaction.

"He's related to your future husband," Lilly had said. "One of Raphael Locke's many cousins, I believe. I swear, that entire family was blessed with exceptional looks."

Her mother had had such great expectations that she would marry the Locke heir. Rebecca had had them, too. From the day she'd first met Raphael Locke when he'd come to one of her mother's garden parties, she'd been enthralled by his handsomeness and charming manner. So she'd been in wholehearted agreement when Lilly had suggested he might do for her husband. Unfortunately, that had been five years ago when she'd been way too young for marriage, whereas Raphael had already been of a marriageable age.

Rebecca and her mother had both worried when he'd gone to London for his first real Season. But then the rumors flew that he wasn't looking for a wife yet. Then more rumors flew about how most of the mamas of the debutantes that particular Season refused to believe that he wouldn't be enamored of *their* daughters. He had tried to put them off by having one brief affair after another, hoping for the title of *rake* rather than *eligible bachelor*.

It didn't work. The mamas still trotted their daughters forward. As the Duke of Norford's heir, Raphael was simply too good a catch to ignore. They hounded him so badly that they more or less chased him out of London and right off to the Continent for a two-year tour of Europe. Which was a relief for the Marshall ladies. They saw it as a reprieve, time for Rebecca to grow up a little more.

But when Raphael returned to the homeland, something unexpected happened. With no rumors to give warning, and not even a courtship, he up and married Ophelia Reed, the most beautiful and spiteful woman in London. What a disappointment that had been. Rebecca had been left floundering without a goal.

Of course Lilly had blamed herself for introducing the subject of marriage when Rebecca hadn't been close to the age for it. She didn't make that mistake again. Marriage was still discussed, but just in a general way that didn't involve any specific names.

But here was Raphael's cousin where she would have least expected to find him. Come to think of it, it wasn't so far-fetched to see him at Buckingham Palace. He was a marquis, after all. At least, she thought he might be a marquis. Hadn't his mother married one, then next they heard, she had become a widow, so the title went to her eldest son? He could certainly have been invited to the palace for one of the entertainments.

Coming out of her daze, she realized that this was the first time she was seeing The Angel when she didn't have designs on his cousin. Previously, she had put aside as inappropriate her curiosity about the man. Besides, he wasn't well known in Norford. His mother, one of the duke's many sisters, had married and moved to London before Rebecca had been born. So she'd never learned his full name, as people referred to him as Raphael's cousin, or Julie's son. He simply remained The Angel to her.

Of course she knew he wasn't an angel. She'd even heard some vague rumors about Julie Locke's son being a notorious skirt-chaser, which was a kinder way of saying he was a rake of the worst sort. She hadn't believed a word of it. How could anything tawdry be associated with *him*?

Alone in the empty corridor, Rebecca started moving again,

but she didn't take more than a few steps before she came to a dead halt again. So utterly distracted by *who* had given her the warning, she hadn't fully processed what that warning entailed.

There was no costume ball tonight? Could Elizabeth really have gotten the days mixed up, or did she lie to make Rebecca look the fool? She would certainly have looked foolish showing up at a social event dressed as she was. Some sort of entertainment must be taking place, or Elizabeth wouldn't have concocted a plan designed to embarrass her in front of others. If it had been a plan.

"Don't jump to conclusions," Rebecca mumbled under her breath. "Give her the benefit of the doubt. She really could have been trying to make amends only to have it backfire on her. It would be a shame then to make accusations only to be wrong and end up looking the fool anyway."

She walked slowly back to her room, all of the ramifications running through her mind of what could have happened if The Angel hadn't passed her in the hall. What would her mother do? She wished she could ask her for advice, but Lilly was probably back in Norford by now.

Rebecca closed the door to her room and leaned back against it. She wasn't sure if she should just retire so she would be fresh for her first full day at the palace, or change clothes and seek out Elizabeth to demand an explanation. The window caught her eye. The offensive window. The silly window draped with her petticoat! The kernel of anger she was trying to ignore couldn't be ignored any longer.

Chapter Five

D ID YOU FIND YOUR room satisfactory this time?"

Rupert St. John, Marquis of Rochwood, reposed in the stuffed chair in an insolent manner, a leg draped over one arm, his back resting against the other. He sniffed the brandy he was handed, but didn't drink it, and he didn't answer the question. The disrespect he showed to his superior was deliberate. But then he despised Nigel Jennings and they both knew it.

The first time Rupert had been asked to reside in the palace for a few days so he could be close to his quarry, he'd been shoved with his servant into a room so tiny it could by all accounts have been called a box. This time he'd been given a suite of rooms that a foreign king had just vacated. So the question didn't require an answer. He hadn't really complained about that other room, he'd merely told Nigel never to ask him to stay in Buckingham again, particularly since his home was no more than a five-minute ride from the palace. But Nigel had stressed how important it was. So Rupert had in fact been a little surprised by the grandeur of his current accommodations.

His pale blue eyes remained on Nigel as the older man poured himself a glass of brandy as well, or half a glass, and began looking for another bottle in the cabinet. Short, wiry, and unassuming, Nigel Jennings could blend into any crowd—which made him all the more deadly. Rupert couldn't do the same. He had a face no one ever forgot. Handsome, excessively so, he'd even been called beautiful on occasion, which could set off murderous impulses inside him, since his beauty was what had gotten him into his present role in the first place.

Not that he didn't like what he did. He enjoyed the danger. It was almost addictive. He enjoyed the thrill of success as well. And he liked being the unknown hero. He just loathed how it had all begun.

Distracted by the search for that second bottle, Nigel asked, "What did you find out, darling?"

Rupert stiffened at the endearment and said precisely, "One of these days I'm probably going to kill you."

Nigel swung around in surprise, and, apparently having realized what he'd accidentally said, he paled slightly. "That didn't come out right."

"Didn't it?"

"I was joking. It won't happen again."

Rupert didn't believe it and said in a hard, thoughtful tone, "You impressed a boy into thinking only he could save his country from doom. You impressed a boy into believing that this face"—he stabbed a finger at his cheek—"was the only thing that would work."

"You *were* perfect for that mission," Nigel insisted. "When I first saw you when you visited George's court with your father, good God, you were the most beautiful child I'd ever encountered. I never forgot that. Years later when a particular mission became necessary, you came to mind for it immediately, so, yes, I sought you out, and at fourteen you hadn't quite matured to your full masculinity, yet you were old enough to decide for yourself—"

Rupert continued as if he hadn't been interrupted, "You enlisted a boy to do the unthinkable—for the sake of his country. And you really wouldn't have given a damn if he had done it your way, instead of finding a different way that didn't tarnish him for life. But that boy is no more."

"For God's sake, Rupert, it was a slip of the tongue!"

"It was a slip of your emotions," Rupert corrected in a snarl as he stood up. "We agreed, long ago, that you would keep those perverted emotions to yourself."

He was being too harsh. Nigel's face flamed with embarrassment. He had cried drunkenly that night four years ago when he'd let it slip that he was in love with Rupert. He said it was something that had just happened, that he couldn't help it. But he'd sworn that he would never mention it again, that he wouldn't let it interfere with their working relationship. By all accounts, Nigel's sexual preferences didn't even lean that way. He had once had a wife, who was now deceased. He had several children. He kept mistresses. All of which could be a ruse—or not. Rupert knew that some men leaned both ways, but Rupert had to give Nigel the benefit of the doubt, or he wouldn't have been able to continue to work for him.

Rupert sighed. "I may have overreacted. Let's drop it, shall we?"

It was as close as he'd come to an apology. Nigel accepted it with a curt nod and, grabbing the half-filled glass of brandy, moved over to a chair as far across the room as he could get. It was a decent-size room. Nigel had called it home since the queen had made Buckingham Palace her home. Here, or at one of the other royal residences, he had the distinction of having served three monarchs now.

Spy, royal agent, whatever one chose to call him, Nigel carried out the business of gathering information that might help or harm the country. Forewarned was forearmed, after all, for good or bad. Some people even thought he was one of the late King George III's bastards, which would explain why he was always in residence with the monarchs. Royal spy just didn't fit the chap, as unassuming as he was.

There was no pay for the people who worked for him. Nobles were enlisted to serve for the good of the country. Pay was reserved for the riffraff who couldn't be trusted unless a coin was placed in their pocket for their efforts. Unscrupulous, though not without some redeeming qualities, Nigel would go to any lengths for the sake of his country.

With the unspoken apology in the air between them, Nigel broached the question again. "Did you find out anything yet?"

"Do I look like a miracle worker? I only just got here."

The older man smiled at Rupert's sarcastic reply. "I wouldn't exactly call them miracles, though you have been known to produce amazing results from time to time."

"I still don't see what warranted my taking up residence here. The prime minister isn't stupid. He isn't going to appoint anyone to the palace who will make him look bad."

With the Whig party in control for so long, Nigel had a long list of contacts among them. He'd even made use, on occasion, of some of the Whig ladies of the court for minor missions. But now that the Tories controlled the parliament, his life would be a little more difficult. Not that Nigel favored either political party. He couldn't really afford to, in his line of work. He would just have to begin from scratch, making new contacts among the court ladies.

"Of course they all come from good families. I have no concern in that regard—yet," Nigel said. "But two of the ladies assigned to the duchess when she reconciled with the queen after the Princess Royal was born were firmly in my camp. They understood the necessity of reporting anything out of the ordinary concerning the duchess. Having lost them—"

Rupert cut in, "Don't tell me you're still worried about the Duchess of Kent? That's old news, under the carpet. She and the queen get along famously now, don't they?"

That had been quite an estrangement during which the queen had not allowed her own mother to live in her household. It was because of John Conroy, the duchess's private secretary and adviser. He was reputedly also her lover, though that had never been proven. But even Victoria suspected as much. When Conroy had had the audacity to try to coerce Victoria into making him *her* personal secretary, she had had quite enough of the domineering pair and had banished them from her household.

Prince Albert, the queen's husband and a nephew of the duchess's, had patched up the rift between the two women after Victoria gave birth to her first child last year. It also helped that Conroy had left the country by then. Rupert was surprised Nigel hadn't just arranged for the man to be assassinated. But Rupert didn't doubt Nigel had had a part in encouraging Conroy's self-proclaimed exile, though Nigel had never admitted as much.

Now Nigel agreed with Rupert's assessment. "By all accounts, the duchess has become a doting grandmother and she and Victoria are close again. But I wouldn't be doing my job properly if I just *assumed* there is no need to keep an eye on that front—particularly since Sarah Wheeler is not being replaced with the rest of the Whig-appointed maids of honor. Smart woman not to declare her politics."

"Did she gain a new position in the transition?"

"Not an official one, but since all the other ladies are new, the duchess has given her authority over the new maids of honor assigned to her."

Rupert knew very well that Nigel had been suspicious of Lady Sarah since she'd first arrived at court. An impoverished noblewoman, the last of her line, she had been part of the duchess's household prior to the queen's moving into the palace and had never actually been given a position. Lady Sarah was merely in the duchess's employ. Then she and Nigel became rivals of a sort. Yes, *rivals* was a good name for the competition that had somehow developed between them earlier this year.

Sarah Wheeler also liked to gather information about people at court. But Nigel had never been able to ascertain what she was doing with it. He was sure she wasn't using it to gain favor with the queen because he'd set several traps for her, and never once had he caught her.

He'd even enlisted Rupert's assistance in determining the woman's motives. Nigel's suggestion had, of course, been for Rupert to become her lover. But Rupert rarely followed Nigel's suggestions. Besides, he'd developed a quick dislike for the lady that had nothing to do with Nigel or his request. She was too impudent, even imperious, for her lowly position. And she called him beautiful. . . .

But all Rupert had been able to surmise at that time was that she posed no immediate threat to the monarchy. Was the woman intent on blackmail? That remained to be seen.

To the matter at hand, Rupert said, "A good half of the ladies who have arrived so far I already know socially. Nothing
untoward there. Good families with no radicals hiding in the
closets. Most are simply delighted by the appointments. A few
are wary because they know that the queen favors the Whigs."

Nigel sighed. "I really wish that *wasn't* public knowledge.
She's been warned to stop corresponding with Lord Melbourne,
yet she persists."

Rupert sympathized with the queen. "I'd be bloody well annoyed if I was told I can't communicate with my friends anymore, too. Melbourne wasn't just one of her closest advisers
while he was in office, he taught her what she knows about
politics, and they've been friends since she assumed the throne.
To just cut that off simply because the current prime minister is
a Tory—"

"You know very well the monarchy must abide by a different set of rules than you and I. She depended on Melbourne,
but she has Prince Albert to rely on now as well as her own
good political instincts—she's learned a lot these last four years.
And as monarch, she knows very well she can't display favorit-
ism to the party out of power."

Rupert grinned. "Let's not forget you've had me deliver a
few of Her Majesty's secret letters."

"I don't presume to advise the queen. If she asks something
of me, I do it without question. As least, she does it in secret
now. She understands she can't publicly undermine Peel a second time."

Rupert almost laughed. The first time had occurred four
years ago, and the incident had become known as the Bedchamber Crisis. Melbourne had resigned and Peel had taken his
place, yet when Peel had tried to appoint Tory wives to the

queen's household, Victoria hadn't just balked, she'd flatly refused. She wasn't giving up her Whig ladies of the bedchamber; they were her close friends, not merely ceremonial puppets. This led to Peel's resigning and Melbourne's returning to office.

But four years later, Melbourne had finally resigned for good, Peel had won the election again, and Victoria didn't make the same mistake twice. Besides, after Victoria married Albert, whom she dearly loved, she no longer relied on her ladies for companionship. So Peel's appointees had begun to arrive at the palace, and Rupert had been brought in to make sure none of them were inappropriate for the job, a task Rupert didn't mind at all. He just didn't think he needed to live in the palace to accomplish it.

Of course he knew exactly why Nigel had insisted. If Rupert had to resort to seducing any of the ladies to find out what he needed to know, Nigel wanted to make sure he had a convenient room nearby to do so.

Chapter Six

THE ENTERTAINMENT WAS TAKING place in the Yellow Drawing room, on the opposite side of the palace from the main state rooms. Rebecca had gone in the wrong direction to begin with, so it took her much longer than she'd expected to find the room. If the queen had made an appearance, she'd already retired, because Rebecca saw only twenty people or so, mostly ladies, standing about chatting. A small podium stood empty in the middle of the room. Perhaps tonight's entertainment had been a poetry recital. Rebecca's mother had told her that the ladies of the court often arranged small entertainments for their own amusement when nothing official was taking place that required their attendance.

Now that it appeared that the recital was over, Rebecca would have left if she hadn't spotted Elizabeth Marly across the room talking with two other girls their age. Dressed in the same gown she'd been wearing when she had left their room, Elizabeth certainly hadn't shown up in costume. Which pretty much confirmed in Rebecca's mind that Elizabeth had set her up for an embarrassing scene.

Without hesitating, she crossed the room and approached her roommate. She nodded at the other two girls, then whispered to Elizabeth, "Why did you lie to me?"

Elizabeth stiffened at the accusation. Making no effort to introduce Rebecca to her companions or even bid them goodbye, she pulled Rebecca away from the others before she replied haughtily, "Don't be absurd, I never lie. And what, pray tell, am I supposed to have lied about?"

"The costume that you went to great lengths to get me to wear to this event? Does that refresh your memory?"

Elizabeth shrugged, though she was unable to conceal the smugness in her tone. "I merely got the days mixed up, easy enough to do around here."

"If that's true, why didn't you come back and tell me?" Rebecca demanded.

"I sent a footman, but apparently he didn't go directly to perform the task. You are quite out of line in suggesting I lied about it."

Rebecca knew that was yet another lie. The girl's smug, catty tone truly spoke for itself. Nor did she look the least bit contrite.

"Let's go find this footman, shall we?"

"Oh, good grief," Elizabeth snapped impatiently. "You really are going to be ridiculous about this, aren't you? You aren't wearing the costume, so obviously you found out in time that it wasn't needed tonight. And how did you manage that?"

"An angel was looking out for me."

Elizabeth lifted a brow, but must have decided not to address such an inane remark and said instead, "So there was no harm done then, was there?"

There could have been and they both knew it. And

Rebecca's anger wasn't cooling. An apology might have helped, but she obviously wouldn't be getting one. And this stalemate wasn't the least bit satisfying. She hadn't thought Elizabeth would simply deny the allegations. As offensive as she'd been from the start, Rebecca had expected her to laugh or make fun of Rebecca's gullibility.

So the only thing left to say was "Don't try to embarrass me again. You won't like the consequences." And for good measure she added, "And you bloody well better not wake me when you come in—this time."

"Or what?" Elizabeth shot back.

That was a good question. Rebecca had to think for a moment before she said, "Or I will develop a fondness for the sun shining into the room quite early in the morning."

As threats went, Rebecca knew it was pathetic, but at least it got her point across. If Elizabeth wanted war, Rebecca was up to the challenge.

Having said her piece, Rebecca turned to leave and found three young women nearby grinning at her. Realizing they must have overheard some of what she'd said, she blushed and moved toward the door. One of them followed her into the hall and fell into step beside her.

"It's about time someone called Elizabeth Marly on the carpet for her deplorable antics. Bravo," the girl said with a bright, genuine smile. "I'm Evelyn DuPree. And I do hope you are Lady Rebecca Marshall?"

"Yes, but how did you know?"

"We were told to expect you tomorrow. You make the fourth maid of honor assigned to the Duchess of Kent. Unfortunately, Elizabeth Marly is also one of us, which means we can't avoid her as much as we might like to."

Evelyn was quite pretty with her sandy-brown hair and hazel eyes, and Rebecca guessed that she was a year or two younger than herself. Not all maids of honor needed to be of marriageable age. Their posts would last at least four years, or until the next general election.

"So I'm not the only one she's made no effort to be friends with?" Rebecca asked as they continued down the hall.

"Goodness, no, I'm sure she dislikes everyone equally. It certainly does seem that way. She got here early and lords it over us, as if it gives her seniority, which of course it doesn't." But then Evelyn frowned. "Actually, she went overboard to be nasty to her first roommate last week, and from what I overheard in the Yellow Drawing Room just now, it sounds as if you have the unlucky distinction of being in that same position now."

Rebecca nodded with a wince. "And there's no way around it either."

"Course there is," Evelyn insisted. "Just ask for another room. She'll end up making your life miserable if you don't. It might take a few days to arrange it, but it would be worth the effort to get away from her for at least a portion of each day."

"I don't dare do that," Rebecca said, and explained what the footman had told her.

"Well, that's too bad, but you're quite right," Evelyn agreed. "Can't have the queen thinking she erred in one of her suggestions."

"I'll make the best of it," Rebecca assured the girl. "Now that I know she's a liar I won't be so gullible again. But what happened with her other roommate?"

"The girl went home in disgrace two days after she arrived. Elizabeth provoked her into causing a scandalous scene. There was shouting, and name-calling, and the poor girl was crying all the while. I've never seen anyone quite that upset." Then in a whisper, Evelyn added, "The girl even insulted Lady Sarah, who tried to intervene, and that was *not* a good idea."

"Would that be Sarah Wheeler? The lady I'm to report to in the morning?"

"Yes, she has been given jurisdiction over us, and a good thing, too. At least she's English. You did know the duchess is not? German is her native tongue. Most people barely understand the little English she speaks."

Rebecca grinned. "Yes, I knew that. German isn't the second language I learned, but I expect we'll learn to speak it while we're here."

"Goodness, I hope not!" Evelyn said with feigned horror. "I was able to escape my last bit of schooling with this appointment, and I'd like to keep it that way! But we won't have much to do with the duchess anyway, other than to spend most of our days in her quarters. Let her ladies of the bedchamber learn German in order to understand her. They're her personal attendants. We're just window dressing, as my mother would put it. If there's an actual ceremony where she must make a public appearance, then, of course, we'll be part of her entourage, but otherwise, we aren't expected to be her companions unless she actually requests our company. Besides, she spends most of her time with the queen or in the nursery." Evelyn chuckled. "She does so adore her granddaughter."

As they continued to walk, Rebecca's thoughts returned to her roommate. Now she understood what John Keets, the footman, had meant with his subtle warning.

"If Elizabeth's former roommate was asked to leave because of a scene Elizabeth instigated, how is it that Elizabeth wasn't dismissed as well?" Rebecca asked.

"There was no dismissal," Evelyn said. "She probably expected to be dismissed, so she flew the coop, as it were, and resigned herself, leaving that very day. Lady Sarah preferred to sweep the whole incident under the rug." Then Evelyn whispered, "We were told never to mention it again, but I felt you *had* to be warned, since by all accounts it appears that Elizabeth is going to try to provoke you into creating a scandalous scene as well. For a moment tonight, I thought she would succeed."

For a moment tonight, Rebecca had thought the same thing. "Do you know why Elizabeth is so provocative? Knowing the cause might help to alleviate it."

Evelyn gave that a moment's thought. "You mean like jealousy or some supposed grudge?"

"Yes."

Evelyn shrugged. "I wouldn't call it a grudge unless she blames everyone for her woes, which would be, well, silly, wouldn't it? Jealousy now, hmmm, if so, my guess would be that it has to do with her lack of money. Her family isn't well-to-do, so she might be feeling the pinch of that now that she's among all the grandeur here. By all accounts, one of her ancestors squandered the family fortune with his gambling. You know, that might be why she gets along so well with Lady Sarah. Sarah comes from an impoverished noble family, too. But I don't really know. Elizabeth might just be provocative because she deplores sharing a room. Her attitude seemed to improve last week when she believed she had that room to herself."

They had arrived at the destination Evelyn had been steering them toward . . . the kitchen, of all places!

Evelyn was laughing at the look of surprise on Rebecca's face and asked, "Hungry? I'm famished. We're allowed access here, of course. One of the first things I did when I arrived was to come here and make friends with the head cook, which I highly recommend you do as well. It's wonderful having fresh pastries delivered to your room each morning. They're rather stale by the time they get to the duchess's quarters, where we take most of our meals."

The huge area was still bustling with activity even at that time of night, with kitchen maids scrubbing dishes and mopping the floors, and cooks' assistants making preparations for the next day's meals. Rebecca thought Evelyn's suggestion about the pastries was excellent, even if she might have to share those fresh pastries with a disagreeable roommate.

"Now that you mention it, I do believe I missed having dinner tonight." Rebecca grinned. "Is the cook about? I'd like to meet him."

"No, but I'll be pleased to bring you back tomorrow for that introduction."

"Thank you, and I mean that sincerely," Rebecca said to her new friend. "You've been wonderfully helpful."

"It's my pleasure. I'm just glad you're not another Elizabeth. One is quite enough!"

Chapter Seven

FLORA WAS AMAZINGLY PERCEPTIVE. Rebecca was able to give her maid the whole account of what had happened yesterday because Elizabeth had flounced out of the room before Flora had arrived. After a brief display of umbrage on Rebecca's behalf, Flora came up with a logical plan of action.

"I'll do her hair."

Surprised, Rebecca turned around on the vanity stool where Flora was working on Rebecca's hair. "You certainly don't have to."

"I know. But your mother didn't expect you to land in a nest of vipers here. She expects you to have a wonderful time, to enjoy this grand come-out to the fullest. You can't do that with a witch plotting ways to make you run home crying to mama as her last roommate apparently did."

"The offer to do her hair may not make any difference, you know," Rebecca warned.

"If it doesn't, then I'll stop. But there's no harm in trying, is there?"

Flora had an optimistic nature. So did Rebecca—except in this case. Elizabeth's unpleasant disposition seemed to be part of her nature, which meant a peace offering wasn't going to improve it. But Rebecca knew her maid was right. It wouldn't hurt to try.

John Keets was waiting in the hall to escort her to the duchess's chambers that morning. Rebecca was grateful and tried not to appear too amused when he asked a few subtle questions about Flora.

The chambers where she and the other maids of honor would be spending most of their time were of a decent size and nicely appointed. Mary Louise Victoria, Duchess of Kent, might have moved into the palace with her finances in a shambles, but the queen supported her now.

Only Evelyn and another young girl, introduced as Lady Constance, were in the drawing room when Rebecca arrived. They were at a tea table, embroidering.

Constance looked a bit older than Rebecca, closer to the queen's age of twenty-two. Yet to have gained the post of maid of honor, she couldn't have been married yet. She wasn't plain-looking, so Rebecca wondered what accounted for her lack of a husband.

"What are you both working on?" Rebecca asked as she sat down next to them.

Evelyn held up her satin square on which a pattern of vines and delicate flowers had been traced. "It was the duchess's idea, and in fact she's working on the larger center square of the blanket. When it's finally pieced together, it will be presented to the Princess Royal. If you have a steady hand, please join us. There are extra squares and thread in that drawer over there."

Evelyn nodded toward a cabinet in the corner next to several chairs and an assortment of large musical instruments. Rebecca hoped she wouldn't be asked to play any of them herself.

She enjoyed embroidering but felt a bit too nervous on her first day at her new post to undertake fine needlework for a blanket intended for the princess.

"Has the duchess returned to the palace?" she asked.

"Not yet, but she's due to arrive sometime this morning. And don't worry, you won't be expected to try to converse with her. She keeps to her private sitting room when she's in chamber. Lady Sarah is in there now making sure everything is in order."

"Terrifying the maids, no doubt," Constance added.

"Nonsense." Evelyn grinned. "She doesn't really have a verbal whip."

Rebecca raised a brow. "Is there something I should be warned about?"

"Not really. Sarah just seems overly abrupt with the servants. But then we've heard how lazy the maids were when the queen first made the palace her residence. Sarah must have heard that, too. The palace was quite dirty, you know, soot everywhere. But Prince Albert rectified all that with the improvements he made. And the servants seem fine to me now. Sarah just insists on perfection."

"It's more'n that, Eve, and you know it," Constance said in a disapproving tone. "She even treats *us* like her own personal servants. Some of the errands she sends us on are highly inappropriate if you ask me."

"Such as?" Rebecca asked curiously.

Constance started to answer, then frowned and closed her mouth. Evelyn chuckled, scolding the girl lightly, "Don't worry, Rebecca isn't one of Sarah's spies. Elizabeth probably is, but then we've seen how chummy those two are. Even now Elizabeth is off doing her bidding."

"What sort of errands is she referring to?" Rebecca asked Evelyn directly.

"Lady Sarah dabbles in palace intrigue, by all accounts. She sent Constance to follow one of the ambassadors when he left the palace and report where he went and what he did. It was harmless enough. We certainly couldn't figure out why she even wanted that information. But while we expect to run errands occasionally, Constance shouldn't have been asked to leave the palace. And unchaperoned!"

"Why didn't you just tell her no?" Rebecca asked Constance.

"You can't tell *her* no," Constance replied, aghast. "One word from her to the duchess and we'd lose our posts here. She does have that power over us."

Rebecca frowned. "And she's abusing that power?"

Evelyn sighed. "We're making too much of this. She is in the employ of the duchess, after all. She never said as much, but the information she gathers *must* be at the duchess's behest, so ultimately it must reach the queen's ear. She wouldn't dare use us for anything untoward."

Rebecca was inclined to agree with that reasoning. But her mother definitely hadn't warned her that she might be involved in palace intrigue. Actually, she thought it sounded rather exciting.

Evelyn was having the same thought apparently. "I find it amusing for the most part," Evelyn said with a grin. "Like tonight at the costume ball, I am to distract a certain lord and then ask him an impertinent question, so that he will have his guard down and answer by rote rather than fob me off. How I am to distract him Sarah left to my discretion."

Constance snorted. "You know very well she implied you should let him kiss you."

Evelyn giggled. "Which I was hoping would happen anyway. He is quite a good catch, after all, and divinely handsome."

The word *divinely* made Rebecca think of The Angel. She certainly hoped that wasn't whom Evelyn was talking about. But she refrained from asking Evelyn the name of the nobleman she was supposed to distract simply because she wouldn't know The Angel's name even if she heard it.

The lady they had been discussing suddenly appeared. Bursting energetically out of the duchess's sitting room, Sarah Wheeler didn't pause, not even for a moment, when she took note of Rebecca's presence.

"Come to my office," she said as she continued through the drawing room, out the door, and into the hallway.

"You'd better hurry," Evelyn suggested. "Or you'll wonder where she disappeared to. Her office is just one door down the hallway."

Rebecca nodded and quickly followed. Sarah had indeed disappeared, though she'd left the door open. Stepping inside a narrow hallway, Rebecca realized this was the duchess's private entrance to her bedchamber.

"In here," Sarah called before Rebecca made the mistake of continuing down the narrow hallway and entering the main bedchamber.

Rebecca turned into the first room to her left, which was the size of a closet. Sarah was seated at a small, cluttered desk pushed up against the wall. The two wooden chairs beyond the desk lacked cushions. Not much else could be stuffed in that little cubbyhole. There were no windows either, just a lamp burning on the desk that left a thin haze of smoke in the room. But the subdued lighting was kind to the lady.

Rebecca thought Lady Sarah could be described as ugly, yet she certainly had an interesting face. She would have been simply plain-looking if not for her oddly close-set gray eyes coupled with her overly long, narrow face. A crooked nose, suggesting that it had been broken at some point, didn't help her appearance. She was perhaps in her early thirties, though her age was rather hard to guess. Tall, even a bit more so than Rebecca, she was so thin she was nearly curveless. And her raven hair was coiffured much too tightly. Bangs would have softened her long face. Did the woman not realize that? She could make herself more attractive fairly easily. Or did she simply not care?

"I assume you are Rebecca Marshall?" the lady said, and barely waited for Rebecca's nod before continuing, "Good of you to arrive on time at the palace. I'm Sarah Wheeler. It's my duty to make sure you do not stray to idleness, but attend all functions expected of you and be available should the duchess require anything of you. Your stay here is to benefit the court as well as yourself. So you and I will get along just fine as long as you bring no shame to your post and do as you're told."

The lady smiled warmly. It was probably meant to put Rebecca at ease, yet something was oddly off-kilter about Lady Sarah's smile, as if it wasn't quite sincere.

"You might have already been informed that there is to be a costume ball tonight? The queen might even attend, though if she doesn't, that is understandable. She is quite far along in her second pregnancy, after all. But you are expected to attend. Do you have a costume?"

"My mother and I overlooked that necessity in our rushed

preparations to get me here on time. But my roommate helped me put a costume together for tonight."

"You're sharing a room with Elizabeth Marly, aren't you? She's a good girl. You can benefit from her advice, I'm sure. But be better prepared next time."

Rebecca had to choke back a laugh at the glowing description of her roommate, but then Evelyn had warned her that Elizabeth and Sarah got along splendidly. "I will be," Rebecca assured the lady. "I have already sent a missive to my—"

"About tonight," Sarah cut in, not interested in any information she didn't ask for. "I may have something special for you to do after the ball begins. It's a matter of grave importance, but I'm not sure you're capable of the task." After a thoughtful pursing of her lips, she added, "I'm sure you're as innocent as you should be, but how naive are you?"

Intrigue. The other girls had warned her, but Rebecca certainly hadn't expected to be called upon for that sort of duty this quickly. Did she really want to get involved? Did she have a choice? Perhaps, since she suspected her answer would determine whether she would be a benefit to her country, or an obscure maid of honor who never met the queen . . .

With visions of being heroic and having Queen Victoria's personal gratitude as a result, she replied, "Only as naive as I need to be."

Sarah Wheeler chuckled. "I like that answer. I think you'll do."

Chapter Eight

REBECCA DIDN'T THINK IT the least bit heroic to sneak into a man's room to search it. In fact, it felt distinctly criminal to her. Yet there she was, dressed in the breeches, fancy jacket, and feathered hat of her rakish cavalier costume, snooping through drawers and trying not to think how she would feel if someone were doing the same thing in her room.

She didn't even know what she was looking for. She didn't think Lady Sarah knew what she wanted her to look for, either. "Letters," the lady had said in ordering her to search the room. "Or anything that looks out of the ordinary."

But absolutely nothing in the room could be classified as out of the ordinary. If anything, it was furnished so spartanly that at first glance it didn't seem that anyone even lived there.

"He never leaves his room unlocked," Lady Sarah had said. "I know because I have it checked often. But today he did. I can't imagine why, unless it's to give one of his agents access to pick up or deliver something. So if it's still open tonight, you're going to find what that something is."

Rebecca had so hoped the door to the room wouldn't be unlocked. She had gone to the costume ball, but had been too nervous about her task to do anything more than keep an eye on Lady Sarah and wait for her nod, which was the signal to begin the intrigue for the night. She had rushed off at that point, winding her way through Buckingham Palace's long corridors, following the precise directions to the room she was supposed to violate. She just hadn't been told whose room it was.

"The less you know the better," Lady Sarah had advised. "Should he ever speak to you, you need to appear genuinely ignorant of his identity. But make no mistake, Rebecca. You're a maid of honor in the queen's court, so listen closely. This is so important that I would do it myself if I could trust anyone else to keep him distracted long enough for the search to be done. But I'm the only one who can keep him occupied for a reasonable time, so you need have no fear of being discovered. But don't dally. Ten minutes and no longer."

When Rebecca discovered the door was still unlocked, she didn't enter the room immediately. Instead she wasted one of the allotted minutes debating whether to lie to Lady Sarah and tell her the room had been locked. But the older woman had stressed the importance of the task. Rebecca might discover a plot against the crown, a planned attack against one of the colonies, or at least evidence that the occupant of the room was a traitor and in the palace under false pretenses.

She found nothing. Riffling through every drawer, she found not one letter, not even a scrap of paper. The heroic zeal that had propelled her earlier had faded, leaving her feeling like a bloody thief.

She was closing the last drawer with a sigh when she heard the door suddenly open behind her. She wasn't supposed to be caught! Sarah had given her no contingency plan for that!

"If you aren't Nigel's lover, you're going to have a lot of explaining to do," a deep male voice intoned.

Some of her panic subsided. It wasn't the occupant of the room, just someone who knew him. But then she felt the weapon in her back and the panic returned in spades.

"You've made a mis—"

"A woman?" The man laughed and withdrew his weapon. "That's priceless. Has you dress like a man, does he? I suppose whatever works."

She didn't quite understand what the fellow was going on about, but she did understand that he'd given her an excuse for being there. She just couldn't bring herself to use it. She decided to take umbrage with his presence instead. Was this room a magnet for snoops?

"You are the one who needs to explain . . . what . . ."

She turned around as she spoke, but the words died in her throat. Him? The Angel. Raphael Locke's cousin? For the fourth time, she was rendered dazzled and speechless in his presence. Like her, he was dressed for the ball in a costume from another century, though his costume was from the more recent past. He was dressed as a dandy in a satin coat and knee-high breeches in a powder blue that wasn't quite as pale as his eyes. An abundance of white lace was at his cuffs and neck. His long black hair floated about his shoulders. He should probably have had a closer shave for the occasion. The foppish look wasn't quite achieved with the dark stubble on his cheeks. He was a little too broad in the shoulders, too. She'd never noticed that before, but then she'd never been this close to him before, either. Usually, all she could do was stare at his handsome face openmouthed, just as she was now doing.

"Dazzled you, have I? Oh, come now," he added with a distinct tone of impatience. "This reaction is typical of young innocents, not sophisticated women of the world like you. Or am I mistaken?"

She couldn't pull her thoughts together quickly enough to wonder what he was rambling about. His halo had arrived, an ethereal glow—or were her eyes just blinded by the bright satin of his coat?

"I'm going to make absolutely sure, you understand," he explained before he reached out and gently squeezed each of her breasts.

That certainly brought Rebecca out of her daze. Aghast, she shoved him away from her only to have him slip his arm around her waist and bring her up hard against him.

"Thought that might work to bring you back to your senses," he said with a chuckle.

"Let go," she demanded rather breathlessly.

He shook his head slowly. "Let's keep in mind who doesn't belong here and who has the upper hand." While his words sounded threatening, he was in fact grinning now. "And while we're at it, let's have a better look at what attracts a man of Nigel's peculiar tastes."

His hand touched her cheek. It was warm, hot actually, and not smooth like a dandy's, but a little callused and wide. Slowly it moved up her cheek in a sensual caress that sent Rebecca into a head spin of dizziness. Fainting was a definite possibility. The Angel was embracing her? She'd never thought she'd even get close to him, let alone feel the whole length of him pressing against her body.

His hand continued moving upward until his fingers reached her hairline, then with one of them, he flicked her hat off. It tumbled to the floor behind her. A man's hat, it hadn't exactly fit her tightly. Her blond bangs tumbled down over her brow. Flora had helped to conceal her hair, but not before she'd arranged it in her usual becoming coiffure.

"Well, well," The Angel said.

His eyes were moving slowly over her face now that it was no longer shadowed by the brim of the hat. He didn't seem the least bit amused now. And without the amusement, he didn't seem quite so angelic either. Brought down to earth, as it were, he was just a man, and possibly—dangerous? *What* brought that to mind? The sudden hard glint in his pale blue eyes? The way he was holding her waist more tightly?

"You're too pretty, and far too young, for Nigel," he said, still gazing at her face. "Though I suppose with the right clothes that would lend itself to the appearance of a young boy. At least, thank God, you bear no resemblance to me. So the question becomes, are you a willing participant in this charade, luv?"

She had absolutely no idea what he was accusing her of now, but his assumption that she belonged there had gone on long enough. Quick-witted when she wasn't bedazzled, she went on the offensive.

"I have no knowledge who this Nigel is that you keep mentioning, but you, sir, need to explain what you're doing in Lady Sarah's room. She sent me here for a scarf. I highly doubt she sent *you* here for something as well. So who are you and what are you doing here?"

"Rupert St. John," he said in an absent manner while his eyes were still slowly perusing her face. Looking for the lie? He must not have been able to find it because he asked, "Do you really expect me to believe that you've stumbled into the wrong room?"

At last she had a name for The Angel, but he didn't look

like a Rupert. No doubt he'd given her a false name, which she found quite annoying.

"You don't look like a Rupert."

Startled, he raised a black brow at her. "Dare I ask what I look like to you?"

"A hungry wolf."

He didn't laugh at the description, but he did abruptly release her. "Wolf, perhaps," he said drily. "Hungry? Not at the moment."

She had enough sense to guess she'd just been insulted. Had she touched a nerve perhaps? Good, because he was certainly touching too many of hers.

Regaining her balance after stumbling back from him, she went to straighten her skirt in an indignant manner, but forgot she wasn't wearing one. How could she appear to be offended while she was wearing britches? She settled for grabbing the hat off the floor and shoving it back down on her head.

The very idea! Not hungry at the moment? As if she didn't know he was implying she wasn't to his taste.

He crossed his arms as he continued to stare at her. She didn't fail to notice that he was standing between her and the door.

"Didn't find a scarf, did you?" he said.

So he was going to test her excuse, look for flaws? "No, but then I'd barely begun to look for one when you barged in."

"You won't find one, either."

"Nonsense. I was told precisely how many doors to count to know exactly which room to enter."

"You're in the wrong wing of the palace, m'dear—if you're telling the truth. Sarah Wheeler, and, yes, I have no doubt that's who sent you on this little errand, is quartered elsewhere."

Rebecca hoped she looked suitably appalled. "You mean I owe you an apology?"

"Not me. It's not my room, but you can be sure the owner will hear of your 'mistake.' "

She sighed. "This is only my second day in the palace. I am not oriented yet with its layout. It was an honest mix-up."

"Was it? Then no harm done. But don't be surprised that now I must say, get the hell out of here."

She blushed, nodded, and tried to hurry past him. He caught her arm for one last warning. "If we meet again in a place where you aren't supposed to be, I will make assumptions more to *my* liking."

"Excuse me?"

He let her go. "Run along, wench. You're too young to understand."

Chapter Nine

I ADMIRE YOUR GUMPTION TO wear a costume like that, 'deed
I do," Evelyn remarked as she walked over to join Rebecca.
"But didn't it occur to you that a woman in breeches isn't likely
to be asked to dance?"

They stood on the edge of the dance floor. The ballroom at
Buckingham Palace was immense. With so many chandeliers
lit, and so much gilt on the walls, the room sparkled brightly.

Rebecca hadn't moved too far from the entrance, though.
She'd been watching the door for Rupert St. John's arrival while
she waited for Lady Sarah to finish her conversation and come
over to her. She'd tried to go directly to the lady to warn her
that she'd been discovered, but a rude flick of Sarah's hand had
warned her not to interrupt.

Rebecca was nervous. The intrigue wasn't over yet. Rupert
wouldn't be put off by any hand-flicking if he decided to question Sarah about the "scarf" excuse. So she really needed to talk
to Sarah before he did.

"This costume wasn't my idea," Rebecca said in response to
Evelyn's question. "I neglected to bring one with me."

"Let me guess. Elizabeth?" At Rebecca's nod, Evelyn rolled her eyes. "She didn't tell you about the costume room, did she? We have access to all sorts of paraphernalia to create a great many different costumes. Why, there must be five shepherdess crooks hanging up in there," she added, tapping the one in her hand on the floor.

Learning about the costume room, Rebecca should have got angry, but she was currently too nervous for any other emotion to take precedence.

"I suppose you could dance with me," Evelyn said with a giggle.

Rebecca grinned. She couldn't really imagine a man asking her to dance either, now that she thought of it, not with both of them wearing breeches. The poor chap would be far too embarrassed, she was sure.

But dancing was the least of her concerns. "It's all right," she said. "There will be other balls."

She actually wasn't displeased with her costume. At least it was unique, dashingly so in her opinion. Most of the other guests were wearing duplicates of the same costumes. Two shepherdesses had danced by while she'd been standing there talking to Evelyn, who was also dressed as a shepherdess. And Rebecca must have seen at least four gentlemen made up to look like pirates.

Rupert still hadn't arrived. Perhaps he wasn't coming to the ball. Perhaps he was only in the palace to spy and was wearing the dandy costume to look as if he belonged here tonight. What was she thinking? He was a member of the Locke family. He couldn't be a spy. She'd seen him in the palace yesterday, too, and he'd been dressed normally.

It was regrettable that she'd met him for the first time under these awkward circumstances, it really was. But what was he doing in that fellow's room? The same thing she'd been doing?

Rebecca paled slightly at the realization that she'd made some wild assumptions about Rupert based on the task she'd been sent to do. Sarah had never told her why she was to search that room, only that it was important. But important to whom?

"Shall we walk?" Sarah said as she approached Rebecca, giving a nod to Evelyn to excuse them.

Rebecca wasn't given much choice in the matter, since the lady put her arm through hers and led her to the back of the crowd. Sarah hadn't donned a costume for tonight, just a black domino mask.

"What do you have for me?" Sarah asked eagerly.

"The information that I was discovered."

Sarah stopped abruptly. "By whom? A servant?"

"No. But he seemed to be well acquainted with the man who lives in the room. However, I had already made my search and found nothing of interest. The room was very neat. I would have thought no one occupied it, if I hadn't found clothes neatly folded in the bureau."

Sarah appeared a bit excited about that piece of information. "If it wasn't a servant, it must have been the agent Nigel was expecting. That would account for his not calling the guard on you, which I assume didn't happen?" When Rebecca shook her head, Sarah nodded. "I need to know who he is. I don't suppose he gave you his name?"

Rebecca didn't hesitate even a second. "No," she lied. She didn't feel guilty about it either. Whether the name Rupert gave her was accurate or false, she wasn't about to brand The Angel as "Nigel's agent," whatever that suggested, unless she knew for a fact that he was up to no good. He was related to the Duke of

Norford, after all! He couldn't be up to anything nefarious or traitorous.

"A description of him will do just as well. What did he look like?"

An Angel, Rebecca thought, managing not to grin. She wasn't sure why she was determined to protect Rupert St. John, if that was even his real name, but she was.

"I'd like to be helpful, Lady Sarah, but he was in complete disguise, dressed for the ball tonight. I've been watching for the exact costume he was wearing and I haven't seen it yet. But that wouldn't be conclusive since he wore a monk's robe with a hood, and a full face mask. His hair was hidden under the hood, and his eyes were shadowed under the mask. He was even of average height. If he changed his costume, he could stand next to me and I wouldn't know it. Or someone else could arrive wearing the same costume. Considering this is a night for hidden identities, it was a perfect time for him to come to the palace, I suppose."

Sarah mumbled something under her breath, then said more loudly, "Total waste of time. If you had used your wits, you would have gotten that mask off of him so that you could recognize him if you saw him again."

Incredulous, Rebecca replied, "I was lucky enough to get out of there with the excuse I used, so how could I have done that?"

"You could have used your wiles and got him to remove the mask to kiss you, that's how. Or are you really so innocent that you don't know how easy that would have been, a pretty girl like you?"

Rebecca didn't respond immediately. She got caught up in the image of being kissed by *him,* which was quite easy to envision since he'd held her so closely in his arms. It really was too bad she didn't possess those wiles Sarah was talking about . . .

"Answer me!" Sarah snapped.

Rebecca pushed the image away, realizing just how angry Sarah had become. Over what? Rebecca's lack of worldly wiles? She was *supposed* to be lacking in that regard!

She felt herself getting angry. Was this how Sarah got the other maids of honor to do her bidding? By browbeating them and making them feel like complete incompetents? With displays of anger to make them think they'd lose their post if they didn't jump to do her bidding? If anyone should lose her post, it was Sarah Wheeler. Rebecca had a feeling the woman far overstepped her authority.

"I'm not so innocent that I don't know that kissing perfect strangers is not one of my duties here at court, Lady Sarah. I was apprised of what this post entails, and playing the thief was not part of the description either. Perhaps we should take this matter up with the queen."

Sarah's face turned livid. "Are you daring to threaten me?"

"Threaten?" Rebecca feigned a wide-eyed look. "Surely you have Her Majesty's approval to use the maids in this manner. So why would you see it as a threat? But perhaps I overreacted. I wouldn't presume to bother the queen with anything this sordid. And I'm aware that the duchess wouldn't understand me if I spoke to her. But . . ."

She didn't really need to mention the names of powerful people such as the prime minister who were acquainted with her mother. Sarah had gotten the idea and was still enraged about it. But Rebecca had probably gone too far. The woman would no doubt have her dismissed in the morning, which was going to so disappoint Lilly . . .

Rebecca sighed and said, "What you have just witnessed is my reaction to feeling like a criminal tonight. I apologize. But if you need to enlist spies for the kingdom, you will have to find someone more heroic next time."

"I see," Sarah said, and pursed her thin lips. "Useless as well as incompetent, but what more can one expect of someone barely out of the schoolroom."

"Precisely," Rebecca replied stiffly. Good grief, making peace merely invited more insults? "By the by, if you should be asked if you sent someone after a scarf tonight, I would suggest you say yes."

Sarah gasped. "My God, you didn't really use my name, did you?"

"The only excuse I had for being in a room I had no business being in was to take umbrage with the fellow who found me there and demand to know what he was doing in *your* room. I forced him to convince me that I was in the wrong room. So my presence there appeared to be no more than a mistake."

"He actually believed you?"

"I'm rather good at taking umbrage."

Sarah almost laughed, having just come under the fire of that umbrage herself. "Very well, perhaps you're not so incompetent after all. But next time—"

Rebecca abruptly cut in, "There isn't going to be a next time, not unless you provide me with a good reason to run one of your errands. Perhaps if you told me more about what tonight's errand was about? Is the queen's life in danger? Is there some plot afoot that requires these unusual measures? I cannot believe that our kingdom doesn't have people trained for this sort of mission."

"Certainly there are such people, but they can't be used for such trivial matters as this."

"Trivial?" Rebecca frowned. "You said this was important, *gravely* important to be precise."

"Important to me," Sarah snapped, and marched off.

Rebecca was left dumbfounded. So her main assumption tonight had been false, too? There was nothing even remotely heroic about what she'd done? She was beginning to not like living in the palace.

Chapter Ten

REBECCA WAS ON HER way back to the front of the ball-room where she'd left Evelyn when a bright powder-blue satin jacket caught her eye. She quickly wound her way through the crowd for a better view.

It was indeed Rupert St. John in his dandy costume. He must have arrived while she'd been talking to Sarah. Even with his back turned to her while he leaned with one arm against the wall, she caught a glimpse of the side of his handsome face. He was with a woman. She could see a wide skirt pressed against his knees as he hovered over the lady. Though his shoulder blocked the woman's face from view, the woman was apparently leaning back against the wall, no doubt looking up at Rupert with rapt attention.

He laughed, then leaned down to whisper something to the woman. Rebecca thought she heard a girlish giggle. He was obviously flirting with the woman. Well, she *had* heard vague allusions to his being a renowned skirt-chaser. It didn't look vague to her, looked quite obvious. Rebecca told herself it was no concern of hers if his halo got a little tarnished in her mind.

She started to turn away, but Rupert straightened up, taking his hand off the wall. That gave her an unobstructed view of the woman he was flirting with. Rebecca just had trouble believing her eyes. Elizabeth Marly? Good God, he was flirting with her roommate?

Rebecca turned about with a huff, feeling—she wasn't sure how she felt. Angry? Certainly not. Indignant? Whatever for? But she couldn't for the life of her think what Rupert St. John could find attractive in such a mean, petty girl. He probably didn't know what she was like. And Elizabeth had looked rather pretty with her adoring expression. Well, more fool him!

Rebecca went back to where she'd left Evelyn, but her new friend wasn't there. She was on the floor dancing. Rebecca waited a few minutes to see if the musical piece the orchestra was playing would soon end, but it didn't, and she really had no reason to stay, she realized. She wouldn't be asked to dance because of her costume.

Feeling a bit forlorn, she made her way slowly to the door. She could stay to listen to the music, at least. The orchestra was the best she'd ever heard. They would have to be exceptionally good, she guessed, to play in the palace.

"Leaving so soon?"

For once, Rebecca wasn't struck speechless by Rupert's sudden presence as he fell into step beside her. He was just a man, albeit an extremely handsome one. Tall, strapping, oh, God, he was beautiful, a pinnacle of perfection in every way—but just a man nonetheless. His tarnished halo proved that.

"Yes, as it happens, I am definitely leaving," she replied tartly. "I feel out of place in this manly costume, which your *friend* arranged for me to wear."

"Nigel?" he asked in surprise.

"No, I told you, I don't know who that is."

"Then which friend are you displeased with?"

"Elizabeth Marly."

"Ah, yes, little Beth. A delightfully artificial chit. She has no knack for duplicity. Quite easy to figure out. You on the other hand . . ."

He didn't finish. He took her hand and led her to the middle of the ballroom. He was going to dance with her? Indeed, he kept her hand in his, put his other hand on her waist, and began to twirl them along to the exuberant melody of the current waltz.

How daring of him! Or did he forget she was wearing breeches? No, she had just mentioned her costume to him, so apparently he didn't care.

"Much better," he said as he glanced at the other couples who were watching them. "It is my bane to be gossiped about. But a dance is irrelevant and can occur for any number of reasons that have nothing to do with choice."

It took her only a moment to grasp his meaning. "So walking with me is a matter of *your* choice, since I certainly wasn't dragging you along with a chain to keep you at my side. But dancing can be no more than satisfying the demands of proper etiquette."

"Precisely! I knew you were smart as a whip, m'dear."

She wasn't sure if she should be wary of that compliment. It could imply he hadn't believed a word of her earlier excuse, and come to think of it, the warning he'd given her before she'd flown out the door of Nigel's room said as much. Yet he'd let her go. Why?

She wasn't going to ask, though. She could be attributing

more intelligence to *him* than he possessed. In fact, much of what he'd said to her could be attributed to his being a skirt-chaser. Good God, he wasn't subtly trying to seduce her, was he?

"So," he began.

He looked down and his eyes met hers now. It was quite disconcerting when he turned his full attention to her like this. And was the hand he had on her waist caressing her there!? He'd placed it under her jacket rather than on top of it, so no one could tell that it wasn't perfectly still as was proper—except her. Was it her imagination? Or was skirt-chasing so ingrained in him that he found it quite natural to caress a woman—any woman—in his arms?

Heat spread through her body. She could feel it on her face, though she didn't think she was blushing. This tarnished Angel was indeed dangerous to her senses!

He continued, "Am I going to have your mentor breathing down my back? For keeping you from finding that scarf?" he added in a tone that said they both knew she hadn't been sent to fetch any silly scarf.

So much for thinking he was on the path of seduction. This was going to be an interrogation! Very well, she was up to the task.

"No, I lied to her. I said you were short, fat, and dressed in a monk's robe."

She realized immediately that she shouldn't have said that. It was a confession that Sarah had wanted information about him. It was also a confession that she'd lied to him.

But his brow went up in surprise, then he grinned. "Did you really tell her that?"

Since the only thing about him that seemed dangerous at

the moment was his seductive charm, she saw no reason to lie. "She makes it sound as if you and your friend are criminals. I prefer to judge for myself."

"I suppose you gave her my name though?"

"When I didn't believe the name you gave me?"

"I appreciate your honesty, but *what* do you find wrong with my name?"

She didn't answer immediately. She asked instead, "Do you realize the sensation you cause?"

She'd noticed how every eye in the room came back to him repeatedly. Men and women alike seemed fascinated by him. Some people were even tripping on the dance floor because they couldn't take their eyes off him.

"Do you really think I could miss it?" he replied drily.

"Well, you see my point then?"

"What point? Am I a mind reader now? Usually a point is made before it's mentioned."

He was being facetious. Mere banter? She wasn't adept at that, not in the least. The socializing she and her mother had done over the years hadn't been with young men, and certainly not with prime seducers like her tarnished Angel. Besides, she preferred real conversation, not pointless repartee that went nowhere and revealed nothing.

But she shrugged, allowing him *his* point. "I would have thought you'd have a more exotic name, one that matched the way you look."

He chuckled. "So now I'm exotic? I suppose that's better than a hungry wolf."

She grinned as well. Maybe she could get used to bantering after all. He certainly made an excellent teacher.

"It's all a matter of perception, isn't it?" she quipped.

"Well, damn me, I find I must agree. You should stop surprising me. I'm becoming quite intrigued."

She finally blushed. He finally lost his jocular air and added, "Do you have anything else to impart about tonight's debacle, before I proceed to my dire warnings?"

She was given pause, not over the "warnings," which she didn't take seriously, but over the question. Was all the banter intended to lower her guard so she'd answer him by rote? She recalled what Evelyn had said about distracting someone prior to asking a serious question. How very spylike.

But Rebecca had already concluded that Sarah Wheeler was the one in the wrong tonight. The lady had even admitted the task had been personal in nature, rather than political, so Rebecca saw no reason not to let him know how serious Sarah was about pursuing whatever it was she was after.

"She thought I should woo you into removing the mask I told her you were wearing."

She'd managed to surprise him yet again, to go by his expression and the lambent look that entered his eyes. "That sounds entirely too interesting. You have my rapt attention. Woo away."

"I wouldn't know how," she admitted, lowering her head and suddenly feeling embarrassed.

"Move a little closer, m'dear. I promise I'll get the message."

Her head shot back up. "You're entirely too bold, Rupert St. John."

"I know. It's wonderful, isn't it?"

She rolled her eyes. She supposed this Rupert was much preferable to the dangerous one she'd briefly met in Nigel's room. But which was the real St. John?

Aware that the dance was going to end at any moment, she said, "Now it's my turn. Are you really a spy?"

"Good God, do you really think I'd say so if I was?" he replied, aghast, which was obviously feigned.

"I thought we were being honest."

"No, you are being honest. I'm merely being delighted by it."

Rebecca gritted her teeth. He'd finally managed to provoke her ire with his evasiveness. She stopped dancing, pulled away from his hands, and walked away.

But she heard him call softly after her, "Wait! You haven't heard my dire warnings!"

"Keep them," she shot back. "I wouldn't believe them anyway."

Did he have to laugh at that?

Chapter Eleven

A LATE NIGHT FOR YOU?" Nigel asked the following day as he nudged Rupert awake.

Rupert sat up instantly, furious with himself for having fallen asleep in Nigel's room, of all places, while he waited for the older man to show up. He couldn't bear the thought of Nigel standing there looking down at him while he slept, and he had no doubt Nigel had done so.

The trouble was, Rupert's current task of investigating the new ladies of the court was simply too easy, which led to boredom. No danger was involved. While he was quite skilled for the task due to his reputation with women, he preferred assignments that involved some risk. He never fell asleep in the middle of the day when he was armed and ready for anything.

"No," Rupert answered, and relaxed slightly. "Sitting around here half the day waiting for you put me to sleep. I suppose I could report in the middle of the night, when I can be assured you're here."

"So I must lose sleep when you could have simply left me a note?"

"There's the rub, notes in your room are no longer an option," Rupert replied, unable to stifle a yawn. He shook his head sharply to finish waking up. "Leaving your room open to give me access to it is no longer advisable either, not unless you're in it."

"I've been busy, or I would have already had that extra key made for you."

"Then keep the door locked until you do. Or do you like having your room searched?"

The only reason Nigel left his door unlocked was so Rupert wouldn't have to wait for him in the hall where someone might see him. He didn't even want the palace servants to link them together in any way. He was fanatic about it. And now Rupert was going to have to confess that someone had indeed found him there.

But Nigel was amused, drawing the wrong conclusion. "Oh, my, you actually searched my room?"

"Don't be absurd. And we might as well get the business at hand out of the way first because the Marly chit is expecting to meet me in the Royal Garden this afternoon."

Nigel nodded. "I have another appointment myself, so we can keep this as brief as you like. You've drawn new conclusions, I take it?"

"Yes, two of the new maids are firmly in Sarah's camp, the same two who fancy themselves in love with me," Rupert complained with a roll of his eyes.

"Already?"

"You expected it to happen?"

"Don't be obtuse," Nigel said. "You know very well women fall in love with you daily. Of course I expected it."

Rupert laughed. "A bit of an exaggeration there, eh, old man?"

"Hardly. Even Sarah Wheeler was in love with you earlier in the year when you turned your charms on her, one of those amazing feats you're capable of." Nigel chuckled. "I never understood how you accomplished that, when you said you didn't have to make love to her."

"I convinced her that I found her fascinating in other ways. It doesn't always have to be about physical attraction, you know. I worked towards friendship. It went on long enough that she began to look beyond that, is all." Rupert didn't add that Nigel should know better than anyone else how the stronger emotions could unexpectedly overwhelm a person, which had happened with Sarah. "Friends lower their guard in the same way lovers do, you know."

"What about the third young lady?"

"Constance? She resents Sarah's 'errands' and has taken a firm dislike to the lady because of it. A prime candidate for you, one would think."

"There's a but in that?"

"Yes, I wouldn't advise taking advantage of her resentment and trying to lure her to your camp. She doesn't strike me as very competent. Not much up here"—Rupert tapped his head—"if you know what I mean. As for Lady Elizabeth, I searched her room before she was assigned a new roommate. There was nothing in it but a god-awful lot of clothes. I suppose I'll have to do so again, now that her roommate has arrived. She complained to me about it last night."

"The newest maid of honor to arrive?"

"That would be my guess and I believe I've even met her. But one last thing about Elizabeth. You'll need to keep an eye on her after I'm gone. She confessed that she caused a scandal to get rid of her last roommate, *just* so I could visit her in her room if I so chose. She might have resorted to drastic measures because of her infatuation with me, but my instincts tell me that she is completely lacking in morals. So she could bring the same underhanded means to her work for Sarah."

"Duly noted. And the last maid you met? Why aren't you sure she is Elizabeth's new roommate?"

Rupert wasn't about to admit that the chit had distracted him to such an extent that he'd neglected to confirm her name. He couldn't imagine who else she could be, though, when she'd been invited to the ball last night and admitted her association with Sarah. Despite the costume she'd worn, he had no doubt that she was a lady born.

"I'm ninety-nine percent sure that she is Rebecca Marshall, who was expected to arrive yesterday. There were too many other things to find out about her, considering how I met her."

Nigel raised a curious brow. "Why does that sound ominous?"

"Because I met her right here as she was rifling through your belongings at Sarah's behest."

Nigel's scowl was immediate. "So Sarah is turning the ladies under her charge into thieves now? How dare she!"

"Careful, the rivalry is showing." Rupert grinned.

"The devil it is," Nigel snorted. "We're talking about stealing. Sarah really is going too far now."

Rupert had to laugh at the spymaster's hypocrisy. "You've turned me into a thief on more'n one occasion, so wherein lies the difference?"

"What you steal is a matter of royal security and you are your own man. You also replace anything you take after examining it. Besides, you could refuse any job you are uncomfortable with. But these are innocent young ladies who don't know any better."

"Would the girl have found any sensitive information?"

"Not unless you dropped off something prior to her arrival, otherwise I never leave anything of import in here even when the room *is* locked."

"I was dropping off the briefing I just gave you, in written form, but after finding the chit in your room, I decided to deliver an oral report. This maid of honor is smart, and adept, which is why I hesitate to make any rash judgments about her. Her excuse came out too readily and was quite believable, the way she presented it."

Nigel sighed. "So she has linked you to me. So much for you being the least bit useful on this assignment, now that Sarah has been informed. She's likely to want revenge now, too, when she realizes that your friendship with her was a farce to gather information."

Rupert steepled his hands and tapped his fingers on his chin a few times before he replied thoughtfully, "I'm not so sure that Sarah was told."

"Are you joking?"

"No, Rebecca Marshall and I had an unusual conversation later at the ball. She claims she gave Sarah a false description of me and didn't volunteer my name. As you know, I'm too well known to try to use a false name unless I'm in another country."

"What reason did she give for protecting you?"

Rupert was given pause and even frowned. "Protecting me?"

"Because if you believe her, that's exactly what she did in keeping your identity from Sarah."

"Ah, but there's the rub, whether to believe her. Keep in mind, I said she's smart. She's too quick with her replies not to have more intelligence than I'm used to encountering in these young chits. She's even quicker to dissemble emotions as needed. She's actually prime material for you to mold, if she was telling the truth."

"What do your instincts tell you?"

"For once, I haven't a clue," Rupert admitted with a sigh. "But I'm not going to discount that she could have a knack for lying and artifice. She surprised me a number of times. I'm not used to that happening."

"Then what was her reason for not serving you up to Sarah on a platter?"

"*If* she really didn't. She claimed that Sarah had made it sound like you and I are criminals, but she'd prefer to judge for herself."

"Meaning she might try to investigate you on her own?" Nigel guessed.

Rupert chuckled. "That actually sounds like fun."

Nigel rolled his eyes. "You're too used to deceit of that sort, since you practice it yourself. Let's remember who she is and that she only just arrived at the palace. Sarah's prime tactic with these young ladies is to make them think everything she does is for the good of the country. Did you assure her that that isn't the case?"

"Our conversation didn't progress that far."

"Well, if that's all last night was about, the chit's thinking she was doing something noble, then there was no harm done. But before we let this matter rest," Nigel continued, "confirm her identity. Second, make sure she's finished with Sarah's intrigues. Third, draw some damn conclusions about Rebecca Marshall. You know the rules. Whatever it takes is acceptable. If she is as adept at deceit as you say she could be, I don't want her in the palace. I'll see that she's dismissed myself."

Rupert had stiffened at the phrase *whatever it takes.* It brought back his worst memory. Nigel had stressed that phrase when he had enlisted Rupert to aid his country. Rupert had been chosen because the French official they needed information from was a bloody deviant. The man had no interest in women, or men, but he was overly fond of pretty young boys. And he was at the root of a plot to kill the French king and have it blamed on King George IV, which could ultimately have led to war.

Rupert had been torn by one of the most horrible conflicts anyone, let alone a boy of fourteen, could face, to sacrifice himself or turn his back on his country. He couldn't agree to do what was being asked of him, yet he would be a coward in his own mind if he refused.

But he'd figured out how to accomplish the goal without making the sacrifice when he recalled one of his mother's parlor maids. Earlier that year, the wench had had him all but slobbering at her feet, she had aroused his lust to such a dangerous level. So much teasing, always teasing, but never delivering. Fourteen years of age and new to amour, Rupert had been ready to promise her the world, he'd been so inflamed.

The wench never did deliver. Neither did Rupert during that assignment. He'd used the maid's tactics to get the job done. He'd promised, but never delivered.

Angry with himself for allowing that memory to surface, he stood up to leave. Nigel might have been hard-nosed in telling him to do "whatever it takes," but Rupert rarely had to resort to that in his work for Nigel. He could use his nobility to his advantage as well as his reputation as a skirt-chaser, as his uncle the Duke of Norford had fondly termed his adoration of women. If a woman expected him to seduce her, well, by all means . . .

Nigel should have figured out by now that Rupert would do things his own way, not Nigel's way. Keeping his anger from showing, Rupert looked directly at the older man and said, "I understand that country comes first. I've always understood that. But country can be served without giving up every sense of decency. It's called finding the balance you can stomach. It's called using your head to find a solution you can live with, instead of the first obvious solution. I'll find out if the lady fed me a pack of lies, but I'll do it my way."

"I don't know why I continue to use you," Nigel said petulantly. "You never do as you're told."

"Ah, but I get the job done anyway, don't I?" Rupert chuckled on his way out the door.

Chapter Twelve

REBECCA TOSSED AND TURNED all night because she couldn't stop thinking about The Angel. She was so restless that Elizabeth had snarled at her, "Be still!" long after they had both gone to bed.

Rebecca knew she ought to find out if Rupert St. John was The Angel's real name. She ought to find out what he was doing in Nigel's room. The same thing she'd been doing? Or just visiting a friend? And who was this man Nigel whom Lady Sarah seemed to be spying on?

There was no chance of sleeping late as she would have liked to do after such a restless night, not with Flora due to arrive early. But then Elizabeth also made an uncommon amount of noise, which Rebecca suspected was intended to wake her. Her roommate's disposition had not improved one jot. In fact, it had deteriorated. Elizabeth mumbled a lot, slammed wardrobe doors, left her clothes lying on the floor, and even pushed her way past Rebecca as they maneuvered in their tiny room.

The first thing Flora did when she arrived was to kick those clothes out of the way, which amused Rebecca, but amazingly drew no reaction from Elizabeth. But then yesterday Flora had made it clear to Elizabeth that she wasn't Elizabeth's personal maid simply because she fixed her hair. Thanks to Flora's efforts, Elizabeth's coiffure was much more becoming to her. So while the lady pretty much snapped everything she had to say to Rebecca, once Flora was in the room with them, she held her tongue.

Rebecca hoped to get answers to her questions if she lasted the entire day. Did Sarah need a reason to have her dismissed? If so, Rebecca could probably stop worrying about it. She was sure Sarah wouldn't want what had occurred last night to come to light. And Rebecca had told Sarah that she wouldn't do anything again that she felt was morally wrong.

An hour later when she arrived at the duchess's quarters, Rebecca considered it a stroke of luck to find Evelyn alone there. She was sure Evelyn could answer some of her questions because the younger girl had been at the palace longer than she had. She grabbed one of the embroidery squares before she sat down next to Evelyn and, after a few words of greeting, asked her, "Do you know who Nigel is?"

"Nigel Jennings?"

Rebecca hadn't heard the man's last name, but she said, "Yes." How many men with that name could be in the palace?

"I've heard he's one of the illegitimate royals, even though he doesn't use the surname FitzClarence as most of them do. Old King William had so many bastards with that actress mistress of his, who can keep count? I haven't met him, so I wouldn't know him if I saw him." Then Evelyn leaned closer to Rebecca and whispered, "I once heard Lady Sarah attach a profane word to his name. I gather she doesn't like him."

Rebecca blinked. "Why not?"

Evelyn shrugged. "Hearing this and that and putting it all together, my guess is that she competes with him to get the queen the best gossip."

Rebecca was incredulous. Sarah had put her in a sordid situation last night simply because she was on a quest for gossip? "But didn't you tell me Sarah's errands involved palace intrigue?" Rebecca reminded the girl. "How does gossip relate to that?"

"It's all one and the same, isn't it? Secrets, if exposed, can become fodder for gossip and scandal. And who is more interested in nipping scandals in the bud than the queen?"

Rebecca simply couldn't believe that gossip was all that Sarah was after. She turned her attention to some stitching, letting a few minutes pass before remarking nonchalantly, "I noticed Elizabeth with a young man last night, an extraordinarily handsome fellow. He quite reminded me of an angel—in appearance."

Evelyn giggled. "Funny you should say that. They call him the Saint, at least I've heard other ladies call him that. As a joke, of course, because he's anything but saintly. It's merely a play on his name, Rupert St. John."

Rebecca knew she should stop right there. She had confirmation of his name. He hadn't lied about it. But she had a thousand questions about him, so she couldn't resist a few more.

"Don't be coy," Evelyn scolded lightly. "I saw you dancing with him. So did Elizabeth. Goodness, you should have seen how jealous she looked! But she's so silly to think she has a chance with him when he delights in spreading himself around. By the by, those are his words."

Ah, a reference to his skirt-chasing! "So he flirts with every-one—equally?"

"Oh, my, yes, even me."

"He's the fellow you were supposed to distract with kiss-ing?" Rebecca guessed.

Evelyn grinned. "You're too perceptive by half, Becky! Yes, Sarah wanted to know if his interest in Elizabeth was serious, since he's often been seen in her company lately. But I don't know why Sarah didn't just ask him herself. I gather they are friends."

Good God, he was friends with Sarah?! No wonder he knew in which wing of the palace she lived.

"And when you asked him if he was courting Elizabeth, he mentioned preferring to spread himself around?" Rebecca queried.

"Yes. He made it sound like he was joking, but considering he is known for doing exactly that with the ladies, I didn't doubt the truth of it. My own hopes were dashed. By all ac-counts, he's never serious about anything, let alone one particu-lar woman. So let me do my good deed for the day with this warning. It's all right that you find him fascinating. We all do. You'd be lying if you claimed you weren't attracted to him, a man as divinely handsome as he is. Just don't make the mistake Elizabeth did and put any stock in his flirtations."

"Duly noted." Rebecca grinned.

"He can be wickedly bold," Evelyn added in a disapproving whisper. Her blush suggested she'd been a target of that wicked-ness. "Try not to be too shocked."

"As you were?"

Evelyn sighed forlornly. "He treats all women alike, scullery maid or lady. I suppose that's how rakes are, but I had *no* train-ing in how to deal with improper gentlemen."

Neither had Rebecca. Surely Rupert St. John didn't treat all women with such risqué boldness as Evelyn was implying. Yet Rebecca recalled he'd treated her the same way last night, when he'd put his hands on her breasts. She blushed at the memory.

"I'm sorry," Evelyn said, assuming she'd embarrassed Rebecca. "I didn't mean to go on about the man's wickedness. Hopefully he won't be a guest in the palace for very long. He is *such* a distraction."

Chapter Thirteen

ELIZABETH ARRIVED AT THE duchess's chambers looking fetching in a pale green gown and the new style of coiffure Flora had fashioned for her. Rebecca wondered if Flora had suggested the pale green gown. The maid had an eye for color, and had removed all the gray and silver garments from Rebecca's wardrobe when she'd first joined the household, claiming they didn't suit her a'tall. Elizabeth must have been pleased with her appearance because she was smiling to herself, lost in her thoughts, until she noticed who was in the room and reverted to a scowl.

Lady Sarah entered the room from the other entrance at nearly the same time. She nodded to Elizabeth with a friendly morning greeting, then summoned Evelyn to follow her out of the room. But not before she glanced at Rebecca and turned up her nose with a humph!

Well, that was encouraging, Rebecca thought. A smirk would have implied that Sarah had arranged for Rebecca's dismissal. That humph! suggested Sarah was afraid other incidents would come to light if she tried it. Rebecca hoped Sarah would refrain from trying to send her on any more errands. While it had seemed exciting when Rebecca thought she would be serving her country heroically, she knew better now.

Unfortunately, Evelyn's departure left her alone with her scowling roommate. Now she understood why Flora's intervention hadn't made Elizabeth behave in a more cordial manner to Rebecca. Jealousy. Over a man Rebecca hadn't even spoken to prior to yesterday. Elizabeth's jealousy over his dancing with Rebecca revealed the girl's insecurity about her supposed relationship with him. But hadn't Elizabeth heard about his skirt-chasing? Surely she didn't take his flirting seriously?

Rebecca knew she wouldn't do anything that silly herself, now that she'd seen and heard evidence of how he "spread himself around."

"If you get bored with that embroidery," Elizabeth said, "I would suggest a swim in the garden lake. Maybe you'll do me a favor and drown."

Rebecca actually laughed, since Elizabeth made that remark with an insincere smile, but a smile nonetheless. "I probably would drown since there are no ponds or lakes near home where I could learn to swim."

"Do I look like I care?" Elizabeth snapped, apparently annoyed that she hadn't elicited an angry reaction from Rebecca. "Just don't do it this afternoon, when I have a rendezvous in the park."

With *him*, no doubt, Rebecca thought, but didn't ask.

"I've tried to be nice to you," Rebecca said, "though I'm beginning to wonder why I should bother. I didn't forbid Flora from assisting you with your hair. It was her idea, you know, though she did say that if it didn't bring about some peace between us, she would withdraw the offer. You might want to keep that in mind because you do look much prettier due to Flora's efforts."

Rebecca was amused to see how a blush from a compliment could mix with indignation on Elizabeth's face. But her roommate stopped making nasty remarks and went over to the corner to pluck gratingly on one of the instruments there. Apparently, playing the violin was not one of Elizabeth's accomplishments either, Rebecca thought with a cringe.

Constance arrived when luncheon was served. Rebecca enjoyed a lively conversation with her about last night's ball and the formal dinner with the duchess that they were expected to attend tonight, in honor of the duchess's childhood friend who was visiting her.

Elizabeth didn't join them at the table. She pulled out her pocket watch at least a half dozen times during the hour. Apparently, she was too nervous to eat, anticipating her rendezvous. Her excitement became almost palpable, which was understandable, considering whom she was meeting. Rebecca decided that a walk in the Royal Garden behind the palace might provide a nice break that afternoon. Not to spy on the lovers, she assured herself. Merely to partake of the beauty in such a grand garden before the weather turned too cold to enjoy any sort of walk there.

Chapter Fourteen

REBECCA COULDN'T BELIEVE SHE was snooping again, and this time of her own volition. How had she stooped so low? She simply couldn't stay away from an opportunity to see Rupert again, even if from afar. She had to determine if he was more interested in Elizabeth than he'd let on to Evelyn. It was no concern of hers, of course, it would just be . . . disappointing if he was interested in her.

As soon as Elizabeth flew out of the duchess's chambers, Rebecca followed her, telling Constance that she needed to step out to speak to her maid about readying one of her evening gowns for tonight. But it wasn't easy to keep up with Elizabeth. The girl was nearly running. By the time the lady finally stopped at a small gazebo, forcing Rebecca to duck out of sight, they were deep into the garden.

Rebecca quickly moved away from Elizabeth, going off to the side where no one would detect her. It wouldn't do to have Rupert come up behind her on his way to the rendezvous. Rebecca could see that Elizabeth was keeping an eye on the path they had come down as she now paced inside the gazebo, repeatedly glancing at her pocket watch. Was Elizabeth early, or was Rupert St. John late? Either way, Rebecca needed to find a spot she could settle into and appear to just be enjoying the peaceful beauty of the garden.

A bench beneath a large silver-maple tree and facing the lake was ideal for her purpose. The wide tree trunk completely blocked her from Elizabeth's view. Sitting on the edge of the bench, she didn't have to lean too far to glance around the tree for quick peeks. But Elizabeth was still alone. No doubt, the girl's excitement and impatience to see Rupert had brought her to their meeting place too early.

While Rebecca waited for Rupert to appear, she took note of her surroundings. The parklike garden was reputed to be the largest private garden in London. Landscaped by Capability Brown and rich in maple, cypress, and chestnut trees, the current garden had actually been redesigned by the famous John Nash back when the Prince Regent had spent a huge amount of money remodeling the palace. Even the great lake had been created several decades ago and was supplied with water from The Serpentine lake in nearby Hyde Park.

Only a few fall colors were showing up so far, but they were lovely mixed in with all the green. She would have to come out here again when the garden was ablaze with autumn foliage and she wasn't so distracted. The day was a little chillier than usual, but there had been no time to grab a coat. She might even catch cold if Rupert didn't hurry up and appear.

Half an hour passed. Elizabeth wasn't giving up, but Rebecca was about to. She stood up to leave, but caught sight of movement from the corner of her eye and sat back down abruptly. It was him. Some hedges, tree trunks, and statues might be in the way, but not for long with that long stride of his that made his black hair sway just above his wide shoulders.

He was dressed today in a tan coat, white shirt, and black pants. When he got to within ten feet of the gazebo, Elizabeth flew out of it and into his arms. Rebecca blushed and started to turn away, but Rupert didn't return the embrace. He was setting Elizabeth back from him.

Hardly loverlike, Rebecca thought as she leaned back against the tree trunk again. Not very Rupert-like either, when by all accounts his roguish ways should have had him taking quick advantage of Elizabeth's ardor. But he did show up. Elizabeth's rendezvous *had* been with him. However, another quick peek showed they were merely talking now. They hadn't even entered the gazebo, which probably had a bench they could sit on. Also, wouldn't lovers take advantage of the privacy the gazebo could provide?

Well, what the devil? Was this grand romance only in Lady Elizabeth's imagination? But then Rebecca chided herself. Rupert had only just arrived. Their rendezvous was hardly over yet.

She took another peek. They were still just talking. No, actually Elizabeth looked upset now. Why hadn't Rebecca thought to hide close enough to hear what they were saying?! Rupert put his hand on her shoulder, but it seemed as if he was merely consoling the girl. About what?

"So you have a knack for snooping, do you?"

Rebecca swung around with a startled gasp. Standing next to her was a rather short, middle-aged man in an ordinary broadcloth suit. *How* had he managed to walk up to her without her hearing him? He wasn't a gardener, obviously. Perhaps he was one of the visiting dignitaries.

However, his remark about her "knack for snooping" implied he knew she had done this kind of thing before, and aside from The Angel, only one man might know about her "errand" for Lady Sarah.

"Nigel Jennings?" she guessed.

He lifted a brow. "We've met? No, I'd remember a pretty lady like you. So you're as smart as he claims then, eh?"

She found herself blushing furiously that she'd guessed accurately. How utterly mortifying and unfair that Rupert had told him that she'd been discovered in his room! She hadn't revealed Rupert's identity to Sarah, so why couldn't he have done the same for her?

But Nigel wasn't interested in lecturing her about that outrageous deed. "Be at ease," he told her. "Since you know who I am, shall we confirm that you're the newest maid of honor, Rebecca Marshall?"

She would have liked to deny it. A maid of honor snooping, lying, caught attempting to steal! The queen might even hear of it.

He waited for her reluctant nod before he continued, "I was led to believe that you did me a service."

Incredulous that he could view her misdeeds in that light, she asked, "How so?"

"In keeping St. John's identity to yourself. Lady Sarah doesn't know of our association and we would prefer to keep it that way."

"I see," she replied carefully. "And that association would be—?"

He chuckled. "None of your business, young lady. But I applaud your attempt to gather information. I can only hope it is for yourself and not for Sarah."

Rebecca sighed. "I thank you for not mentioning what occurred, but I really *must* apologize. I was told next to nothing about the task Sarah sent me on, merely that it was important. So considering how highly improper it was, I convinced myself that it was of great importance to the crown, that you were a suspected traitor of some sort."

"Let me guess," he said in an amused tone. "You were being heroic?"

She nodded. "But I began to feel terrible about entering your room and looking around it. And the bad feeling remained, so I lied to Sarah about who entered your room, and—"

"He had that much effect on you?" Nigel cut in curiously.

"Effect?" She frowned, then chuckled as she guessed, "Oh, you mean because of his angelic looks? No, it was because I know he's the nephew of my neighbor the Duke of Norford. To think that any relative of the duke would do something treasonous is ludicrous."

"Quite so. Pray tell me, are you here at Sarah's behest today, or merely satisfying your own curiosity?"

Rebecca managed not to blush this time, but she didn't want to own up to her interest in Rupert, either. Fortunately, she came up with a ready excuse, "Yes, I'm keeping an eye on my roommate who's been rather difficult. I merely wanted to find out why Elizabeth was so excited earlier today. You needn't worry that I will be doing any more snooping for Lady Sarah. I warned her last night not to use me like that again, that I would take the matter to a higher authority if necessary."

"That's too bad."

She blinked. "It is?"

"Yes, I was hoping an intelligent girl like you could keep me apprised of anything unusual that Sarah might ask of you again."

He said it so nonchalantly, yet she didn't doubt he was serious. "You mean spy for you?"

"No, my dear. I'm not talking about eavesdropping or peeking through keyholes—or sneaking into places where you don't belong. Nothing of the sort. But if Sarah asks you to do anything else out of the ordinary, I would appreciate a warning beforehand. Just a note, sent by your maid or a trusted servant, to myself or even to Rupert, since business sometimes takes me away from the palace and he usually knows where I can be found." Nigel paused and shook his head. "Sarah's antics are usually harmless, but she really has no interest in helping the crown, you know. I had her investigated so I'm sure of that. Everything she does here at court is to better her own position. And the day may come when she goes too far."

Had he not mentioned Rupert, Rebecca would probably have flatly refused and walked away, no further discussion. But she was intrigued by the idea that she might occasionally have a *reason* to seek Rupert out. It really was too bad that, as Nigel had put it, she had pretty much burned her bridges with Sarah.

"She's not going to ask me to undertake another of her 'errands.' The way she greeted me this morning pretty much confirms that she now views me as a useless member of the duchess's entourage."

"Useless to her," Nigel agreed, giving her a thoughtful look. "But you might still be of use to me."

Rebecca stiffened slightly, annoyed that he thought he could use her for his own purposes. How was that any different from how Sarah had treated her?

"How so?" she asked carefully.

"Don't look so suspicious, m'dear. I merely meant you will still be in a position to hear and see what is going on and make your own judgments in that regard."

He was quite right. Evelyn seemed not to object to Sarah's little errands and didn't mind talking about them either. But Rebecca wasn't about to commit to anything of this unusual nature again, especially when she knew so little about Nigel Jennings.

"We can agree that Sarah works for her own interests, not those of the crown," she said, then bluntly added, "Whom do *you* work for?"

He seemed surprised, but that could easily have been feigned. "Do you really need to ask?"

She nodded. "You are cloaked in secrecy. No one I questioned could provide anything but rumors about you. So I would need—"

He appeared amused again and cut in, "You were checking up on me?"

"Of course. I was hoping to find out that you are here at the queen's behest. I wanted to have more ammunition for my mother to take to the prime minister, should Sarah try to dismiss me over this matter. The Marshalls do not go down without a fight. If Sarah wants a battle, she will find that she is the one who will likely get dismissed."

She had no doubt that Nigel's surprise was genuine now. "You have floored me, indeed you have. And damn me if that doesn't sound promising and worth more thought. But in the meantime—"

"There is no meantime. Don't ask me simply to believe everything you say. That sort of naïveté is what led me astray last night. Before I can do what you ask, even as minor as it seems,

I would need proof that what you do, your intelligence gathering, is in the service of queen."

"You mean proof other than that I am her illegitimate uncle?"

Rebecca raised a doubtful brow. "Taking advantage of a rumor? Fie on you, sir. No, I don't think that will do."

He laughed. "Touché. Would you believe Rupert if he vouched for me?"

Rebecca knew she would enjoy *any* contact with Rupert, for whatever reason, but she shook her head. "While I am certain that he could not be involved in anything that might harm our country, I can't discount that you may have him fooled about your own motives."

Nigel smiled, even though she suspected her stubbornness was beginning to annoy him. "Well said. Your determination not to be gullible again I find even more useful. We will not ask the queen to interrupt her busy schedule to have a word with you, especially now that she is being hounded to rest more often during these last few months of her pregnancy. But her husband occasionally has time on his hands. Will you believe Prince Albert if he corroborates that I am a loyal servant to our country?"

Oh, my, the prince? "Indeed," she said immediately.

"Very well, I will mention it to him before I leave for my appointment today. Give him a day or two to find an opportunity to approach you in a manner that will not draw undue notice. Once you are satisfied that my devotion to the crown is without question, you can keep me apprised of anything untoward you may learn of at court."

She was amused that he was taking it for granted that she *would* assist him as long as she received proof that he was a legitimate royal supporter. Not that she minded. He wasn't asking her to do anything she was morally opposed to, as Sarah had done.

"Just don't shove any notes under my door if I'm not there. Hand deliver only. People seem to be breaking into my room lately," Nigel said drily. "In fact, Rupert could serve as a go-between for us, since the ladies do visit him at all hours of the day—and night—and this meeting I'm going to today may result in a sudden trip out of the country."

Rebecca blushed instantly at his remark about Rupert, but she tried to cover it up by asking, "A short trip?"

"It's often impossible to know how long I'll be away from the palace."

Preparing to leave, he glanced around the tree first. "They're gone," he said with a sigh. "I was hoping to catch Rupert alone here, and I really don't have time left to search him out." He pulled an envelope from his pocket. "I wanted to give this to our mutual friend. Perhaps you can deliver it for me, since you are likely to see Rupert socially before I will."

Rebecca chuckled as Nigel walked away. Did he really think she didn't realize that this was a test and he would no doubt ask Rupert if the seal had been broken prior to delivery? As if she cared what was in the missive. But Sarah would probably like to see it. That was the test. But then Mr. Nigel Jennings was a spy, she was sure of it, so, of course, he wouldn't trust everything she'd told him. He no doubt wanted proof of her honesty just as she wanted proof of his.

And then it struck her and she smiled. Nigel hadn't just handed her a test but also a reason to seek Rupert out.

Chapter Fifteen

REBECCA LEFT THE DUCHESS's chambers early to prepare for the formal dinner that night. She didn't notice Rupert leaning against the wall in the hallway outside the chambers since she set off at a brisk pace in the opposite direction. Her mood had soured. She told herself that she was returning to her room early so Flora wouldn't feel rushed in getting both her and her roommate ready for tonight, but in fact she just wanted to know if her roommate had made an appearance there.

When Elizabeth hadn't returned to the duchess's chambers, Rebecca guessed that she and Rupert had gone off someplace where they could really be alone—to make love. The thought had put her in a bad mood for the rest of the afternoon, and she *really* wanted to be proven wrong, to find that Elizabeth had spent time alone in their room instead.

"You're a hard lady to find."

She nearly tripped on her skirt when she heard Rupert's voice and she turned to see him walking alongside her. She really had to stop having this immediate bedazzled response to him. It wasn't quite so bad or so long now, but still, she'd seen and spoken to him enough now that it shouldn't be happening at all to her anymore.

As for his sudden appearance, she wondered if he had been waiting outside the duchess's chambers for Elizabeth to come out. Perhaps he hadn't spent the entire afternoon with her after all. Rebecca's mood brightened a little with that thought.

But she didn't believe for a minute that he'd been looking for her. "Nonsense," she said as she continued down the hall. "If you wanted to speak to me, you could have knocked on the door."

"No, that wasn't an option."

"Why not?"

"For the same reason we couldn't have had more'n one dance last night. Tongues will wag."

She doubted that was his reason. When he spread his charm around so much, *who* could keep track? It was more likely that he just didn't want Elizabeth to know about it. That might even have been why the girl had appeared upset with him earlier. She might have been upbraiding him for dancing with Rebecca last night.

She rounded the corner at the end of the hall. He hadn't gone away, was still keeping pace with her. She was starting to feel a little too thrilled by the encounter.

To temper her excitement, she said, "Is this to be another interrogation, then? Or those dire warnings you mentioned?"

Instead of answering, Rupert abruptly stepped in front of her. She wasn't quick enough to stop in time and slammed into him, which he must have known would happen. Surprised, she nonetheless pushed away from him. He didn't try to stop her, he just extended an arm to make sure she moved to the side of the hall, with her back against the wall. He put his hand against the wall to block her from the direction in which she'd been heading.

The position so reminded her of how she'd seen him standing with Elizabeth last night that she guessed it was a practice of his, to trap women this way for his flirtations. Most were probably delighted. She wasn't.

"You do have a lot to say about nothing, don't you?" He said it huskily and so close to her face that she could feel his warm breath on her cheek. Standing *this* close to him set her pulses racing! Maybe she didn't mind the position after all.

"Cat got your tongue now, Becca?"

Rebecca realized he was probably also used to women being so surprised by his boldness that they didn't react to it as quickly and indignantly as they should. She was no exception. It didn't occur to her to wonder how he had come by her name when she hadn't given it to him.

All she could think to say was "Don't call me that."

"Then you aren't Rebecca Marshall?"

"Yes, but we haven't known each other long enough for you to be so familiar with me."

He laughed. "Putting on indignant airs again, luv? I thought we established that I never do anything in a proper fashion. It's *such* a waste of time, you know."

"No, it isn't," she disagreed hotly. "It's how things are done!"

"If you want to be boring. Can you really imagine me being boring?"

Proper etiquette certainly wouldn't make him boring! Did he not realize how exciting his mere presence could be? But she grasped the point he was making. He must think women expected him to be outrageous because of his reputation. Or maybe he just liked to shock women because it gave him an advantage. And maybe she ought to stop making excuses for him. A rogue was a rogue, and in his case his behavior might simply come naturally to him.

But she did allow herself to admit, "I don't think it's possible for you to be boring even if you tried."

To go by the slight widening of his pale blue eyes, she'd surprised him. Why? Oh, good grief, had she just complimented him? She blushed and hoped he wouldn't notice with his tall form casting a shadow over her.

"Are we having this conversation for a reason?" she asked, hoping to change the subject.

He grinned. "Aren't you the impatient one. You don't want to simply bask in my undivided attention? I'm wounded, 'deed I am."

She rolled her eyes. Excellent! At least she'd recovered from that compliment after all.

He leaned a little closer to add, "D'you really think I need a reason to talk to a beautiful woman? Let me assure you, I don't. But *as* it happens, it occurred to me that you might need my help."

The mention of help made her immediately think of Nigel Jennings and what he had asked of her. Had Rupert seen him and been told he was to be their go-between? And that letter she was to give him!

"Yes," she said, "and I have—"

"If you're going to continue to do Sarah's bidding," he cut in, "you may need to woo some lucky chap to distraction as you implied the other night. Having admitted you don't know how, I have decided to offer my help in that regard."

With his gaze turning decidedly sensual, she would have had to be stupid not to realize he was about to kiss her. Paralyzed with anticipation, she couldn't have said anything at that point even if she wanted to. Nor did she realize that she was missing the opportunity he'd just given her to deny any further involvement with Sarah.

And he did kiss her, oblivious of servants appearing and disappearing in the distance. Rebecca certainly didn't notice them. His kiss was so much more than she was prepared for, in touch, in taste, in the wonder of discovery. She wasn't overwhelmed—well, she was—but it seemed more that she just willingly succumbed to the gentle pressure of his mouth as his lips caressed and aroused all of her senses.

She really wished her mother had explained as much about kissing as she had about lovemaking when they had finally discussed that enlightening subject last year. Was her entire body supposed to be as involved as Rupert was involving it as he pulled her so closely into his arms? Was she supposed to feel so much of him and be so thrilled by it?

"What a delightful surprise you are," he said as he slowly rubbed his cheek against hers in such an intimate manner that it felt like a caress.

Rebecca would have preferred not to come out of that sensual daze. But it was necessary in order to concentrate on what he was saying. She didn't want to miss a single word.

But his remark smacked of insincerity, and she didn't doubt dozens of women had heard the exact same thing from him.

"You don't need to use your typical blandishments on me, you know."

"Typical, eh?" He leaned back with a grin. "It's true that I find most women delightful, but believe me, luv, I rarely am surprised by them. You, on the other hand, have been one surprise after another."

She couldn't imagine how she'd surprised him, but that remark did sound more sincere. Yet she felt he was still just telling her what he thought she wanted to hear. Were the lines ingrained in him after so many years of skirt-chasing? Or were they a deliberate, contrived part of his seduction routines? She wanted to believe him, however, and that didn't surprise *her* at all.

Her attraction to him was over-the-top, far, far beyond anything she'd experienced before. Not that she had much experience of men to draw on. But for Rupert to feel even a small measure of delight about her would thrill her beyond measure.

"Now that your mind is clear again, shall we continue the lesson?"

Lesson? Oh, good God, she'd completely forgotten that this started with his offer of help. She began to blush for having read so much more into that remarkable kiss than he had intended. But he hadn't finished.

"You need to be able to do this without any emotion involved," he warned her. "So I think we should practice till you get it right and it becomes so mundane that you are in complete control."

Was that how it was for him? Just a mundane prelude to his lovemaking? She was hurt *and* insulted, a powerful combination that she was quick to react to. "Do us both a favor and don't do *me* any more favors. You, sir, are a rogue!" she snapped, and marched off.

"You don't think that puts me off, do you?" he called after her with a chuckle.

She didn't answer, but she did swing around to toss Nigel's

envelope at him. Too bad it didn't hit him and only fell at his feet.

He just laughed all the more as he picked up the note without even glancing at it and stuffed it in his pocket. "If you wanted to hit me, luv, a slap would have been more in line, don't you think? Though you might have been amazed by my reaction to it."

She wasn't going to ask. She didn't need to. He was looking entirely too wicked as he said it. And he had resorted to a raised voice to be heard. She wasn't about to raise hers. Turning about, she was determined to get far away from him.

She thought she heard him say "Coward," but she just wasn't sure.

Chapter Sixteen

ALTHOUGH THE DUCHESS OF KENT was still quite a vigorous woman in her midfifties, her dinner party turned out to be boring, with only her ladies and maidens invited to celebrate the arrival of the duchess's dear old friend. Even though most of the women present were English-born, the duchess didn't even attempt to converse in English. Which resulted in the ladies chatting about nothing of particular interest in a desultory fashion so the duchess wouldn't feel excluded. Rebecca found her mind wandering to the events of the day.

Elizabeth had apparently returned to their room much earlier than Rebecca and had dressed for the duchess's dinner. When Rebecca arrived, the girl did no more than shove past her through the doorway, giving her a fulminating glare as she departed. Rebecca had sighed. Was she going to have to start guarding her back or worry about sleeping in the same bed with the lady? Whatever had started it, Elizabeth's animosity toward Rebecca had intensified with the added jealousy over Rupert.

After Elizabeth left the room, Rebecca turned to Flora and asked, "When did she return here?"

"Less than an hour after the gentleman showed up."

"Someone came here looking for one of us?"

"No, he came to the wrong room, even managed to say so as he backed out of the door in embarrassment. His surprise was understandable, though. He probably didn't expect to find a maid in the room sitting here doing nothing."

"Are you scolding me? You don't have to stay in the room all day, you know. I doubt I'll require a change of clothes for luncheons. Mornings and evenings should be all that's necessary."

"I know my duty, and it's to be available *if* I'm needed, not sitting in my flat doing nothing either. Besides, the man's showing up definitely livened up the day. Never seen a fellow so far beyond handsome. I sat here with my mouth hanging open even after he'd closed the door."

Rebecca was bemused. Only one man she knew fit that description. "Long black hair, very pale blue eyes?"

Flora gasped. "You actually know him?"

"It sounds like it. Rupert St. John, a nephew of our most illustrious neighbor, the duke. Rupert and Elizabeth are— friendly."

"No," Flora replied doubtfully.

"Yes. And they did have a meeting today, so he must have been mistaken about the location if he came here first."

That would explain why it had seemed as if he'd been late to his meeting with Elizabeth. Could he really have made such an unlikely mistake? But she was forgetting that he probably had many assignations every day!

"It must not have gone well," Flora speculated.

"What?"

"Their meeting today. The lady was crying when she came back to the room. I could tell. Not one word did she say. She just sat at the vanity all glassy-eyed."

Now that was a surprise, but Elizabeth might not have been upset about Rupert. Rebecca recalled that earlier when she'd seen them by the gazebo, she'd thought Elizabeth had been sharing some bad news with him.

"Well, that's their business, not ours," Rebecca said. "And she wasn't so upset that she couldn't spare me another of her nasty looks on the way out the door. As for your boredom, I was thinking of going into the city tomorrow to buy some books—it gets quite boring in the duchess's chambers, too, you know. We can get some for you, too, or maybe some knitting materials, or whatever you'd prefer to pass the time with."

Flora had stopped complaining after that as she was looking forward to the shopping trip. Rebecca was, too. The only excitement in the palace so far had been one costume ball that she hadn't even been prepared for, and the antics of Nigel and Sarah. Of course, she'd only been here a few days. But for the "grandest come-out of them all," she couldn't help but notice the definite dearth of young men to meet. Just Rupert. He was more than enough in her opinion, but still . . .

She wondered if her mother realized that most of the men who would be invited to the palace entertainments would be middle-aged officials and even older dignitaries. The prime bachelors of the realm probably didn't even come to London during the off-season. Would she have to wait until the winter Season to meet them? Would they even be invited to the palace?

Rebecca left the duchess's dinner early, dissatisfied with her thoughts and her mood. These up-and-down swings of emotion weren't the least bit normal for her. She hadn't experienced them until she'd met Rupert—and it was confirmed without a doubt what a rake he was. He generated too much excitement. If she hadn't discovered how exciting life could be, she was sure she wouldn't be so unhappy with her lot when he wasn't around.

Rebecca didn't escape the dinner unnoticed. Well, she might have, but she couldn't very well ignore Constance, who was standing in the hallway crying. Two upset maids of honor in the same day? Rupert wasn't spreading himself around *this* much, was he? But that was an unfair thought. She was just still highly annoyed with him for trying to add her to his tally and so blatantly, with his ridiculous offer of help.

Evelyn had confided to Rebecca that Constance had waited three years for her fiancé to return to the country, only to have him end their engagement when he finally came home. If Constance appeared bitter occasionally, it was because of that. It was also responsible for her being quite the pessimist now.

"Constance?" Rebecca began.

She saw that she had startled the older girl, who quickly wiped her cheeks with the back of her sleeve. "It's nothing."

"Then would you like to talk about—nothing?"

Constance didn't see any humor in the question. "No—yes. Sarah has asked me to go into the city again in the morning. And I haven't heard back from my mother yet about whether I should be doing this sort of thing. I was so afraid the first time. I've never been anywhere by myself before, you know."

"Take a footman with you this time."

"I thought of that and mentioned to Sarah that I would do so, but she said no. She doesn't want anyone to see me delivering the note to Lord Alberton on Wigmore Street."

Rebecca managed not to laugh at how Constance had just

told her what Sarah had wanted to keep secret. In her mind, she could hear Sarah complaining, "I should have done it myself!"

"Isn't that just a few blocks north of New Bond?" Rebecca asked, recalling her mother had a friend who lived there.

"I have no idea."

"I'm pretty sure it is. And as it happens, I am going into the city tomorrow myself to Bond Street to shop. Would you like to join me?"

"We could stop by Wigmore Street?"

"Certainly. And don't hesitate to ask me to accompany you to the city, should the need arise again. I really won't mind getting out of the palace now and then, and my maid will go with us."

Good God, Rebecca thought, had she just *that* easily decided to become Nigel Jennings's spy?

Chapter Seventeen

RUPERT WAS QUITE PLEASED that Rebecca Marshall was his final assignment in his investigation of the new ladies at court. That she presented a challenge made the task much more enjoyable. The other maidens had all been too easy to figure out. Evelyn, a charming chit, found a titillating excitement in Sarah's intrigues. Constance, a timid mouse, would do exactly as she'd been told even though she had quickly come to despise Sarah. She might still be a wild card if she was pushed too far and decided exposing Sarah's machinations would be her only out.

Elizabeth, while a tad amusing in how easy she was to read and play, had become a nuisance, so it had been necessary yesterday to put an end to what she had assumed was a dalliance. She was simply too pushy about wanting to get him into her bed. He knew her kind. If he had accepted her invitation, in a month she'd be telling him they *had* to get married. He wasn't about to fall into that trap.

He supposed he ought to warn Rebecca to be on her guard.

Simply because he had danced with Rebecca at the masque ball, Elizabeth had refused to believe that Rebecca wasn't responsible for his putting an end to his meetings with her. And he knew Elizabeth had a vicious streak; she had bragged to him about provoking her last roommate into causing a scandal that had led to her quick departure from the court.

Getting *to* Rebecca seemed to be his only problem now. She seemed to be keeping herself barricaded in the duchess's chambers all morning. It had been much easier to encounter the other maids of honor as they'd been sneaking down to the kitchens, walking in the garden, enjoying the art gallery, and running Sarah's numerous errands. Waiting outside the door to the duchess's chambers as he'd done yesterday just wasn't a good idea. He'd been lucky that Rebecca had been the first to come out, but that wasn't likely to happen again. She might be wary of departing alone if she expected him to be waiting for her. He definitely didn't regret his attempt to intercept her though. He had even gone to bed last night smiling, remembering their encounter.

She'd melted in his arms. No surprise there. But he'd found himself enjoying that kiss too much. When his desire had abruptly shown up in full bloom, he'd been incredulous. He had been working her! He never lost control like that with a mark. So the advice he'd given her about not letting her emotions get involved while kissing had been as much a reminder for himself as it had been the perfect excuse to allow her to continue. Yet she'd taken it as an insult instead. How amusing! She had probably wished she'd had something more damaging to throw at him other than that envelope containing a piece of paper hawking a new tailor on Bond Street. And what the deuce had she been doing with *that* in her pocket?

He found himself eager to see her again and annoyed that it wouldn't be soon enough to suit him. But the evening entertainments seemed to be the only opportunities he would have to see her. And his impatience was entirely personal, since Nigel wasn't around to prod him to finish his task anytime soon. Nigel had had to make an unexpected trip to the Netherlands. One of his contacts had warned that war was being discussed again in secret there.

The Netherlands had never been happy with Belgium asserting its independence, and this wouldn't be the first time that country had invaded Belgium to get it back. The treaty that had finally been signed was only a few years old! And Queen Victoria was personally involved since her dear uncle Leopold had become the king of Belgium when it gained its independence. Nigel was hoping to calm the waters, as it were, before the treaty was broken. That could take weeks, even months.

With Nigel gone from the palace and Rebecca no doubt beyond his reach for most of the day, Rupert had decided to visit his family that morning. Since they lived with him, they noticed his absences, and his mother wouldn't refrain from demanding to know where he'd been. But it would be easy enough to allude to being holed up with his current mistress. It was the one excuse his mother never doubted.

But as Rupert exited the palace, he wasn't expecting to see Rebecca climbing into a coach. He didn't hail her. He ran to the stables, where earlier he'd sent a footman to get his horse. He was in luck. Mounted, he had no trouble catching up with Rebecca's rented hack and following it at a discreet distance. When it turned onto Old Bond Street, he grinned. No errand for Sarah after all. A shopping trip, obviously, and a lady shopping could take all day! What a prime opportunity to spend the day with her.

He no sooner concluded that than he castigated himself for being as bad as Rebecca at making assumptions. Her coach didn't stop as he'd thought it would. It continued past Old Bond Street onto New Bond Street and kept going past the shops. A few blocks later it turned onto Wigmore, a street he'd never had occasion to navigate before. Halfway down the street, the coach stopped at the curb.

Rupert moved his horse behind a carriage parked at the curb a few houses away; not as much concealment as he would have liked, but unless Rebecca actually glanced in his direction, she wouldn't notice him. He wasn't going to guess what she was doing here given the assortment of reasons that had nothing to do with Sarah. Her family might even own the town house she'd stopped in front of. Or she could merely be visiting a friend.

But Rebecca wasn't alone as he'd thought, and she wasn't the one who got out of the coach and knocked on the door. It was the maid he'd found in her and Elizabeth's room yesterday when he'd kept Elizabeth waiting in the garden so he could search their room. He hadn't been all that disappointed that he'd lost the chance for a thorough search because he hadn't really expected to find anything revealing.

He still wasn't jumping to conclusions. The maid could have been sent to the door merely to find out if a friend was at home.

A servant answered the knock. Rebecca's maid wasn't invited to wait inside the house. A few minutes later, the owner of the house came to the door, Rebecca's maid handed him a note, then the maid hurried back to the coach—and Rupert felt as if he'd been poleaxed.

He knew the man, not personally, but he knew him by sight, the same Lord Alberton that Nigel had investigated last year after young Edward Oxford had tried to assassinate the queen while she was riding in her carriage in London. The boy had been tried for high treason, but had been acquitted on the grounds of insanity. Nigel, with his suspicious nature, hadn't let it go as the act of a deranged young man, and suspecting a plot, he had investigated everyone known to be acquainted with Oxford.

One of those acquaintances was Lord Alberton, who had been seen talking to the boy. While Alberton claimed he'd been castigating Oxford because the boy had tried to block his coach, Nigel reserved his doubts, mainly because Alberton was a Tory who had disagreed with some of the queen's policies at the time. For six months Nigel had carried out that investigation fanatically. Rupert hadn't been asked to help, which he was glad of. He didn't favor hard work going nowhere, which is where that investigation had gone.

But just because Nigel had found no proof of a conspiracy against the queen, it didn't mean there hadn't been one, just that it hadn't been discovered. Apparently, Sarah was involved with the man if she was having notes delivered to him. It could be no more than one of her power schemes. Or not. Alberton was a bachelor, after all, so Sarah's interest could even be of a romantic nature. But regardless, Nigel would have to be warned as soon as he returned to the palace.

Damn, Rupert didn't doubt now where Rebecca's loyalties lay. She was obviously firmly in Sarah Wheeler's camp after all. He was surprised to find himself disappointed with that conclusion. Very disappointed.

Chapter Eighteen

THE BOOKSTORE WAS QUAINT and cluttered with a wide variety of volumes. Nonetheless, Rebecca made her selections quickly. Flora, who didn't read as fast as Rebecca, was taking longer in deciding which book to buy. But they were in no hurry. It wasn't yet eleven o'clock. They could be back at the palace in time for lunch. Or perhaps they could find a restaurant nearby instead. That might be fun. At least it would guarantee no dour Elizabeth being present to spoil one's appetite.

Constance wasn't interested in books and had accepted a cup of tea from the shop's owner, a friendly older chap who had coaxed the timid girl into a lively discussion about the palace when she had mentioned they were maids of honor there.

Not wanting tea herself, Rebecca moved on to their next stop, the yardage store across the street. This much larger establishment was filled with all sorts of materials for clothing, and a small section of yarns. No sooner did Rebecca open the door and hear the bell above it tinkling than she was pushed farther inside.

With an indignant gasp at such rudeness, she swung around to see Rupert's engaging grin. She certainly hadn't expected to see him on Bond Street. That bubbly excitement his presence generated came instantly to the fore. But at least she wasn't utterly bedazzled this time. It was getting easier and easier to look at him and not lose all of her thoughts.

Still, it took her a moment to notice that he was wearing a satin, burgundy coat with his black pants. The white undershirt was normal, the pants were normal, the lack of a fancy cravat was normal, and the boots were normal, but that coat stood out like a sore thumb at this time of day. She was too flustered to mention that, though.

"Fancy finding you here," he said jauntily.

Nothing about it was fanciful, and she suspected he might have followed her. Why else would he be there?

"You've taken up knitting, have you?" she countered as she walked to the yarn section of the shop.

"No, I've taken up finding you alone. Nice of you to accommodate me."

His answer pleased her more than she could say, but she warned him, "I'm not alone."

"For the moment you are."

She'd stopped in front of a table that was tightly packed with spools of brightly colored yarn. He leaned in close behind her to point at a pink bundle of wool yarn. "That one would suit you."

Rebecca barely heard him. All she could do was feel him pressed against her back and try to deal with the new excitement that caused. The clerk across the room smiled at them. Apparently, having determined they were a couple because they had come in together, the clerk considered it normal for them to be standing so close to one another while examining the goods.

Rebecca used that excuse herself for not moving away from Rupert. It was naughty of her. She knew she should have pushed him away immediately. But she simply didn't want to break the intimate contact, not quite yet.

"You have exciting eyes, Becca. Too dark to read, which cloaks you in mystery. Pink would offset that, don't you think?"

How was she supposed to think a'tall?! Her pulse was racing out of control. She could even feel him pushing himself against her hips!

"If we really were alone right now, I think I'd have to lift your skirt."

Whispered in his low, masculine voice near her ear, the outrageous remark made her draw in her breath so sharply she almost choked. It completely saved her and brought her to her senses. He'd stepped back as she coughed. She swung around, glaring at him, and was met with a cheeky grin.

"Will you throw yarn at me if I kiss you again?" he asked with a twinkle in his pale blue eyes.

She understood now. He was teasing her. Just teasing, although in the most outrageous, seductive way. But at least he hadn't *really* been attempting to seduce her in a yardage shop. His approach, however, was still highly inappropriate. Was he so used to sophisticated women that he'd forgotten how to deal with young innocents who were likely to swoon over such indecent advances? Or did he just not care to make the distinction between sophisticates and innocents? More likely the latter. He was a skirt-chasing rogue, after all. But entirely without scruples? She'd have to reserve judgment on that.

In response to his question, she warned, "There will not be

any more kissing. You were an excellent teacher. I graduated from your class."

He laughed, though he was quick to rejoin, "How disappointing. You were supposed to claim ineptitude and ask for further guidance. I don't offer a position in my arms to just anyone, you know."

She tsked. "Of course you do. *That* is a well-known fact."

She turned back to the yarn table. Staring directly at him was detrimental to clear thought. And he still hadn't said what he was doing here.

"So you were just passing by and noticed me?" she asked casually.

He moved to stand next to her. Too close. Their arms were touching now. He pretended to be examining the yarns for a moment.

Then he said in the same casual tone she had just used, "No, actually, I had to pick up a package down the street. This is my second stop for the day. I was winding my way back from the first when I saw your coach on Wigmore Street and we ended up going in the same direction, so I knew you were around here somewhere. You were visiting friends on Wigmore?"

She knew immediately that nothing in that question was casual. Good grief, he was interrogating her again! She could have sworn they had moved beyond that. Annoyed, she decided not to satisfy his curiosity, particularly since Nigel must have told Rupert that he'd asked for her cooperation. Nigel obviously trusted her enough to do so, but Rupert didn't?

"I don't have friends in London, but my maid does" was all she said.

It wasn't exactly a lie as she suspected his excuse for seeing her coach on Wigmore Street had been. One of Flora's old loves had moved to London, so she *could* have visited someone in town. Would Rupert now claim that the house they had stopped at belonged to a lord who certainly wouldn't be one of Flora's more intimate friends?

Before he could, she posed a question of her own. "What do you do for Nigel Jennings?"

There was no pause at all. "I'm his tailor," he answered immediately.

"You're nothing of the sort."

Rupert gave her a cheeky grin. "Meant to say, he's my tailor."

She cast him a thoughtful look. "Interesting that you would lie about it."

"You call joking lying?"

"Evasion is a form of deceit."

"Interesting that you would see it that way." He gave her back her own words. She almost laughed.

While he hadn't answered her question any more truthfully than she had answered his, he surprised her by not pursuing his inquiry about why she had been on Wigmore Street. Fingering a white silk yarn within his reach, he said, "I'll take a vest in this if you run out of ideas to ply your needle toward."

She couldn't help but grin. "Will you indeed? But that implies a gift—"

He cut in, "Consider it an early Christmas present," and actually sounded serious.

"I don't make presents for mere acquaintances."

"We're more'n that."

"We aren't."

"Of course we are, or do you make a habit of kissing mere acquaintances?"

She huffed. "You did the kissing, not I."

He was grinning again. "You fully participated, Becca. Don't even try to deny it."

He'd finally managed to make her blush. She wondered if her cheeks were as bright a color as his coat. Reminded of his unusual apparel, she asked, "Do they actually have costume balls this early in the day in London?"

"Not to my knowledge. Why do you ask?"

She glanced pointedly at the sleeve of his brightly colored coat. "A satin coat during the day? Surely you do know that this dandyish fashion went out of style decades ago?"

He chuckled at her dry tone. "Don't use the plural, m'dear. It hasn't been *that* long. But this coat is for my mother."

"Your mother wears men's coats?"

"You know, I think she would if she thought she could do it without provoking endless commentary from the ton, but no. I wear it for my mother because it irritates her more than you can imagine to see me wearing satin."

She raised a brow at him. "And that pleases you?"

"Absolutely."

He said it with a grin, so she didn't know if he was teasing again. But she realized he must be returning home if he was going to see his mother today. For good? She was terribly disappointed. She wouldn't see him anymore at the palace? She couldn't imagine how boring that would be. And how was he supposed to be her go-between with Nigel if he wasn't nearby at the palace? Surely they didn't expect her to find him at his home in London.

She wouldn't usually be so bold, but she had to know, "Will I see you later at the palace?"

"Your eagerness overwhelms me." A corner of his mouth tipped up in a roguish smile.

She sputtered over the conclusion he'd drawn, "I was merely curious, since it sounded like you were going home. But perhaps I drew the wrong conclusion and you aren't actually a guest at the palace?"

"For the moment I am, but I don't need to be a guest to visit—and you miss me already, don't you? Admit it." She rolled her eyes over his continued teasing, but then he assured her in a husky tone, "You know very well you and I aren't done, Becca."

He was no doubt referring to his being the go-between for her and Nigel, yet she got flustered anyway, reading more into those words than he'd intended.

Chapter Nineteen

THE ST. JOHNS HAD always been city dwellers, according to their long, distinguished family history. The original home of the St. Johns had been in Old London town, though it had been destroyed centuries ago by a city fire. Much later, they had acquired some property in the country outside of Plymouth that was associated with the Rochwood title that had been earned centuries ago, but it had never been developed. As London had expanded, the St. Johns had moved with it.

The title Marquis of Rochwood had come to Rupert when his father, Paul St. John, had died. The current house, a mansion on Arlington Street built by Rupert's paternal grandfather, was his as well. Although its façade resembled those of most other London town houses, inside it was extravagantly appointed.

Just north of the palace and a block east of Green Park, Arlington was no longer the quiet street it used to be. When Victoria made Buckingham her official royal residence, the first monarch to do so, all of the streets near the palace, including the narrow ones, became secondary routes for city dwellers who wished to avoid the major thoroughfares congested with deliveries to the palace. Residential or commercial construction was usually going on, too, since the entire area had become much more valuable with the royal residence nearby.

Rupert arrived home at noon, in good time to share luncheon with his mother and his two brothers if they were all available. He always missed his family when he was away too long on one of his missions, and in particular his mother's amusing attempts to whip him into shape, since she went about it so dramatically. He'd only been gone a few days this time, but his mother would still no doubt complain.

His brother Avery, who was two years younger than Rupert, didn't actually live with them anymore. As soon as he'd reached his majority, he'd talked Rupert into turning over to him one of the St. Johns' many rental properties in town, for him to transform into a bachelor flat where he could keep a mistress if he was lucky enough to find one. Rupert would have been a hypocrite to deny him that luxury, though he had never wished for such a place for himself. Too many bedroom doors were opened for him, so he didn't really need a home away from home.

Their mother had objected, of course, to Avery's moving to his own flat. She'd thought she'd succeeded with her two younger sons where she'd failed with Rupert, and with Avery's departure it appeared as if he were following in Rupert's footsteps. But the lad just didn't have Rupert's knack for debauchery. He'd been appalled when he'd lost his first fifty pounds at the card tables, so he certainly hadn't taken to gambling. He did have a passion for horse racing, though not riding them, and he frequently entered his stallion at the races and won. And Avery kept his amorous pursuits within social dictates. He'd had a few mistresses, but those affairs had never lasted long and he hadn't moved any of the ladies into his flat. He kept that part of his life quite private, as most young lords of the realm did.

Because Avery lived fairly close to Arlington Street, he still tried to take lunch and dinner with his family, though it appeared he wasn't doing so today. Rupert's youngest brother, Owen, though, at sixteen, was still being tutored at home, so he was usually around. Julie St. John's youngest and quite unexpected last child, Owen, had been born the same year that Julie became a widow, so Owen had never had a chance to know their father as Rupert and Avery did. Already as tall as his two older brothers, Owen was the quiet one, and the most studious of the three.

No sooner did Rupert appear in the doorway to the dining room than his mother demanded, "Where have you been?"

Rupert took the seat across from her, gave Owen a conspiratorial grin to warn that the battle was about to begin, and replied, "Do you really need to ask?"

"Who is she?" Julie shot back.

"No one you would know."

She humphed, "When are you going to stop dallying and find me a daughter-in-law?"

He laughed. "What was my last answer to that question? Do you really think it's changed, when I'm having far too much fun debauching my way through the ton and leading vestal virgins astray?"

"Virgins!" she gasped.

Damn, he'd even surprised himself. Where the deuce had that remark come from? As if he didn't know. He'd entered the room with Rebecca still on his mind.

But before he could backtrack on that comment, Julie warned, "If you weren't joking, I'd shoot you m'self before some outraged father does."

His mother merely complained—a lot—about his sordid skirt-chasing career, as she saw it. She wasn't really *that* impatient for him to marry and carry on the St. John line, any more than he was eager to do so. All in good time. He was only twenty-six after all, and she had two other sons who could carry on the line. So as long as he didn't go beyond the pale and add seducing innocents to his social misdeeds, she confined her disapproval to grumbling complaints.

Julie Locke St. John was still quite a striking woman in her midforties, but then all the Lockes had those remarkable good looks. Although Julie was blond with blue eyes like most of the Lockes, all three of her boys had taken after their father and had much paler blue eyes and black hair.

She was a proud woman, and stubborn. When her husband had died, she didn't run home to her family in Norford. She'd been determined to raise her children herself, without remarrying. She often claimed that she'd been lucky in her marriage to Paul St. John to have found a man she loved, and that sort of luck was too rare to encounter twice in a lifetime, so like her brother Preston, the Duke of Norford, who'd lost his wife, Julie didn't seek another spouse either.

But that had left her with a dilemma, three young sons, ages one, eight, and ten, with no male role model other than their tutors, which wouldn't do at all in her mind. This was one reason she often took her children to visit their uncle Preston.

To fill the role of *both* parents in her sons' lives, Julie had transformed herself. The change had occurred gradually, but Julie had turned into a male bully in skirts! While their father had never been gruff or bossy, this was Julie's interpretation of masculinity, and she mastered it quite well. While she provided her sons with love and emotional support, her tone and manner reflected how she thought a man would deal with his sons. Her style of child rearing was comical, but no one had the heart to point that out to her. She thought she'd done the right thing.

Rupert was more aware of this than anyone else, and he loved his mother all the more for it. She had made this huge sacrifice for him and his brothers. So he'd taken it upon himself to make sure that she never came to feel that she'd done it for naught. By being a rebellious rogue he gave her a purpose in life and would continue to do so as long as he could, because if she didn't have him to browbeat and try to whip into shape, he was sure she would flounder.

His brothers knew his outrageous behavior was a ruse on his part, which was why he'd box their ears himself if they ever tried to emulate him. Rupert found it rather easy never to do exactly as his mother wanted. She wanted him to wear his hair short, which is why he wore it long. She wanted him to dress discreetly, which is why he wore some pretty outlandish outfits—just for her. She'd like him to marry and settle down, but they both knew there was no real hurry for him to do that. She wanted him to stop flittering his life away on nothing but amusements. She knew absolutely nothing about his work for the crown. She didn't know, either, that he kept on top of their family's finances and wasn't just leaving to factors as she assumed.

One of his ancestors on his father's side had got into trade and other financial endeavors to recoup the family fortune that an earlier marquis had squandered. Future generations of St. Johns never talked about him, frowning on his sullying his hands in commerce, so no stories had been handed down about this enterprising great-great-grandfather of his. Rupert was even named after him, a name he'd always been proud to bear, which is why he'd been rather annoyed when Rebecca had made so much about the name not suiting him.

Rupert considered his relatives' scorn absurd. The man should have been dubbed a hero instead of thrown into the closet with the rest of the family's black sheep.

Rupert fit well in that closet himself, he'd thought on more than one occasion. And his mother thought so, too!

"Rest easy, Mother. I really was joking," he assured her now.

"In poor taste," she said with a scowl. "But I'd rather not shoot you, if you must know the truth."

"Glad to hear it! But you worry too much."

"As if you don't give me cause," she replied grouchily.

"Nonsense, I've only worked my way through half the women in London. Besides, I've heard there's a cure for the clap."

"There's no such thing!" she sputtered.

"No? You're certain? Gads, I may be devastated to discover you're right—one of these days."

Owen hooted with laughter. Julie gave her youngest a quelling look. Rupert waited until his mother looked at him again, then winked at her and grinned. So their lunch went, nothing out of the ordinary in this household.

Rupert was cheered by the meal. He loved teasing his mother in this fashion. As he had no need to remain at the palace any longer now that he'd drawn his conclusions, other than that he was enjoying his encounters with Rebecca, he assured his mother that he would be home again in a few days. Reporting his results to Nigel would have to wait until the older man returned from abroad.

Nigel would no doubt be disappointed that none of the new maids of honor were likely candidates for his camp, including Rebecca, but Nigel would make do as he always did. Rupert had concluded that Rebecca was the most dangerous of the lot, with her flawless lying. He'd given her the chance to come clean when he'd asked her what she'd been doing on Wigmore Street, but she'd evaded the opportunity. But as long as Rupert warned Nigel, he would have done his job.

He almost wished Nigel would ask him to investigate Rebecca further. She was the prettiest maid of the lot and the most intriguing, which was a tempting combination to play with.

Although she took on maidenly airs, Rupert was beginning to suspect she wasn't quite the innocent she ought to be. This had first occurred to him after he'd kissed her in the hallway. Even though she'd been outraged—or had pretended to be outraged after the act—she'd fully participated during the kiss, so much so that she'd aroused him much more than he'd seemed to arouse her! And earlier today at the yardage shop, she hadn't protested when he'd stood so close to her and pressed his body against hers in such a suggestive manner. She certainly didn't seem too innocent in that, had seemed to even like his bold advances.

Rebecca Marshall was turning out to be a little too tempting. Perhaps it was just as well that he'd drawn his conclusions and finished his investigation of her.

Chapter Twenty

Iʼve no doubt you will be asked to sing, once they find out what a splendid voice you have. Donʼt be shy. Itʼs a gift you have. Be proud to share it."

Rebecca really wished she hadnʼt remembered her motherʼs words when she and Constance returned to the duchessʼs chambers after their trip to the city, and Sarah immediately asked if either of them could sing something soothing. The duchess, apparently, had a headache and wanted soft music to help her through it. Evelyn was already playing the violin. Constance moved over to the harp to join in. Rebecca recognized the song and sang a few verses.

"That will do nicely!" Sarah had exclaimed, seeming genuinely pleased. "I will be sitting with her until she feels better, so I will let you know when to stop or if she falls asleep."

But Sarah didnʼt return to the room, and Rebecca ended up singing for the rest of the day, such a long time that her voice was now quite scratchy. Finally, one of the duchessʼs personal attendants came out to thank the maids for the entertainment and mentioned that the duchess had left her chambers over an hour ago to join the queen for dinner. The other girls laughed about Sarah's not having bothered to tell them sooner. Rebecca didn't think it was an oversight. Sarah was simply a vindictive witch.

A full orchestra was playing that evening and the maids and the ladies had been invited to enjoy the event. Rebecca had had quite enough music for one day, but she couldn't very well not attend, especially when the royal family might make an appearance and the prince could use that opportunity to speak with her about Nigel Jennings.

Which wasn't the case. A number of gentlemen had also been invited, and the dinner was formal with eight full courses that lasted for hours! But the royal family dined privately that night, close enough to hear the music, but still, just family. Nigel had said it might take a few days before the prince spoke to her, which had been fine at the time because she hadn't expected to come across information so soon that Nigel might be interested in. But now she did have intriguing information!

Although Rebecca had decided to help Nigel, she still wasn't going to tell him anything until the prince vouched for him. However, she felt she could trust Rupert in regard to matters of state. After all, his uncle was the Duke of Norford. At any rate, Rupert, who seemed to be a friend of Nigel's, would know whether the information she had was important and if it should be relayed to Nigel.

Rebecca knew she'd had her chance to ask Rupert what to do with the information this morning on Bond Street, but instead she'd taken offense at his not-so-subtle interrogation. She also had to admit she'd been thrown off-balance because of his well-practiced seductive charm. How foolish was that!? Now she'd have to find Rupert.

She looked around the grand dining room again. He wasn't at the dinnertime concert. Had he even returned to the palace yet from his visit home? Or had he changed his mind about returning at all? His being a guest "for the moment" as he'd said could end at *any* moment, she realized.

Now she was furious with herself for not taking care of business while she'd had the chance. She decided the whole matter could wait until the morning. It would have to. But what if it couldn't? What if Sarah was cooking up some kind of scheme with Lord Alberton that was imminent and there was no time to waste? With so many possibilities, Rebecca worked herself frantic during dinner, thinking about it all. So when she saw the footman John Keets standing at duty in the hallway as she walked back to her room after dinner, she fairly pounced on him.

He was happy to oblige her. No, the footman told her, the marquis had not yet vacated the palace. John prided himself on knowing such things. Yes, he could show her the way to Lord Rupert's room, but he was hesitant to do so, even mentioned it would be scandalous for her to be found there. Embarrassed over what he must be thinking of her for making such a request, she assured him she wasn't going to be there long. He pointed out that Rupert might not even be in his room this early of an evening. Early? It was ten o'clock! Or did John know something he'd rather not relate to an innocent maid of honor? Was Rupert dallying with some woman somewhere private? That would explain why he hadn't been at the dinner concert when he was still a guest in the palace.

She told John she would take her chances, that the matter was important. He warned her he wouldn't be able to stay to escort her back. Which wasn't necessary anyway. Rebecca no longer found the palace a maze of corridors. She could find her room with no difficulty now.

It was still a long walk to Rupert's room. The light coming from under the door indicated he was there, so she thanked John for his help and knocked as soon as he walked away. There was no answer. She knocked again, but still no answer. Had Rupert fallen asleep and left the lamp burning? She knocked several more times. Louder. Her impatience was kicking in. He had to be in there and was just sleeping. But she couldn't keep knocking so loudly. Someone else in one of the rooms nearby or a servant was going to hear her, and she didn't want to have to explain why she was knocking on a man's door this late at night. Darn! But at least she knew where to find him now.

She turned to leave, disappointed at not having been able to resolve what had been weighing on her mind tonight. She tried to ignore her disappointment at not seeing Rupert again, especially since he'd indicated he wouldn't be a guest in the palace much longer. But the importance of her mission still nagged at her, too. She supposed she could come back later tonight—no, that wasn't a good idea. Leaving her room once she was in it was going to be too difficult with a roommate in it. Slipping a note under Rupert's door wasn't a good idea either. Nigel had warned her not to leave notes.

She was halfway down the corridor when she did an about-face. She hadn't even tried his door! She should at least have done that. If he was such a sound sleeper that knocking at a door wouldn't wake him, surely she was justified in entering his room to wake him. It would only take a few moments for her to tell him about Lord Alberton, then she could go to bed with her mind relieved, the matter out of her hands and into his.

Back at the door to Rupert's room, Rebecca turned the knob. The door was open! She understood immediately why

Rupert wouldn't have heard her knock. His quarters were large! There was even a separate bedroom and no light coming from under that door. She set about knocking on this bedroom door, four times before she tried the latch and pushed the door open. It was dark inside, too dark to make out a bed, and she wasn't about to go in there. She fetched the single lamp that had been left burning and, bringing it to the opened door, was met with the same disappointment as before. The bed, and the room, were empty.

"Why am I not surprised?" came a sarcastic voice from behind her. "Let me guess, you're looking for a scarf again?"

Chapter Twenty-one

Rebecca swung around so fast, the lamp tilted in her hand. She immediately raised up her other hand to keep the glass from falling off its base, too flustered to realize she would have burned herself. But her hold on the lamp balanced out before she did and she quickly shoved it onto the table next to the door.

By the time her eyes lit on Rupert, he was already walking toward her, and he looked as daunting as he sounded. "I can explain," she quickly told him, completely unaware of how huskily seductive she sounded with her voice still so scratchy from her long performance that afternoon.

He seemed amused now. "When explanations aren't necessary? You've obviously recalled I warned you what would happen if I found you where you don't belong again. I don't doubt you were counting on it. So let me assure you that nothing else needs to be said, dear girl."

She had no idea what he was talking about. His remark that night in Nigel's room had been something about assumptions—

what was it? "If we meet again in a place where you aren't supposed to be, I will make assumptions more to *my* liking."

She drew in her breath sharply. Knowing what she did about him now, she realized he had meant something of a sexual nature. Was he serious? Did he really think she meant to encourage him by showing up here tonight?

She had to correct him. "You're going to laugh when you realize how far off—"

She didn't get a chance to finish. He cupped her face with both hands and drew her lips up to his. That quickly it happened again, those amazing new feelings welled up inside her at his very first touch. But, oh, God, that was nothing compared to what she felt as he tilted her head just so, to accommodate a kiss that was so deeply stirring.

It was no lesson this time. Rupert wasn't even trying to coax her along. His lack of restraint was passionate enough to burn. For a long moment she was completely overwhelmed and simply thrilled to be in his arms again.

"I never laugh during a seduction," he said as he wrapped an arm about her waist and pulled her up to him so tightly, her feet even left the floor. "Afterwards I'll laugh with you all you like, luv, but beforehand—I take this very seriously, you know."

What was he saying? How was she supposed to hear anything with her heart pounding so wildly. He took this seriously? How ridiculous. He did nothing of the sort! He was too carefree in chasing after every skirt around to take any of it the least bit seriously. And he was moving them! With his mouth pressed against hers again, he was slowly walking them farther into that darkened bedroom.

Desperately, before she lost all will to stop him, she tore

her mouth away from his. "You've got the wrong idea!" she gasped out.

"Oh, no, there's nothing wrong about this." He grinned down at her. "*This* couldn't be more right. Besides, disclaimers don't work a'tall when said in such a sexy timbre. Should I warn you just how highly arousing your voice is, Becca? But I suppose you already know that."

She had meant to sound urgent, not breathless. That darn singing all afternoon, who would have thought it would be her undoing. Her back and legs had come up against—not a wall, his bed! She put up both arms to stop him from closing the distance between them again, but there wasn't enough space to really make the effort, and her arms ended up around him instead of pushing him away.

"Wait," she cried before his lips slanted across hers again. She didn't think she'd be saying any more. She didn't think she'd want to. She just didn't think . . .

The wonder of a man's body pressed down on hers for the first time was a unique pleasure all its own, yet it wasn't just any male body. Perhaps that's what it was, him, *his* body, his weight, his mouth making such a passionate claim on hers that made her relinquish the last traces of resistance and let the pleasure take over.

Suddenly her senses seemed more alive. Or was it just her own desire that was guiding her? She was too innocent to be sure of anything regarding what was happening to her body, but there was no discounting how wonderful it all felt.

"I knew you were going to be dangerous, I just didn't realize to what extent," Rupert said as he rolled them to the side so he could get at the fastening at the back of her gown. "But I've never been more delighted to surrender."

He was surrendering? What did that mean!? He probably didn't know what he was saying. He ought to just shut up and she told him so.

"Why don't you shut up?"

He contradicted his own statement about laughter. He let out a burst of it now. "Yes, why don't I?"

The constraints of her yellow off-the-shoulder gown were gone. It felt loosely out of place now, but not for long. He nudged her to her back again and suddenly the gown was whisked off her completely. Another hard kiss from him and the embarrassment she'd started to feel faded away.

She still felt the chill in the room. It wasn't cold enough for a fire yet, but it wasn't warm enough to lie there in her under-clothes, either. But even that became barely noticeable when his hand settled over one of her breasts. He was unlacing her che-mise, but in such a slow manner. A touch here, the trace of his fingers along the upper edge of the thin chemise, a kiss on one shoulder to lower the strap there, a long caress to her waist to pull open the strings of her petticoat. All the while his mouth kept returning to hers. If she even thought about protesting this undressing, it was too fleeting to fully form in her mind.

But she did think that she'd like to see some of his skin as well. Fair was fair. Enough light was coming in through the open door to offer a clear view of him, now that her eyes had adjusted. But she couldn't mention this desire aloud.

She picked at the shoulder of his jacket instead, until he noticed and removed it. She then picked at the shoulder of his shirt. He got that message, too. Much, much better. But he didn't stop there, and she wasn't prepared to see *all* of him.

Her breath caught in her throat and stayed there. In no way could she think of him as an angel now, but the rogue was mag-nificent. No wonder his conquests were legion. Beautiful face *and* body, his black hair skimming his shoulders, he went so far beyond temptation in just looks alone, before he said a single sensual word, before he applied his skilled touch. It was incredible how enticing this man was. Was it even possible for a woman to resist this much visual stimulation?

He moved back in range of her hands so she didn't have to try. She couldn't get enough of touching him. The silky steel of his long arms, the thick, corded neck, the powerful, hard muscles on his back, the sinewy ripples on his chest under her fingertips. She didn't realize he was watching her in suspended wonder.

She couldn't imagine the myriad emotions that crossed her face as she touched him, or how her fascination aroused him. With a groan, he lowered his head and his mouth found hers again, his tongue thrusting inside for a long kiss before his tongue was suddenly laving at her breast, then surrounding it with his mouth, and she did some groaning of her own. He was like a furnace, his heat surrounding her.

Her petticoat was lifted out of the way, her drawers tossed aside, and suddenly she had more heat than she bargained for as his body covered hers and he thrust inside her. Her cry was caught by his mouth. She knew what it was, she had just forgotten to expect it, which was probably a good thing.

Without any anticipation to make her tense, the discomfort was minimal and too brief to interfere with all the other sensations inside her clamoring for notice. He might have gone dead still at her moment of pain, but he was still deep inside her and touching the most sensitive spot he could have found. He didn't have to move at all for her orgasm to suddenly burst around him, and yet another soft cry escaped her, this one of immense pleasure, which sent him over the edge as well.

It was the most sublime moment. Oh, how she wished it could have remained so.

Chapter Twenty-two

"YOU SAVED ME FROM embarrassment my first day here," Rebecca said shyly. "When you told me that there was no costume ball that night, after Elizabeth had convinced me there was. I never did thank you for that warning."

She was lying in Rupert's arms, a thin sheet draped over their entwined legs. He'd pulled her there and was holding her rather tightly, which was all right, since he was also caressing her most tenderly. She was loath to end the embrace, though she knew she would have to return to her room soon.

"That was you?" he replied. "Yes, of course it was. I should have remembered the hat."

That easily, the tenderness was gone. It was the hat. It must have reminded him of the second time he'd seen her wearing it—in Nigel's room. She'd thought they had moved beyond that, but apparently not.

He stopped caressing her. He didn't push her away, but she had a feeling he'd like to. She sighed to herself. She'd behaved outrageously. She'd let herself get completely carried away by a rogue's seduction. She should have known better than to put herself in a position where it could happen, but she didn't regret it. However, she would now leave, before he spoiled what had been for her the most wonderful experience of her life.

She sat up, started to move her legs off the bed, but couldn't. The bed was situated oddly in a corner of the room. She hadn't really noticed it before because she'd been facing Rupert. But now she encountered a solid wall blocking her exit, leaving her with the options of scooting slowly to the foot of the bed—or climbing over him. Had he purposely positioned his bed this way to make it more difficult for his conquests to leave him until he was ready to let them go?

Of course not. She was being silly. The bed had no doubt been in that position when he'd moved into the suite and he hadn't bothered to move it.

Having lost the warmth of his body, a sudden chill reminded her that she was half-naked. Her chemise was bunched about her waist. Feeling some belated embarrassment, she pulled up her chemise. Her petticoat was in the same position, and with the strings untied would slide off her hips the moment she stood up, so she corrected that, too, before she started to slide toward the foot of the bed. At least her coiffure was still mostly in place, thanks to Flora's skill. She only needed to adjust a few hairpins so that nothing would look amiss.

"Giving up such a prime advantage?" she heard him say behind her. "I'm disappointed, 'deed I am."

He didn't sound disappointed, he simply sounded sarcastic. Why was he being so unpleasant after what they had just shared? She should be the one outraged that he'd made love to her instead of listening to her. But how could she be angry over something so beautiful that she still felt the bubbly glow of it?

She said nothing until she was on her feet and had snatched up her dress from the floor and tossed it over her head. "I don't know what you mean, but then you say a lot of things that make no sense to me."

"You're mumbling."

She sighed and pulled the dress down off her face, then condensed her remark to "What advantage?" as she slipped her arms into the quarter-length sleeves.

"Your bare breasts of course, as if you don't know. A very pretty distraction."

He was just being his usual naughty self, she supposed. A little more tact would have been appreciated considering her highly emotional state. All positive emotions, but still, it wasn't every day one lost her virginity to a rogue . . . good God, this was what John Keets had tried to warn her about! If anyone found out, it wouldn't just result in her losing her post at court, it would be her ruination! But she quickly tamped down the fear that started to rise. No one was going to learn of this, and it could instead lead to something even more wonderful. . . .

She gave him a shy smile, but it was a mistake to look at him again. He was lying there facing her in sublime repose, raised up, leaning on one elbow, his wide, bare chest in full view, the thin sheet barely covering the hip his other arm rested on. The long, lean hardness of his body, the perfection of his face, his silky black hair in sexy disarray—my God, did he even know what a feast he was for her eyes?

"Stop it!" he snapped. "Ah, a better advantage after all, I see."

She blinked. Another ambiguous remark was just too much for her. "Why would I need an advantage?" she asked in genuine confusion.

"Don't you? Hmm, I suppose you could reason that such an extreme sacrifice for the cause was enough. I'm impressed at your sense of dedication. Tell me, is she getting desperate now that Nigel is out of the country? Can't figure out what he's up to?"

"She?"

"Don't play ignorant now, Becca. It doesn't become you. You know very well we're speaking of Sarah."

She drew in her breath sharply, beginning to understand. "*We* are doing nothing of the sort. You've made some ridiculous assumptions tonight. Is this yet another test? Or are you looking for a means to assuage your guilt?"

He snorted. "What guilt? I took what you offered. I gave you ample time to bolt, but you didn't. You don't think I would have tried to stop you, do you?"

"I had information for you," she said, her voice rising in indignation. "I couldn't leave before I gave it to you, and you *didn't* let me do that!"

"Did I tie a gag over your mouth?"

"You know very well you kept interrupting me!"

"Rubbish. You were sent to pry information out of me—by any means. Did you really think I'm so stupid that I wouldn't figure that out?"

His derisive tone hurt her the most and prompted her to reply, "No, you're just stupid! Nigel told me you could be trusted to pass information to. That's why—"

He cut in, "Nigel wouldn't have said anything of the sort. He knows very well I can't be trusted with any woman."

She could believe that! But his doubt made her so angry she just wanted to get out of there. Furiously, she glanced around the floor for her last article of clothing, which she refused to leave behind.

"Looking for these?" he smirked.

He was twirling her drawers about on his finger. She snatched them out of his hand with a gasp and turned around to put them on. Hearing his tsk behind her because she was denying him a view of her bare legs just infuriated her all the more. She was halfway to the door when she realized her dress wasn't fastened and she couldn't do it herself.

Gritting her teeth, she marched back and sat on the bed next to him.

"Fix it!" she said angrily.

He didn't play dumb. How could he when she was presenting him with her gaping dress?

He did sigh though as he sat up and said, "I suppose I must."

He ended up taking ten times as long to fasten the gown as he took to undo it. Deliberately, she didn't doubt. But when he finished, he planted a soft kiss on her bare shoulder. It was the last straw.

She shot to her feet and turned around. "How could you turn this into a battlefield? You know very well I've agreed to help Nigel. I gave you his note, didn't I?"

"What note?"

"After you kissed me in the hall." When he still looked confused, she shouted, "The one I threw at you!"

He didn't look confused now, in fact, he looked angry. "Nice try, luv, but that was nothing that Nigel would have sent to me."

"It wasn't? Well, whatever it was, *he* asked me to give it to you."

"That's about as far-fetched as it can get. I'm sure you can think of something more believable."

"Do you realize you're calling me a liar?"

"Was I not obvious enough for you to be sure? A liar, a thief, oh, and now I suppose I must add—tempting seductress. How the hell did you develop *that* trait and remain a virgin this long?"

Rebecca was incredulous. He thought all of that and still he'd made love to her? What a despicable rogue.

With a fulsome glare, she told him, "I'm going to say this only because I feel I must. Nigel assured me the prince would vouch for him. I had hoped that would happen tonight, but it didn't. And while I have already come across the sort of information Nigel asked for, I don't feel I can give it to him without hearing from the prince first. But you, for some stupid reason I can no longer fathom, I trusted you to at *least* not be a detriment to our country. And Nigel did say that you could be given whatever oddities I found out about. So I came here to let you decide if the information I have warrants immediate attention, or if it can merely be passed along to Nigel at your leisure."

"What information?"

"Lady Constance was sent to the city this morning to deliver a note for Sarah. The girl was so upset about having to venture into London alone again that she ignored Sarah's warning to keep the task secret and told me about it. If secrecy hadn't been stressed, I might not have thought it was anything out of the ordinary. But in either case, I couldn't let her go alone when she was so clearly upset about it, so I offered to accompany her. And that is what I was doing here tonight. I came to tell you about Lord Alberton and Sarah's interest in him."

Rupert didn't appear the least bit surprised or concerned, and the reason became clear when he said, "I'd think an intelligent young woman like you would surmise that I already knew this, since I saw your coach at his house. I must congratulate you, though. That really would have been a splendid excuse, all quite plausible, except for one thing. I'd already asked you what you were doing on Wigmore Street and you gave me quite a different answer. Or are you admitting that you lied to me this morning, when you told me that your maid was visiting a friend?"

"I merely said she had friends in town, not that she had any on that particular street."

"You implied it."

"You were interrogating me again!" Rebecca shot back. "I took offense."

"So let me get this straight. Not only did you lie instead of taking that perfect opportunity this morning to deliver your information, but you're also saying that you let a little indignation take precedence over something you now deem important enough to warrant your breaking into my room? Does that about sum it up, m'dear?"

"No, but this does. After the horrible treatment I've had at your hands, I'm done with this whole affair. I won't be helping anyone anymore, least of all someone who calls you a friend. *You* can tell Nigel that and lay the reason for it at your own door. Good night, Sir Rogue," she ended scathingly. "You've earned your title well."

She marched to his door, but at least she had the presence of mind to recall her earlier concern about a scandal and look both ways down the corridor to make sure it was empty before she hurried away. Rupert didn't try to stop her. In a daze of angry thoughts, she got lost after all and ended up running up a grand staircase and down the queen's corridor! Two royal attendants turned her back around right quickly, and she took better note of her directions after that until she was safely in her room. Elizabeth's snoring didn't even bother her. She was mired so deep in hurt and angry thoughts over what had happened tonight that the palace could have fallen down around her without her noticing.

Chapter Twenty-three

R EBECCA NEVER RECOVERED FROM her last encounter with
Rupert St. John. Weeks went by, but the hurt and anger she
had experienced that night remained with her. Nothing would
distract her from it for long.

A trip to the theater with the duchess and her full entourage
had been the most successful of the distractions. Rebecca had
actually enjoyed that. Finally meeting the young queen had
been exciting as well, but too brief. Few palace entertainments
took place now as Victoria got closer to her term. The few words
Prince Albert had spared for her offering his reassurance that
Nigel Jennings was a devoted servant of the crown had come too
late.

She no longer cared that Nigel's devotion to his queen and his
country was so long and so superlative that it was above reproach.
She was never again putting herself in a position to be called a liar
or labeled a thief. So she closed her eyes and her ears to whatever
Lady Sarah was up to. She simply didn't care anymore.

The boredom of her days left her too much time to think

about, and revile, *him*. Rebecca had walked away from Rupert a number of times at evening entertainments. Why couldn't she have done so that night, before it became so fateful?

She'd kept tears to herself, but her snappy temper she wasn't as successful at hiding had embarrassed her more than once. She no longer had any tolerance for Elizabeth's vile disposition, which had culminated in a veritable screaming match that Rebecca wasn't the least bit proud to have been a part of. But it did have one positive outcome. Elizabeth, in high dudgeon, had packed up her things and vacated the room. Too bad she hadn't left the palace as well.

Rebecca knew that she couldn't blame all of her emotional swings on Rupert—well, she could, but another situation had begun to take precedence, and this one she couldn't ignore.

She needed her mother's advice, but she'd have to go home for that. Actually, she needed her mother's advice about going home, too. What a mess she was in, needing advice to get advice! But having made the decision that she needed to go home, it still took her three days to broach the subject with her maid, the only person at the palace to whom she was close enough to discuss such a delicate matter.

She waited until she was sitting at her vanity and Flora stood behind her, running a comb through her hair. She kept her eyes off the mirror. Her cheeks were already growing warm, but then embarrassment was to be expected.

"There's something I'd like to talk to you about, Flora, if you wouldn't mind."

"The baby?"

Rebecca's eyes flew up to the mirror to see the maid with a raised brow looking directly at her in the glass. "How did you know?"

Flora snorted and went back to combing her hair. "Who takes care of you, eh? Did you think I wouldn't notice you've been filling the chamber pot with food you can't keep down? You might have asked me to arrive later of a morn so I wouldn't witness it, but the evidence was still there."

Rebecca's morning sickness was horrible. She'd even had to run out of the duchess's chambers several times now to find a quiet place to throw up her breakfast. But at least it was only a morning malady that didn't trouble her beyond those early hours.

"I thought the maids were taking care of that," she said with a wince.

Flora snorted again. "I've never let those uppity palace maids in here to clean *your* room. That's my job."

"If you had guessed, why didn't you say anything?"

"You weren't ready to discuss it." Flora shrugged. "Now you are."

Rebecca sighed. "I no longer have a choice. It's been five weeks since . . ."

She had a hard time saying she'd actually made love, but Flora understood and was already ahead of her. "And three weeks overdue for your monthlies," the maid said with a nod.

"Yes. So you see why I can't wait any longer. I could actually start showing in another month or so."

"Some women don't show at all until quite late in their pregnancy."

"And some don't have morning sickness either. I'm not that lucky. I was hoping you could help me decide what to do. Do I tell my mother and let her find a solution if there is one, or do I tell the baby's father?"

"Do you like him well enough to marry him? Never mind, you must to have let him—"

"Let's not discuss that, please. It was a foolish mistake. And, no, I'd rather not marry him. If I'm sure about anything, it's that he'd make a terrible husband. I don't know what sort of father he'd make though."

"Well, surely you realize that your mother's options for solutions will be very limited. She will either have to buy you a husband, which she can certainly afford to do, or find a good home for your baby."

"I can't bear the thought of giving my baby up to strangers," Rebecca said instantly.

"Then—"

"But I can't bear the thought of having a paid-for husband, either."

Flora rolled her eyes. "If you've already made up your mind to let the father deal with it, then why'd you ask for my advice?"

"I've done nothing of the sort."

The Angel was quite tarnished in her mind now, beyond redemption, without a single sterling quality. He was just a rogue, after all. And this was the father of her child?

"In fact," she continued, "I'd as soon never lay eyes on him again. But I was hoping you might think of some other alternative."

"You could go away, not just to have the baby, but for good. Live abroad and pretend to be a widow. Your mother would probably even go with you."

Rebecca hadn't thought of that and didn't want to now. It would be a tremendous change in their lives. How could she suggest that to her mother when Lilly had lived her whole life in Norford? All her friends were there and she was quite happy with how socially active they kept her. But of course, Lilly would pack up and go with her if Rebecca opted for that plan. That's how much Lilly loved her. But the guilt Rebecca would feel at over-turning her mother's life would be more than she could bear.

None of her options were palatable, but that was to be ex-pected after such a huge leap down the wrong path. She'd done the one thing that was absolutely unforgivable in the eyes of her peers, which was why those peers could never know.

"I can't do that to my mother," Rebecca said. "I really can't."

Flora ran the comb through Rebecca's hair a few more times before she said thoughtfully, "You still ought to tell your gentleman—he *is* a gentleman, correct?"

"An aristocrat by birth, yes."

"There's a distinction?"

"In his case, most definitely."

Rebecca said that so sourly, Flora was quick to ask, "Who is he?"

Rebecca had no reason to keep his identity a secret, at least not from her maid. "Elizabeth's *friend* who mistook this room for their trysting place all those weeks ago and left you all agog."

"So Lady Elizabeth wasn't the only one who—oh my God, Becca, *him*? Marry him!"

"No."

"How can you not want to?"

"Because he's probably the worst skirt-chaser ever to be born. Women flock to him because of his extraordinary looks and he takes full advantage of it, seducing them all!"

"All?"

"All of them who are as foolish as I was."

Flora sighed and patted Rebecca's shoulder sympathetically. "This is so much more understandable now. A man who looks like that can whittle away all defenses, especially if he *tries* to."

"His capabilities don't matter. The situation he's left me in does."

"There's one other option, you know."

"That's why we're having this discussion, to explore every option. Which one did you forget to mention?"

"Well, it's not ideal, but if you *really* don't want to marry him—"

"We've established that."

"And you don't want to buy a husband, go away, or give your baby to strangers . . ."

"Yes?"

"Give it to him instead. He certainly wouldn't be the first lord to own up to his responsibility and raise his bastard himself. He'll probably prefer that alternative to marriage, if he's as bad as you say. And you could become a 'friend' of the family so you can visit all you like, although . . ."

"What?"

"I'm not so sure that'd be a good idea, after all. If you get too attached, it might end up being even more painful for you, and how could your heart not get involved, when it's your own baby? But in either case, you really must tell him, and you might as well do so before you go home. If you don't, your mother will, and she won't be very nice about it, I'm sure. She'll put the whole blame where it belongs, on him. *She* will probably even demand he marry you. So if you don't want it coming to that, deal with him yourself. He might even have some other alternative we haven't thought of."

Chapter Twenty-four

Finding Rupert wasn't the simple matter Rebecca had thought it would be. Although she'd caught a glimpse of him at a couple of palace events right after that fateful night, she'd heard that he'd moved out of the palace. He hadn't even returned for the celebrations after the queen birthed her first son in early November, the new heir apparent to the throne.

But she knew Rupert lived in London, she just didn't know where and didn't have any acquaintances in town that she could ask. She tried several hacks, hoping one of the drivers might know where the Marquis of Rochwood lived. That didn't work. She asked another to take her somewhere she could find a book of addresses, but that driver said he only knew of gentlemen's clubs that kept addresses of the nobility, and neither he nor she would make it through the door of one of those establishments.

She could have asked Nigel Jennings, but she hadn't seen him since he'd given her the letter to deliver to Rupert, and she certainly didn't want to talk to him now. Besides, Rupert must have told him that she couldn't be trusted, which might account for why Nigel hadn't sought her out again himself.

Finally she told Flora of her difficulty, and an hour later the maid came back with the address. John Keets again. What a resourceful man!

Rebecca waited until the next morning so she could arrive at Rupert's home early enough to be assured he wouldn't be out and about for the day yet. She should have told Flora to come to the palace early so she could accompany her. But a chaperone wasn't really necessary when she was only going straight to Rupert's house and then coming straight back to the palace, hopefully before her morning sickness showed up.

Arlington Street was much closer to the palace than she'd thought, too. She could probably deal with this dreaded conversation with Rupert before she got sick. But as she stepped out of the hack and walked up to his house, her nervousness returned. She dealt with it, though, by reminding herself of all the reasons she should be furious instead. That worked. She was halfway to high dudgeon when the door opened, but within a few moments she was filled with dismay.

The marquis wasn't home, the butler informed her. In fact, he wasn't even in the country. Perhaps she could return in a few weeks. He *might* be back from France by then, though that was doubtful, since his ship, the *Merhammer,* had sailed just this morning.

That's when Rebecca felt a tiny shred of hope amid the panic. Had his ship actually sailed yet, or did his butler just assume it was gone? In either case, she had to find out which port the *Merhammer* was sailing to, so she had to go to the docks anyway. She walked briskly back to the hack and informed the driver of her new destination. Waiting several more weeks for Rupert to return to London was out of the question. She didn't have much time to spare at this point. She'd have to send someone after him right away, that very day! Perhaps John Keets could be persuaded to take a small vacation. . . .

"What in the bloody hell are you doing here?"

"How nice to see you, too," Rebecca replied curtly before she turned to the young deckhand to thank him for showing her to Rupert's cabin.

She'd experienced every sort of anxiety on her race to the docks. It would have been much worse though if they hadn't quickly found out at which dock the *Merhammer* had been berthed. But it all went away as soon as she saw that the *Merhammer* hadn't yet sailed. Well, not quite all. There'd been enough left for her to spill her guts into the Thames before boarding the ship.

How embarrassing that had been, but none of the sailors who might have witnessed it had commented on it. As bad as the river smelled at dockside, they were probably used to seeing men and women do the same thing.

Rebecca couldn't believe her good luck. The ship hadn't sailed as soon as the tide rolled in because some of the ship's cargo was late in arriving. But the ship would sail as soon as it did, so she was warned to keep her visit brief.

With that in mind, Rebecca moved past Rupert into his cabin and said, "You might want to cancel this trip."

She was keeping her eyes off his face. Having not seen him in—it was closer to six weeks now than five—she didn't want to risk that old bedazzlement she used to feel.

"Might I indeed? I suppose I should ask why, but since I'm not likely to believe anything you say, I think I'll contain the urge."

He'd closed the door. He was leaning back against it, his

arms crossed over his wide chest. He was casually dressed in buff-colored pants with a dark brown jacket and his white shirt open at the neck. Did he actually sound amused at her suggestion? Amazing how he could raise her ire so easily, but at least it allowed her to look directly at him and not be affected by his dazzling handsomeness—too much.

"Fine," she said stiffly. "If you can make your decision quickly without giving it much thought, then I can be on my way all the sooner. You are merely an option at the bottom of my short list, after all, and it wasn't even my idea to put you on the list. Someone pointed out that—'

"You can stop right there, Becca," he cut in tersely, his amusement gone now. "I've heard enough to recognize that your confusing tactics are in full swing, so let me warn you I no longer have any patience where you're concerned. Spit it out or get out. *That's* the only option you have right now."

She glared at him. "Do you treat your family in this abominable manner, too?"

He was momentarily caught off guard to go by his expression. "My family? Where the deuce did that come from? Never mind. *That's* none of your business."

"Actually it is. And if you can't answer that one simple question for me, then I have nothing further to say to you."

"Good," he said in a satisfied tone, and turned to open the door wide for her.

She drew in her breath sharply. He was serious! He wanted her to leave without even finding out what had brought her here. Had she really thought she could deal with him again as nasty as he'd become *after* he'd bedded her? It hadn't occurred to her until now that this might be how he treated all of the women that he seduced and then discarded. All sweetness and charm beforehand, then the veriest cad afterward. It certainly was an effective way of making sure that they wanted nothing more to do with him.

He didn't even deserve a final retort. She couldn't help the look of contempt she gave him as she marched past him. She was halfway up the steep steps to the deck when he yanked her down them and dragged her back to his room. He even slammed the door shut behind them this time before he let go of her.

"You've got two minutes to explain yourself," he growled at her.

"You've got two seconds to get out of my way," she snapped back.

"Or what?" And now he actually smirked. "D'you really think you can get past me?"

His absolute confidence tipped the scale on her anger. She flew at him with her nails bared. The hard kiss he gave her in return so surprised both of them that it took a good ten seconds before they realized it shouldn't be happening and pushed away at the same moment. Rebecca was left panting and horrified by her slow reaction. She didn't hesitate though to wipe the taste of him off her lips.

Rupert's pale blue eyes gazed at her hotly. "Oh, that hurts. 'Deed it does."

"Spare me your sarcasm and just move aside. The decision I came here to discuss with you is no longer yours to make, it's mine, and thank you for helping me make it. So you see, we have nothing further to say to each other."

He raked an angry hand through his hair. "I suppose you know that's one of the oldest tactics around? I've even used it myself on occasion. Good God, did Sarah actually take you under her wing? She's personally teaching you duplicity now? You were good before, but you've definitely graduated to much better."

"Sarah be damned. *You* be damned. But my baby isn't going to be damned to your care now," Rebecca cried furiously, "*That's* why I came here, to find out if you might want to raise the child yourself instead of seeing it go to strangers. But giving it up is my last resort. My mother might be able to buy me a perfectly acceptable husband and then I won't have to give it up a'tall. So you see, your answer in either case wasn't really important. I was merely advised to consult you before apprising my mother of my condition, since her first reaction will probably be to demand you marry me, which you'll agree is out of the question."

His immediate response was to clap his hands—slowly. "Bravo. You've really mastered the knack of manipulation, haven't you? Gad, you almost had me buying it. It was almost like standing back and watching myself in action. Fascinating—until you blew it with the mention of marriage. You should never put your ultimate goal on the table, luv. You must let your mark think that the idea is his own, or it just doesn't work."

She almost laughed at that point. He really thought she'd made all that up to get a proposal out of him? He couldn't be more wrong, but it would be a waste of her breath to say so.

"Good-bye, St. John," she said with as much contempt as she could muster, and headed for the door again.

But the ship chose that horrible moment to dip dramatically in the water, and Rebecca swayed both ways with it. It wasn't a movement her delicate condition could come even close to handling. Eyes widening with dread, she started to gag.

Chapter Twenty-five

Ox THE SLIM CHANCE that Rebecca really was about to puke all over the floor, Rupert leaped across the room, snatched up the empty chamber pot, and thrust it into her hands. It wouldn't be the first time he'd seen someone get seasick before the ship even sailed, but this one *was* under way. His small cabin contained no windows, but he'd been on enough sea voyages to recognize the signs.

He still couldn't believe that Rebecca had come here. Actually, he couldn't believe that his first thought upon seeing her was that Nigel must have sent her. But then Nigel had stressed that a "wife" would make his current mission easier, and he'd been thinking about spending a day or two in France trying to find a suitable wench to impersonate a spouse for him.

But it had been crazy to think that Rebecca had been sent for the task. Nigel knew that Rupert thought Rebecca was a duplicitous schemer. He'd made that clear in the condemning report he had given Nigel when Nigel returned to London. Rupert had visited his superior after Nigel had had a chance to review the report.

"Well, old boy, I'm glad Rebecca Marshall gave you my note about the tailor," Nigel had told him. "I think you're ready for a few new coats."

That might have been something Julie would have said to him, not Nigel, and he was shocked at Nigel's cavalier reaction to the report. "Did you even read my assessment?"

"Course I did, I just think you've made too much about nothing. I'll look into Lord Alberton again, but I very much doubt that Rebecca was being duplicitous. I was testing her with that note she gave you. I also told her to use you as a go-between for her and me, since I suspected I would be away from the palace for a while, so she wasn't lying to you."

"You realize by doing that you gave her the opportunity to lead us astray?"

"Only if she's still on Sarah's string, but I honestly don't believe she is. My instincts tell me she's trustworthy. I actually like the girl."

Rupert had snorted. "That's how good she is, Nigel. She's got you completely fooled."

"I disagree. If her behavior seems odd to you, perhaps it's simply because she gets a little flustered around you. Don't you realize the effect you have on women?"

"This is different," Rupert had insisted.

Nigel had given him a questioning frown. "I've never seen you overreact like this before. I wonder why. And over this particular girl. You haven't developed feelings for her, have you?"

That hadn't deserved a response. The one thing Rupert had left out of his report was the location Rebecca had chosen to deliver her information about Lord Alberton—his room, late at night—and what had occurred because of it. He'd nearly mentioned it at that meeting, but had held his tongue. Those details were too personal to share. But without doing so he couldn't explain why his judgment had been so harsh.

Rupert knew he'd been duped, royally. But never again. He'd warned Nigel that he was done with palace intrigues and he'd meant it. He'd left Nigel with no doubt about how angry he was when he'd added that if he was ever asked to do anything so ridiculously trivial again, they would be finished—for good. Which was possibly why Nigel hadn't called on him for anything this last month, until now.

Rupert was still furious over that whole affair with Rebecca and how easily she had manipulated him. He'd let himself get emotionally involved with this girl, and because of that she'd been able to ply her tricks on him. And now she had the gall to toy with him again? Had this been her plan all along, to trap him into marriage?

Not for a moment did he believe there was a baby. If there was, she would have told him sooner and not waited to confront him until his ship was about to sail. Actually, she wouldn't have told him at all. Her *mother* would be demanding that he marry Rebecca.

Rupert sighed. He couldn't take his eyes off Rebecca. He had to resist the urge to put his hand on her shoulder, had to tamp down all sympathy for her. She was faking! He bloody well needed to keep that uppermost in his mind.

When she was done hacking up what looked like no more than spit, he said drily, "How unpleasant. Was that supposed to prove that you're carrying my child?"

"You're still an insensitive bore, aren't you?" she said, then wiped her mouth. "That was the sway of the ship. While I do suffer morning sickness, I'm pretty sure I got rid of most of it before I stepped aboard. The strong odors of the river brought it on."

He could say one thing about Rebecca: she was consistent in *sounding* plausible. If he didn't know better, it would be so damned easy to believe her, that's how good she was at deception. Dealing with her had been a challenge he'd actually enjoyed—until she'd won. Which was why he was also furious with himself. She'd exploited the one thing he couldn't control—his desire for her.

He still wanted her. He could deplore it, but he couldn't deny it. She was the first woman he'd ever come across who was more adept at pulling the strings than he was.

"I must apologize," she said, setting the chamber pot back on its stand. "I wasn't expecting that to happen. But I'll leave now, since we really don't have anything more to discuss."

He raised a brow. "You're impressing me again. Walking on water is one of your amazing skills?"

Her eyes widened briefly, but then the doubting look showed up. "That isn't even remotely funny."

"You're quite right, it isn't, especially because this is the only cabin available on this ship. This isn't a passenger ship, you know. The captain keeps this single cabin empty for emergencies only and charges a ridiculously exorbitant price for its use. I'm afraid I gave him the idea of renting it out the first time I needed a fast trip abroad."

"I don't believe a word you're saying," she replied huffily on her way to the door. "I don't know why you're trying to delay me, nor do I care, but it won't work. Good-bye."

Rupert moved to the single stuffed chair to await her return. It was a comfortable chair. The captain had at least included some amenities that a nobleman would expect for the extortionate price he charged. The bed was a decent size and the sheets might not be as soft as the ones he was accustomed to, but they were clean. Even a small, round table and a chair were nailed to the floor for dining in case the trip across the Channel took longer than usual.

Rebecca was in high dudgeon when she returned, to go by the virulent glare that she directed at him. "This is unacceptable! I left a hack driver back on that dock who hasn't been paid yet! I assured him I wouldn't be long."

Rupert shrugged indifferently. "Should have paid him."

"And have him hie off and leave me stranded? I wanted to be sure he'd still be—"

"That's the least of your worries, Becca, so stop going on about it."

"I know that! My maid is going to be out of her mind with worry when I don't return to the palace. She'll be forced to send for my mother!"

He felt a twinge of discomfort over that predicament. He'd never had to deal with an outraged mother before—other than his own. But the discomfort warned him that he was starting to believe Rebecca's performance, so he indulged his skepticism again.

"I'm sure you'll do just fine in explaining how you got stuck on a ship you shouldn't have been on to begin with."

"You know something, Rupert?" she replied scathingly. "You give new meaning to the word *dense*."

"I suppose you're going to tell me why you think so?" he said with a sigh.

Much to his disappointment, she did. "I'm concerned about what my disappearance is going to put my mother through. She's going to be told I'm missing! Do you know what that will do to her? I'm her only child, I'm all the family she's got. You have to tell this ship to turn around!"

He had a feeling she was serious, so he managed not to laugh. Well, he tried—and failed. "I'm sure the 'ship' won't listen to reason. No, really, I'm positive it won't."

"You know what I mean!" she shrieked at him.

Course he did, but his answer was still the same. "The captain doesn't listen to reason either, m'dear. If you want to apprise him of your presence on his ship, be prepared to pay him for it. But don't expect a return trip until after he's disposed of his cargo. This ship is a trader. The cargo on it comes first, passengers a very distant second."

"I'll buy the cargo!"

"Not unless you brought your bank with you, you won't. I did mention the captain is a moneygrubbing bastard, didn't I? He charges me fifty pounds just for a one-way trip. You realize how outlandish that is? But he doesn't care if he rents the cabin. His cargo, however, is his lifeblood."

Her shoulders slumped and her lower lip quivered. She looked as if she was about to cry, which had Rupert shooting out of his chair. "Don't you dare try to make me feel guilty over something you set in motion! If I'm stuck with you, so be it, but I won't tolerate any more theatrics."

He slammed out of the room, determined to speak with Captain Overly himself. If there was any way to get the *Merhammer* turned around short of holding a gun to the man, he would do it.

Chapter Twenty-six

Iт тоок several hours for Rebecca to calm down. Three more unpleasant dashes for the chamber pot helped her at least to stop thinking about her mother's anguish when Rebecca could do nothing about it. She just hoped that Flora wouldn't be too hasty in contacting Lilly. If Rebecca was really lucky, she might even be able to get back to England before Flora did so.

Rebecca also felt a little better now that Rupert wasn't making any more of his snide remarks. At one point he'd handed her a cold, wet cloth for her face and led her to the bed, where she'd curled up. That had been decent of him, though one act of decency didn't erase such a long list of despicable behavior. Otherwise, he was ignoring her and hadn't said anything to her after he'd made a few blistering remarks when he'd stormed back into the cabin.

"You're going to France and that's the end of that discussion!" he'd informed her.

"You asked—?"

"I even took your suggestion and offered to buy his bloody cargo. He knows I'm good for it."

"The captain refused? Why, when he'd make the same profit either way?"

"He refused because he could. He refused because he found it much more enjoyable to laugh in my face. I should have known better, when I am quite familiar with his type. He hates aristocrats. He'll take my money, but once at sea he'll grab any opportunity to lord it over me that he's 'god' and I'm just a pissant under his feet."

Rupert was so furious about that he didn't say another word, but she didn't give him too much more thought when her own misery was uppermost in her mind. She was pretty sure now that her nausea wasn't due to her morning sickness, but to the pitch of the ship. As she lay on the bed, she opened her eyes a few times to take note of where he was in the room.

He'd paced for a while, but she'd merely heard that and hadn't actually looked, too nauseated to open her eyes. When the pacing stopped, she did locate him in the one comfortable chair. He was sprawled out so much with a leg dangling over the arm that she thought he might be trying to take a nap there.

It had to be approaching noon. Shouldn't they have arrived in France already if the *Merhammer* was only crossing the Channel? She'd never sailed before, but even she knew how close the two countries were. At least she was feeling a little better, well enough to sit up and find out.

"How soon before we can get off this ship?" she asked.

"Not soon enough," Rupert mumbled without opening his eyes. "France is a very big country. Were you thinking this was just a short hop across the Channel?"

That's exactly what she'd thought. "It's not?" she asked with dread.

"Not even close. The ship's cargo is bound for Rouen, which is much farther down the coast and still another twenty to thirty miles along the river Seine. My own destination is inland, and farther south as well, so it didn't matter to me which port she was headed to."

"*How* many days?"

He opened his eyes now and looked at her. "*If* you were as desperate as you pretended to be, why didn't you just jump ship while we were still in the Thames? So you would have returned to the palace a bedraggled mess, but at least you would have done so today and not next week."

"That was never an option," she said in a small, horrified voice, her face completely blanched. *Next week?* "I never learned to swim."

"Wonderful. That had to be the one skill you don't possess, didn't it?"

How could he be so sarcastic when her panic was soaring again? "When do we reach port?"

"If the weather holds, probably sometime tomorrow."

She glared furiously at him. "You couldn't say that instead of 'next week'? Do you like seeing women faint?" she added scathingly.

He raised a curious brow. "You've figured out how to fake that, too, without hurting yourself?"

"Go to the devil!"

"This room has already become hell, so I'd say I'm close enough."

"For once we agree."

She wasn't going to say another word to the odious man.

That decision lasted for all of ten minutes. She could wish it were otherwise, but he possessed information she needed.

"I can expect a return trip sometime tomorrow then?" she asked hopefully.

"On the *Merhammer*? No, it travels farther south before it heads back for the return trip. If you can afford the price to keep this cabin for that long, you're looking at a minimum of six days."

"What about another ship in Rouen?"

"You can try, but if it were that easy to travel by sea on the spur of the moment, I wouldn't find it necessary to use cargo ships like the *Merhammer*. But who knows, you could get lucky."

"Then I'll just have to get lucky, won't I?" she replied with a determined nod.

He actually chuckled. "We'll see. I usually try the port in Calais myself, where ships offer that short Channel hop you were thinking of. If you can't get a cabin, most of the ships leaving for Dover will rent you deck space because the trip is so short. Actually," he amended, "they'll do that for a man. I'm not so sure about an unchaperoned woman. But at any rate, renting deck space isn't a good idea if it's raining or snowing, which is often the case this time of year."

Did he have to add yet another obstacle? "When will you be returning?"

"Not as soon as I'd like to. I'm going to have to waste a couple days finding an . . . acceptable . . . wife."

Her eyes widened. "You're going to France to get *married*?"

He didn't answer immediately; he was in fact giving her such a thoughtful look that it began to make her distinctly uncomfortable.

But he finally answered, "Not a'tall. While that might delight my mother, I think even she would prefer an English daughter-in-law. Fortunately, I'm in no hurry to delight her. It's not a real wife I need, just a woman to play the role for a few days."

"A fake wife?"

He smiled enigmatically.

"Exactly."

"Whatever for?"

"If you're offering to play the part, we can discuss it further. Otherwise, it's none of your business."

She snorted and had to wrestle with her curiosity a bit before she could tell him, "Real or fake, I find marriage to you so detestable that my answer isn't just no, it's a *resounding* no."

He shrugged, closed his eyes, and made another attempt at that nap.

Rebecca lay back on the bed, closing her eyes as well. It really was none of her business what he was up to. But she simply couldn't imagine why anyone would need a fake wife, and her frustration was rising by the minute. Curiosity of this sort was overwhelming—no, she refused to ask him again and that was that.

At least an hour passed. She'd almost gotten it out of her mind when she heard him say, "You'd probably get back to London quicker with me than on your own. There is the possibility that none of the merchant captains will deal with you simply because they don't want unmarried women on their ships. It wasn't so long ago when sailors considered women aboard their vessels bad luck, you know."

She'd never heard anything so silly, but she knew exactly what he was up to and said drily, "Did I not say no? Yes, I'm sure I did."

"I'm not joking, Becca. If I had a woman posing as my wife with me, I could probably be in and out of my destination city in a day. Even if I'm delayed trying to find an appropriate partner, I have a feeling I'll still beat you to Calais and be home long before you are."

"Nonsense. If I must make that trip, I'll do so in all haste."

"If you can find a coach willing to take you that far, you might. But my guess is you'll be stuck using the public coaches, and they offer one delay after another. They don't travel unless they're full, you know. Are you going to wait for them to fill up at every town you pass through? Come to think of it, weeks instead of days is a more reasonable guess."

"All right!" she shouted to end his dire predictions. "If you can guarantee that I'll be back in London in three days, then I'll do it. If you can't, then I don't want to hear another word about it."

"Done," he said.

Chapter Twenty-seven

Rᴇʙᴇᴄᴄᴀ ᴡᴀs ᴜɴᴀʙʟᴇ ᴛᴏ eat lunch that day at sea, despite being hungry. The smell of food in the cabin had made her break out in a cold sweat and had put her back in front of the chamber pot until the sharp aromas were gone. Sailing was smoother later in the day, and by dinner she was able to sit at the tiny table with its one nailed-down chair, which Rupert had offered to her while he sat with plate in hand in the stuffed chair.

"Enjoy every bite of that meal," he told her. "It cost me five bloody pounds."

She nearly choked hearing that, but she continued to eat anyway, she was so famished. "He's a thief," she said of the captain with a nod of commiseration. "But I had no idea you were so low on funds that you'd feel the pinch of five pounds. I will certainly reimburse you."

She wasn't being flippant. He'd complained so much about the cost of this trip, naturally she'd concluded that he was light in the pockets even though she probably *should* have kept it to herself.

He gave her a hard look. "It has nothing to do being able to afford it or not. No one likes to be robbed, plain and simple. But it wasn't the captain in this case, it was the cook. He didn't like being inconvenienced when I asked for bland food because of your onboard malady, since he had a splendidly rich meal already prepared."

She felt horrible after that. It was the second thoughtful thing he'd done for her that day, neither of them expected. "I'm sorry."

He didn't even acknowledge her apology with a simple nod, leading her to think she might have hurt his feelings. So while she hadn't satisfied her curiosity yet over why he needed her to pose as his wife, she couldn't bring herself to question him further.

She was silent for the remainder of the meal. Returning to the bed, she didn't lie back down, she just sat there staring at the floor.

The number of emotions that crossed her face was probably quite telling, but one finally prompted him to ask in a gentler tone, "What are you stewing about now?"

A better question might have been, what wasn't she stewing about? But her thoughts had just briefly touched on his earlier remark about her swimming back to London. The results could have been disastrous in unexpected ways, and her expression had probably reflected that.

"You would really have let me jump overboard this morning in my condition, when it might have hurt the baby?"

He looked annoyed. "Let's be quite clear about this, Becca. I don't believe a word of that nonsense you were spouting about a baby. I *do* believe you had a motive for coming to me today. If you'd like to make a clean breast of it . . . ?"

That was it! He'd called her a liar one time too many. "What I'd like is for you to shut up now, you've insulted me quite enough for one day."

"Is that always going to be your response when you get backed into a corner?"

"This bed might be in a corner, but it's quite roomy, thank you. I simply don't feel a need to convince you when I've already told you that your opinion no longer matters to me. You lost your chance to be involved with this baby, and there's not a thing you can do to change that now."

Good God it was satisfying to tell him that and see his unexpected reaction. He actually looked furious.

"*If* you were enceinte, no, I would not have let you jump overboard, but since you aren't, a little cold water wouldn't have hurt you if you were as frantic to get back as you pretended to be."

So he thought her worry over her mother was a pretense, too? He was despicable. He didn't deserve another word from her on any subject. In fact, she lay down determined to let him think she had gone to sleep without giving him another thought.

Actually, she didn't have to pretend to fall asleep. With a meal in her belly she did go right to sleep. But then her body had been racked throughout the day with dry heaves, which had exhausted her more than she'd realized.

The only thing that Rebecca could be thankful for before the *Merhammer* docked the next morning was that Rupert had made no attempt to claim his bed back from her. He hadn't even mentioned their sleeping arrangement. He'd simply spent the night in the stuffed chair.

The next morning Rupert had no sooner left the cabin with

his portmanteau in hand after telling her they'd arrived in Rouen, than she was diving for the chamber pot again. The ship had been anchored near the docks. But having arrived in the middle of the night, it had had to wait for the harbormaster to show up in the morning to assign it a berth.

She found Rupert on the deck, standing at the rail. She thought he was waiting for her there, but when she joined him, he made no move to leave the ship. She didn't bother to ask why. Solid ground was in sight and she raced off the ship herself. He followed her down to the dock.

"Better?" he asked.

"Much," she replied, and found a crate nearby to sit on. "The morning sickness I'm used to already, but that *plus* seasickness is a bit too much."

"I'm sure," he said drily.

She sighed. He simply didn't believe she was having a baby. He had really made that perfectly clear last night. He'd developed a bad opinion of her because of all that nonsense with Sarah, so of course he assumed she was lying about this, too. The trouble was, the more she tried to convince him that he was wrong, the more he was likely to think he was right.

Time wouldn't tell either, since she didn't expect to ever see him again after this trip. He might think he could check on her in a few months, but that would be too late. She'd either be out of the country in seclusion where *he* certainly wouldn't find her—or married to someone else. She was leaning toward the latter. Giving up her baby, even to Rupert, was, well, it was ripping her up inside every time she thought of that now.

Chapter Twenty-eight

REBECCA THOUGHT SHE MIGHT start to cry right there on the dock, so she pushed her bleak thoughts aside.

"Can we go now?" she asked Rupert.

"As soon as my coach is on the dock."

"You arranged for one to meet you here?"

"No."

When he didn't elaborate, she realized with some surprise why he hadn't been so eager to leave the ship. "You brought a coach along?"

"And a driver. A first for me. I much prefer a swift mount. But I was warned that a 'wife' wouldn't travel by horseback. Arriving at my destination with some flair and pomp will get us in the door sooner as well. You can't exactly rent crested coaches, even at home."

Of course you couldn't, but she was reminded that he hadn't explained yet why he needed a wife or some pomp. It was time to correct that.

But before she could broach that subject, he added, "Don't

worry. I managed to scrape up enough pounds to pay for the coach to be unloaded first, prior to the cargo."

She blushed. She had a feeling he was never going to forget her thoughtless remark about his being low on funds. But she wasn't going to apologize again. Instead she asked, "What's this all about, your unusual requirement? Are you here to seduce some unlucky lady, and just to make sure she doesn't ask you to marry her, you want to bring a fake wife along?"

"That's not a bad excuse, now that you mention it." He put a hand to his cheek, as if he were actually giving it some thought. "Shall we leave the explanation at that?"

"If you do, I may help *you* to jump into the water."

He lifted his foot and rested it next to her thigh on the crate and leaned down to say, "If you're done with empty threats and pointless sarcasms, I will explain. I wasn't planning on keeping you in the dark. I've been tasked with concluding an investigation that's been going on for several years now. Since you're so fresh out of the schoolroom, I assume that you're aware of just how far our empire has spread?"

"Certainly."

"Then you know that expansion hasn't been without casualties or military occupation. In India, for instance, there have been uprisings of one sort or another caused by some of the smaller displaced rulers. But one attack was of particular note because some of our soldiers stationed there were killed with British rifles."

"Stolen?"

"Yes, but not from the army's supply in India as you might think. It's taken nearly two years to follow the trail back to this side of the world to shipments that hadn't even left England yet."

"Why so long?"

"Because only one or two crates were being stolen at a time, so no one noticed."

"And our armies are spread out in so many countries that the rifles could have come from numerous other places," she guessed.

"Exactly." He nodded "But the trail ends in Le Mans, at least we hope that it does. The thief in England was finally caught and persuaded to volunteer the name of the man who'd hired him."

"So the French are actually trying to get back some of the land they lost to us in India, without actually revealing that they're instigating the attacks?"

"A good guess, Becca, but no. Samuel Pearson is supposedly the man who masterminded the theft, but we need more evidence than just the word of a thief. But Pearson does have a good motive. He's the second son of a minor English lord, an aristocrat, but untitled. He obtained an officer's commission in the army and was in fact stationed in India for most of his military career. That was also where he earned his dishonorable discharge for some underhanded dealings with the sepoys under his command."

"Aren't they the local Indians who comprise most of our infantry over there?"

Rupert appeared impressed and nodded. "That's quite a teacher you had in your schoolroom."

"Tutor," she corrected. "Mother kept me close to home. But, yes, he was very well traveled and enjoyed sharing what he'd seen and learned firsthand of the world."

"Your mother allowed such a broad curriculum?" Rupert asked curiously.

"She encouraged it. My father died when I was young, so my mother raised me as she saw fit.

"Interesting. Quite a radical approach with a female child. But then she wouldn't be the first widow to go a tad overboard in her newfound freedoms. My mother did the same when she was widowed, not where her children were concerned, but for herself."

Rupert's team of horses were finally being led off the ship, one at a time, so he excused himself for a few minutes to help. The harbor wasn't that big, so it was surprising to see that it had a crane vessel, which had already maneuvered next to the *Merhammer* to unload the larger cargo, and the coach was the first item it lifted to the dock.

Before Rupert returned to Rebecca, the horses were hitched to the coach, and he escorted her to it, then climbed in behind her. The roomy vehicle was comfortably upholstered in dark brown leather, with the floorboards highly polished. Thick curtains could be drawn over the windows. From the outside, it was obviously the coach of an aristocrat, not gaudy, but with dark brown wood that made the gold crest of the St. Johns stand out more prominently, so it would serve as "pomp" she supposed.

"Brace yourself," Rupert said as he leaned back into the seat across from her, "I told my driver to make haste. He's rather good at following orders."

He'd no sooner said it than she was bounced a few inches off her seat. The timing, as precise as it was, set them both to chuckling for a few moments. It gave Rebecca an odd feeling. She shouldn't be laughing with him.

She sobered and reminded Rupert that he hadn't finished his explanation. "What exactly is Mr. Pearson's motive?"

"Considering it was his former unit that was attacked with these stolen rifles, and more'n once—"

She cut in with a frown, "You're talking about murder, aren't you?"

"That's a better conclusion than any other. He did bear a few grudges. The scandal of his discharge so disgraced him at home, he was forced to leave England for good and settled in Le Mans with his immediate family. But that's all we have to go on. What we need now is some proof that he was receiving the stolen rifles, or that he was shipping them on to India. A receipt or a manifest will do."

"Your involvement in this investigation has been requested by your tailor, I presume?"

"Who?"

"Mr. Jennings."

Rupert chuckled. "Pearson's not going to let just any Englishman in his door. An aristocrat was required, so, yes, Nigel did happen to think of me. And since I have time on my hands, I agreed."

"You're going to let Pearson know who you really are?"

"Of course not. We'll use false names—Lord and Lady Hastings."

"So what exactly is your plan?"

"I need to get into his house. If he didn't have such a large family, I'd just sneak in and be done with it. But between servants, his many children, and even some of his wife's relatives who live with them, there must be thirty people under that roof, and it's not that big a roof."

"Did you think of knocking on the door to get in?" she said tongue in cheek.

Rupert grinned. "You'd think that would be an option, wouldn't you? And it is, but not without a wife in tow."

"Why?"

"Because although Pearson is as rotten as they come, a

bloody thief, a suspected murderer, he has one good quality—he's a devoted family man, even took his whole family to India with him. In fact, he prizes family so much, he appears to distrust any man who isn't married or who doesn't value his own family as much as he does."

She scoffed, "No one could be that eccentric."

"Pretty much my own words when I was told what I just repeated to you. But apparently it's true. At any rate, the plan is to show up at his door as a married couple, just passing through town, heard another Englishman lived there, and having been gone so long from England on our grand tour, we were eager to make his acquaintance. Actually, we should probably change that to an extended wedding trip, considering how young you are."

"You're saying your entire plan is that simple? But don't you still have to snoop through his belongings to find your proof?"

"That's where you will come in. You aren't just going to be window-dressing. It will be up to you to cause some sort of distraction so I can search a few key rooms in the house. But then that's one of your fortes, isn't it, luv?"

Chapter Twenty-nine

REBECCA HAD NEVER MET anyone else as sarcastic or insulting as Rupert St. John. She was beginning to wonder if his rudeness came naturally or if it was a stratagem he reserved for women to keep them from falling in love with him. After he charmed them into his bed, of course. Actually, in her case he'd made it perfectly clear that he thought she'd done the seducing and he despised her for it. Did he even realize how hypocritical that was of him?

But the man could at least have warned her what her "role" in his mission entailed. He hadn't even volunteered any suggestions on how she might distract the Pearsons so he could search for some proof of the man's crimes.

His only additional remark had been "It's not a quick trip. We'll be lucky if we arrive before dark, so you have plenty of time to figure something out."

She supposed she could, and it was certainly a better way to pass the time than brooding about the silent man sitting across from her. She just had to try to forget that Samuel Pearson was a suspected criminal and concentrate on his one oddity, that he was a devoted family man. An aristocratic wife and children . . . surely she could find something she had in common with these people. It still seemed bizarre to her that a man who loved his family so much could be guilty of treason and the deaths of his countrymen. Was his extreme devotion to his family a result of guilt from his crimes? Or was this trail that had led to him false? Perhaps he wasn't a criminal at all.

But how would she distract him? Fainting was out of the question. She wasn't going to deliberately take a fall that might hurt her baby. Knocking over something like a vase might work. She could pretend to be a clumsy wife. If the first accident didn't distract Pearson, at least he would keep his eyes on her to make sure he didn't lose anything else of value to her clumsiness.

Satisfied that she had a plan of action, she settled back into her seat and gazed out the window at the landscape. That got boring rather quickly since they were between towns and all she could see were brown fields. Rupert was taking a nap. Had he had trouble sleeping in that chair last night? She didn't feel bad about that. It was his fault she was in France, his fault she was having a child out of wedlock, his fault she couldn't keep her eyes off him for long. With him sleeping, she didn't even try.

He had changed clothes before she'd woke up that morning. She had none to change into, but at least the pale lavender outing dress she had been wearing yesterday when she left the palace was warm and didn't wrinkle easily. It showed no signs that she'd slept in it last night. Rupert's garb today clearly presented him as a rich aristocrat. The satin, brocaded waistcoat with the extravagant jeweled buttons, the flashy rings on his long fingers, the perfectly tailored fit and the quality of the materials, it all clearly indicated that no expense had been spared to turn him out in grand fashion.

She sighed to herself. Why did a man who looked so angelic have to be such a despicable rogue? And why didn't this knowledge end her attraction to him? She should feel nothing but loathing for him over the way he'd treated her, yet she looked at his supple lips and thought only of how thrilled she had been by his kisses, looked at his fingers and remembered the excitement of his caresses, looked—well, no, she wasn't looking there, but, was her pulse beginning to race?

She forced herself to close her eyes. He wasn't even awake! *How* could he have such a powerful effect on her?

With a short stop for lunch, they still weren't going to arrive in Le Mans before dark. The city was so old that it had been established even before the Romans had conquered Gaul. Rupert had never visited the city, and he had greatly underestimated the time it would take to get there by coach.

After obtaining the latest set of directions, the driver, Matthew, opened the door of the coach and informed Rupert, "Another eight hours, m'lord, at least. The horses won't hold up that long at this pace."

She wasn't going to be back in England in three days after all? Her expression must have reflected how disappointed she felt about that alarming news.

After glancing at her, Rupert told the man, "We can't afford that long a delay. Give me a few hours to get some sleep, then I'll take over the night drive so you can sleep."

"Very good, m'lord."

Matthew might find this arrangement acceptable, but Rebecca, who was still concerned about being away an extra day, pointed out, "You've already slept the entire day. Why not take over for Matthew now?"

"You really think I could sleep with your eyes devouring me all day?"

Her face turned red with rage and mortification. That faker! She *had* been staring at him at various times throughout the day. She probably had his face so memorized that she could sketch it without his being present. But he couldn't keep his knowledge of that to himself? He had to make sure she was embarrassed right down to her toes?

But he didn't rub it in further. At least, she thought he was done with the subject when he lay down on his seat and turned his back to her. "Get some sleep yourself," he ordered. "You'll need to be at your best tomorrow, too."

She was just lying down when he added, "And keep your eyes off my arse."

Waves of heat crept up her cheeks. That pretty much guaranteed that she wasn't going to get any sleep until *he* was out of the coach.

Chapter Thirty

SAMUEL PEARSON DEFINITELY WASN'T what Rebecca had been expecting. He was in his late thirties, tall, with a military bearing, but he was also so gregarious that she immediately began to suspect that Rupert had lied about the man and hadn't revealed the real reason why they were there.

They had arrived in Le Mans early enough to have a leisurely breakfast before going to the Pearsons' house at a decent midmorning hour. Rebecca even managed to keep her meal down, though for once she wished it were otherwise, since worrying about when her malady would act up just added to her nervousness about her part in the plan. But as soon as Rupert had introduced them as John and Gertrude Hastings—she was sure he'd picked that name for her because he thought she wouldn't like it—and related their "wedding trip" tale to Pearson, the man had beamed in genuine welcome, invited them into his parlor, and sent for the rest of his family to make their acquaintance.

Pearson's nine children ranged in age from one to fourteen

years, and apparently Mary Pearson wasn't done adding to that count, since she was in her sixth month of yet another pregnancy. The couple were so obviously devoted to each other and their children. They were such amiable people, treating Rebecca and Rupert like old friends. Rebecca could see nothing even remotely nefarious about Pearson to support Rupert's contention that the man was killing his former comrades in India for revenge.

"How do you like living in France?" Rebecca asked during a brief lull in the conversation.

"The climate is warmer," Samuel answered.

"And not so much rain," Mary added with a grin. "I've actually come to love this city."

"And some of the people are even friendly," Samuel continued with a chuckle. "Though as in any town in any country, there will always be those who prefer to keep to themselves. But we expected more hostilities carried over from our last war with Napoléon and were quite surprised not to encounter much in that regard."

"I tried to tell him enough time had passed for that not to matter," Mary said. "It's not as if that was the first war our country has fought with France. Goodness, can we even count the number of conflicts there have been over the centuries between the two?"

"True," Rupert agreed. "If we're not fighting on the home front, then it's over new territories both countries covet. But trade is flourishing again between us. Money tends to bridge the gap, eh?"

"Quite right," Samuel said, then asked curiously, "Do you dabble in trade yourself?"

It was a most impertinent question for one aristocrat to ask another, even if they had just been talking about trade, yet Rebecca was surprised to hear Rupert reply, "I don't, but my grandfather did extensively. It was either that or let the family go on being paupers after his father had squandered their entire fortune at the game tables."

"Not an unknown occurrence," Samuel replied, sounding sympathetic.

Rebecca didn't doubt that tale was just another of Rupert's lies, but the lie was meant to put him and Pearson on a more equal footing, she realized. Had he said that in case he couldn't find any written evidence of Pearson's crimes and needed to find some other means of proof such as going into business with Pearson? After he took her back to England, of course.

Rebecca just wanted to get this over with so they could be on their way. With that in mind, she asked if a room was nearby where she could freshen up, Three of the children quickly volunteered to show her where to go.

No flower vases were displayed throughout the house, of course, at that time of the year. Silly of her for thinking there would be. But having noted the pretty, delicate-looking glass figurine that was nearly a foot tall on a table she would be passing, Rebecca was determined to knock it over on her way out the door.

She easily accomplished the maneuver, but she didn't count on one of the children so close to her skirts catching the figurine before it hit the floor. She was still able to turn and apologize to her host with the explanation "I'm sorry, but I seem to be plagued with this unusual clumsiness ever since I realized I was enceinte. I am so hoping this will quickly pass."

The man actually laughed. "No need to explain. Mary can tell you many such stories when you return. With her it was cravings, and while I tried to prepare ahead each time to have plenty of what she wanted on hand, it was pointless. With each pregnancy she had a different craving!"

Rebecca smiled to acknowledge the humor, though she didn't find it the least bit amusing. Easy for a man to laugh when he wasn't the one experiencing the odd sensations. She also bent down to thank the little girl who had rescued the figurine. And got a strong whiff of an unpleasant odor in doing so. The child was young enough to have had an accident, but Rebecca's constitution wasn't strong enough just then to stomach the smell of it.

She gagged, her hand going immediately to her mouth, her eyes widening in horror that she was going to vomit right there on the parlor floor. Her first thought was to run outside, but Mary Pearson was already rushing toward her.

"Come, let me take you upstairs where you can be made comfortable."

Rebecca didn't really think she would make it that far, but that wasn't going to be a problem. One of the children actually shoved an old chamber pot in her hands. Earlier she'd thought it was a flowerpot filled with big, colorful flowers made of embroidered cloth.

As they rushed up the stairs, Mary was explaining, "Since my first pregnancy, I made sure there would be a container available in every room for the early months. You will likely wish to do the same when you return home. The sickness may only last a few weeks or a few months, but still, you should not have to worry about something so natural."

What a perfect idea! Of course, she would only be returning to the palace to pack so she could go home. But in Norford, an empty container in every room could easily be arranged.

Upstairs, Mary opened a few doors before she found a room that wasn't overly cluttered with her children's messes and ushered Rebecca inside. "You may have some privacy here," the lady said. "And please use the bed if you will feel better lying down."

Rebecca knew the only way she'd feel better was to try emptying her stomach, and having made it that far, she didn't try to hold it back any longer. She only vaguely heard the door close behind her and Mary's voice in the corridor telling her children, most of whom had followed them upstairs, to be quiet and go clean their rooms!

Chapter Thirty-one

RUPERT COULDN'T HAVE ASKED for a better distraction than the one Rebecca had set in motion, particularly since all of the Pearson children had followed the ladies upstairs. Left alone in the parlor with Samuel and his wife's grandfather and two of her older male cousins, Rupert waited a few moments for the conversation to perk up again.

Then looking toward the empty doorway with a worried frown that he made sure Pearson noticed, he said, "This difficulty with the baby is all new to me. I feel it is all my fault, but I simply must help her through it. I will be back in a moment."

He didn't give his host a chance to assure him that Rebecca was already in good hands. He rushed out of the parlor. Playing the inexperienced husband and father-to-be wasn't something he was exactly familiar with, but it must have been an acceptable performance since he only heard a few understanding chuckles behind him.

He had no time to spare since the children could all come marching back downstairs at any moment. But the staircase began farther back in the hall and he had to pass two other rooms before he reached it. With all the doors in the hallway open, he saw that one of the rooms was a study and he quickly slipped inside it.

He went directly to the desk. He knew very well a systematic search would be impossible. He hated being rushed. He actually preferred to work in the dead of night with no light, but with time to spare. He didn't dare close the door, either, since that would be a visual giveaway. So all he could do was quickly stuff his pockets with every scrap of paper he could find and simply hope one of them turned out to be what he was looking for. Pearson would notice the papers were missing and Rupert would be suspected of stealing them, of course, but hopefully he'd be halfway to the coast by then. Just in case his plan didn't go well, he'd had Matthew park the coach in the road in front of Pearson's house with the family crest facing the street instead of the house.

It was Rebecca's fault he was being rushed. This task should have taken a couple weeks at least, allowing him to become a friend of the family's, get invited into rooms he wouldn't have access to otherwise, gain the man's trust. But, no, Rebecca had to be back in London in three damn days. What had possessed him to agree to her terms when he knew it would limit him to this single chance to get what he needed? Because he couldn't bring himself to leave her alone in a foreign country?

He knew from experience what a superb actress she was, and though he'd been right there, he'd love to find out how she'd faked vomiting. One finger down her throat when she covered her mouth with both hands?

"You shouldn't be in here." A male servant was standing in the doorway frowning at him.

"I just needed a moment to cool off since I sweat when my wife embarrasses me with her morning sickness," Rupert told the man.

The servant wasn't amused. He still looked stern and suspicious, but Rupert had given his improvised explanation while walking toward the man and was within reach by the last word. He tried a punch first, grabbing the servant's shirtfront as he did so the man wouldn't land out in the hall. If that didn't work, he wasn't sure what would. He certainly didn't want to seriously harm the fellow, just knock him out and dump him out the window for the time being.

Half of that plan worked. The man did drop immediately and Rupert's hold on him kept him from falling loudly to the floor. He even got him to the window with ease, but the plan ended there. Priceless. The window frame was nailed shut for the cold months to minimize drafts. Bloody hell, it wasn't that cold yet. There were no large pieces of furniture to stick the man behind either. As a last resort, he dragged him back to the hall wall and just laid him down alongside it, so he'd be less noticeable to anyone passing by the room.

Rupert dashed up the stairs finally and ran into Mary Pearson backing out of one of her children's rooms. Seeing him, she smiled in understanding and nodded toward the next door beyond her. It was closed, and he closed it again after he entered the room.

Rebecca was on her knees in the corner, groaning over a chamber pot again. He was finding her in that position all too often, and while it usually aroused him to see a woman positioned that way, the gag she added for effect quite ruined it.

"Nicely done, Becca. But we have to leave now."

She glanced back at him, but only long enough to give him

a fulminating glare before she faced the chamber pot and groaned again.

He sighed. "I wasn't joking. I will use the excuse that you have discovered that fresh air helps you to get past this, and that we should have left immediately to find some." When she still didn't get up, he added testily, "No one is walking in behind me to witness this performance, and we have to—"

He paused as he realized that the large size of this room in such a small house indicated it was the master bedroom. And there was a desk. He marched over to it and saw what looked like a leatherbound diary or ledger. As he flipped it open, he found it was definitely a record of transactions, with dates, volumes for goods bought and sold, a running tally of costs, and even the names of Pearson's employees and how much he was paying them *and* for what service.

He almost laughed when he saw the name of the thief who had volunteered Pearson as his employer. He preferred to keep the book intact for evidence, rather than rip out the needed pages.

"Think you can hide this under your skirt long enough to get out of the house?" It was a little too wide for one of his pockets.

She glanced at the book in his hand and said, "Certainly, but I'm not going any—"

"I had to disable a servant downstairs," he said sharply. "The man could wake up at any moment to raise the alarm. There is no time to discuss this, we leave now."

While he usually enjoyed this type of challenge and risk, it was a whole different game with Rebecca along. He was even starting to feel an odd sort of panic—because of her presence. While he found her to be annoying in the extreme, confusing, frustrating, the thought of her being hurt started a cold sweat he wasn't used to at all.

He didn't hand her the ledger after all, just grabbed her arm and headed for the door, slipping the book in the back of his pants under his coat. "You don't stop for anything, just go straight out the front door and into the coach. I'll make the excuse for our host if there's still time, or fight my way out. . . . That's good, that pale look is perfect, keep it up."

Rupert was reasonably sure that Rebecca wasn't pretending any longer and realized now that the situation was perilous. But there really was no more time for discussion or assurances. At least Mary Pearson was no longer in the upper corridor, so he quickly got Rebecca downstairs and pushed her toward the front door before he stopped at the parlor again.

He almost expected to be facing a room full of pistols, but apparently he'd hit the servant harder than he'd figured. The men were still conversing, Mary was back on a sofa with four of her youngest children, and he made quick work of his excuse to leave so abruptly, suggesting they might return for another visit tomorrow afternoon prior to resuming their trip.

Rebecca was still quite pallid when he joined her in the coach, but he was able to assure her, "Unless Pearson goes immediately to his study, it could be an hour or more before he discovers the servant I knocked out. We should be fine now. But we will still make haste to the coast."

Rebecca said nothing, but her expression said a lot. She was still angry about something, probably that he'd put her at risk like that, and he certainly couldn't blame her. But the danger was over, and the last buildings of Le Mans were behind them. He'd no sooner had that thought when the first shot was fired.

Chapter Thirty-two

RUPERT YANKED REBECCA OFF her seat to the floor! If that weren't bad enough, he dropped down on top of her, not with his full weight, but enough to make it uncomfortable.

Rebecca had, of course, heard the gunfire that had prompted Rupert's actions. She wasn't deaf. Still, annoyed, she asked, "Do you *really* think a shot is going to get through the back panel of a coach this sturdily built? And fired from a moving vehicle? Anyone aiming isn't likely to hit us a'tall."

"They're on horseback" was all he said.

"Even worse. Have you ever hit what you aimed at while racing along on a horse?"

"Yes."

She snorted, not believing him at all. But she did grasp the implication of the pursuers being on horseback. Even though Matthew had immediately picked up their pace to a reckless degree, it still wouldn't take all that long for horses to catch up to a coach.

"Highwaymen?" she asked, and couldn't hide the hopeful note from her tone.

"In the middle of the day?"

"So they're desperate."

Being robbed wouldn't be pleasant, but it would actually be preferable compared to an angry criminal running them down for his stolen property.

"That would be the logical assumption, Becca, if we didn't just leave the house of a *confirmed* mass murderer."

"So you did find the evidence you were after?"

"It's in the book I asked you to smuggle out. Considering how quickly we left, my guess would be that Mary Pearson immediately mentioned to her husband that she'd put you in their bedroom, and that I entered it as well. Samuel would have gone straight upstairs in that case to check on the incriminating ledger he'd carelessly left lying on the desk."

"And found it gone," she said with a resigned sigh.

"Don't sound so aggrieved. We'll be fine."

She could have screamed at him like a harpy for that ridiculous assessment. With two more shots fired at them, her fear was rising fast. It had been the same back at the Pearson house. The moment Rupert had warned that he'd disabled one of the servants, meaning they could be found out at any moment, her nausea had abruptly ended. Incredible. Did the sudden rush of fear do that? Not that she was going to seek out things to frighten her just to get through this pregnancy a little easier, but it was an interesting side effect. She could at least test the theory at home by having Flora try to startle her or . . . what the deuce was she doing thinking about things that might never happen when she could end up dead in minutes?

"Aren't you alarmed at all?" she demanded of Rupert.

He had the audacity to say, "Not really, at least not as long as *you* stay down flat on that floor. They were probably on our tail before we even left the city."

"Then why didn't they fire at us sooner?"

"Because of the evidence. Shots fired with witnesses lining the streets will have to be explained, and they can't very well commit murder with citizens watching them. Well, they can, but since Pearson lives in that city, he wouldn't want to expose himself in that way. So they waited until we were beyond the city. Out here on the empty road, we're fair game."

She did screech at him this time. "I don't see how you can *not* find that alarming!"

He leaned down and said by her ear, "I'm not going to let you get hurt, I promise you I'm not."

His tone was so soothing she could almost believe him. Almost.

"I have one of the fastest teams of horses around," he continued. "I wouldn't be surprised if we reach the next town before they get close enough to try to board us."

She wished he hadn't added that. It pointed out clearly that the pursuers would be trying to disable poor Matthew first, which would immediately slow the coach down if not halt it completely—or wreck it.

But before she could point that out, Rupert said, "Excuse me," and leaned off her.

She glanced behind her to see him raising the boxed seat he'd occupied. He reached into the compartment under it and lifted out a rifle. Her eyes flared wide with her first conclusion.

"You're going to kill someone over this?!"

"You don't think he deserves it? But, no, that's not my intention. I'm an excellent shot. I'm just going to help them decide to turn around."

Just like that? And said with such complete confidence? Whom did he think he was kidding? But she watched him open the window in the door nearest to her head. Braced on his knees because he was too tall to stand up in the coach, he got his head, half his chest, and the rifle though the window, no easy task. The window was wide, but his chest was wider. Then he took aim.

The sound of the shot so close to her left her ears ringing. She barely heard Rupert swear, but then the coach did just bounce as his first shot was fired, probably making it go wildly off the mark. She covered her ears with her hands for the duration. It didn't help much, but over the next five minutes, Rupert only sent off three more shots, the last one from the other window.

"You can get up now."

She dredged up some indignation as she crawled back onto her seat so he wouldn't notice how frightened she'd been, not just for herself, but for her baby. "It took you three shots to change Pearson's opinion? Not such an excellent shot after all, eh?"

"He had two others with him. All three are wounded now."

Her blush was only slight, her fear still present. The shooting might have stopped, but her trembling hadn't. Nowhere in his description of what they would be doing in Le Mans had he mentioned running for their lives.

Sitting opposite her again, his arms crossed, Rupert remarked after a moment of studying her face, "You know, I think this is the first time in my adult life that I have been ensconced with a female in a comfortable coach and haven't tried to maneuver her onto my lap for a more enjoyable ride. Aside from my mother, of course."

"Is that remark supposed to have some hidden meaning?" she snapped.

"Thought it was rather clear m'self," he said with a roguish grin as he reached for her hand and drew her onto his lap.

"What are—?"

"You've had a bad scare," he said in a low tone by her ear, his hot breath sending a shiver down her spine. "This will get your mind off it, don't you think?"

Her mind was already off it! She couldn't imagine why he'd want to soothe her when he saw her in such a despicable light, but he wasn't waiting for her answer. Putting a hand to her cheek, he maneuvered her lips to his, and within seconds that kiss became hot and explosive. Their brush with death had caused some heart-pounding emotions in them both that were now being released in a burst of passion.

God, how could he keep doing this to her, making her want him so badly that nothing else mattered? It was bad enough when she just looked at him, but tasting him, feeling him! And remembering their lovemaking—if she didn't know what this was leading to, she might have had the will to stop him, but she did know, and she didn't want to stop him.

Her fingers threaded through his silky hair. A lock brushed against her cheek as he changed her position slightly without ending the kiss. Her head now rested in the crook of his arm, while his hand, spread wide, moved slowly from her neck to her stomach in a long, delicious caress that only paused a moment before she felt his fingers press ever so slightly where her legs joined. Her clothes were in the way!

A hard bounce of the coach broke that kiss and cleared her head enough for her to realize she had to try one more time to convince him about the baby before she let this go on. They would both regret it afterward if she didn't. Or maybe this was his way of telling her that he did believe her!

She put her fingers to his lips before he could kiss her again so she could ask him, "Do you believe me now?"

"About what?"

He really was confused, to go by his expression. But then his mind had been on only one thing and the passion was still in his eyes. So she clarified, "About the baby."

That quickly extinguished the fire—for him, anyway. He put her back on her seat, raked a hand through his hair, and pinned her with a scowl. "Your timing is deplorable, Rebecca. I thought I made it clear I wasn't falling for that trap."

That doused the sensual flames for her. If he still thought that, he shouldn't have kissed her! It didn't matter that he'd managed to make her forget her fear over being shot at, what was left now was pure frustration.

She ought to try one last time to convince him that he was wrong about her, but all she ended up saying was "You know, when we're both old and gray-haired and looking back on our lives, only I will have the memories of this child we created. I think at that point I will pity you."

She definitely struck a nerve, to go by the dark look he was giving her now. She didn't care. That prediction was no more than he deserved.

He said no more.

She'd said too much.

Then Rupert shook his head. "What a fool I am to get taken in by you again and again. You are a master manipulator. So you want to marry me that much? Fine, I'll have the captain marry us at sea on the crossing back to England. But don't think you're getting what you want, Becca. This won't get you in my door. It will be in name only until it is proven you aren't pregnant, and then we'll have the marriage annulled. You will have to leave your position at the palace, of course. Maids of honor lose that title when they marry, and they certainly aren't allowed to have babies. So you will go home and hide yourself away for the duration."

How dare he dictate his despicable terms to her! "I was already planning to return home because it's getting harder and harder to hide my morning sickness. If there were another option, guess what? I'd take it just to spite you! But marriage to the most unfaithful skirt-chaser in London *isn't* an option, and you've already had my answer. It's *not* going to happen."

"It will," he insisted.

"Ha!"

"You don't think so? Then I guess you won't mind when your pregnancy is announced in the newspapers."

She sucked in her breath, livid with rage. "*Why* would you do that?"

"Because you've finally inserted some doubt in my mind, and as long as there's even a speck of it, let me assure you, I will be damned before I allow any child of mine to go to strangers."

"*Why don't you just be damned!*"

Chapter Thirty-three

Hᴏᴡ ᴄᴏᴜʟᴅ ʏᴏᴜ ʜᴀᴛᴇ someone and still feel bad about wishing them damned? Yet she felt bad! Rebecca actually had to grapple with herself to keep from apologizing to Rupert. She was certain that Rupert also had only spoken in anger and that he wouldn't really marry her.

But he did.

The shock was tremendous and wouldn't go away. Standing there on the deck of the small ship that Rupert had gotten them passage on, the cold wind in her face had dried her tears so quickly she didn't even know she was crying. Such a horrible way to be married, and all because she couldn't resist the tarnished angel. She was trying to think what this "marriage" would mean to her and couldn't. It had no meaning!

A bigger ship would take the coach and horses as well, but only Matthew would be traveling on that one, since it wasn't sailing until the next day. The smaller ship didn't offer a cabin but was leaving immediately and would get them to Dover within the hour.

She only sensed him when he came to stand next to her at the rail. She couldn't bring herself to look at him. The English coast was in sight by then and she kept her eyes on it.

"Let me give you a few assurances, Becca," Rupert said in a calm, soothing tone, as if he were actually doing her a favor. "I won't touch you again. This marriage really will be in name only."

She might have thanked him for that if she could have managed to speak. Then again, she would as soon not talk to him at all at this point.

But he hadn't actually finished his last remark and added, "I'm not going to take the chance of you *really* getting with child."

If she were prone to hysterics, she'd be having some. And he still wasn't done pounding her self-esteem into the ground. Although his voice remained calm, he was insulting her at every turn.

"You won't even have to see me again until enough time has passed to prove that you are lying about the baby. In fact, I don't need to show up for that. I'll send one of my brothers to check on you in my stead, and I'll get our marriage annulled immediately thereafter. So no harm done, at least from my perspective."

"My, how nice for you," she said scathingly under her breath.

"While I don't doubt this marriage is exactly what you wanted all along, despite your silly protests to the contrary, too bad. No one is going to know about this, or should I be more explicit?"

"Yes," she replied sharply. "I am brilliantly cunning and stupidly dense at the same time. Do continue treating me like a child."

"Your sarcasm is uncalled-for."

"I disagree. Actually, I will probably disagree with you henceforth whether I agree with you or not! I *can* behave like a child if you insist on treating me like one."

She hadn't looked at him yet, but she did look down to see his knuckles turning white as he gripped the rail beside her. Good. Why should she be the only one angry about this deplorable situation?

"Have it your way, the explicit version then," he bit out. "No one had *better* find out about this marriage-in-name-only that you say you didn't want, and I know damn well I didn't want."

Now he was threatening her? With what? Marriage to him for life? She might just get hysterical after all.

"You can tell your mother, of course," he went on. "I don't want to have her pounding on my door if you're foolish enough to try to convince her that you're enceinte. But you will tell no one else and warn her of the same."

"Is that so? And what makes you think I'm going to do anything you say?"

"Because for the time being you are legally mine, and that means you *will* obey me."

She nearly choked she drew in her breath so sharply. "Do *not* count on that, St. John. I don't care what rights you think this mockery of a marriage gives you, as far as I'm concerned, you don't even exist. Do *I* need to be more explicit?"

"No, I believe we have come to a mutual agreement to forget about each other, which suits me just fine. As long as you do nothing to gain my notice, which means you stay at your home for the duration."

"Your threats don't scare me."

He lifted a brow at her. "No? Then you really must have

some odd notions about marriage, if you think you can do as you please now. Ask your mother if you doubt me."

He walked away, and she didn't bother to look where. They were man and wife and would be until he got their marriage annulled. What a rude awakening that was going to be in three or four months' time. For him.

Chapter Thirty-four

*W*here *have you been?!*

Rebecca winced at Flora's screeching tone, even though she had been expecting no less. It had taken so long to rent a coach in Dover and hie it back to London that it was now near dark. But the maid didn't have to be quite that loud in expressing her relief.

"Not where I wanted to be," Rebecca replied tiredly, and moved to sit down on the bed.

"Four days have passed!"

"I'm lucky it was only four," Rebecca grouched. "It's not exactly easy to catch a ship at a moment's notice, you know. No, I suppose you wouldn't know. But let me tell you, I found that out firsthand."

Flora's eyes widened. "Just where did you think you were going by ship? And alone? Without me?"

"It wasn't by choice. The ship sailed while I was telling my husband that marriage to him would be out of the question."

"So you married him?"

Rebecca blinked now at Flora's suddenly calm tone. "Why doesn't that surprise you?"

"Because it was the right thing to do, all things considered."

Rebecca snorted and, with some of her anger returning, leaped to her feet again. "Not when he didn't want to marry me. Not when he thinks that I seduced him. Not when he's so bloody sure that I'm lying about having his baby."

"Then—how did you end up marrying him anyway?"

"A speck of doubt was how he put it."

"A speck?" Flora choked out.

"Yes, just a speck."

"You spent four days with him and didn't vomit once to prove—"

"Course I did. Every morning." Rebecca sighed. "But he's not counting something he thinks I faked. Besides, on board ship, it wasn't just the morning sickness I was beset with. I'm quite sure the only proof he'll accept prior to the actual birth is a widened girth. But as it stands, he intends to annul the marriage, since he's *so* positive I won't start displaying some proof that I'm pregnant in the expected period of time."

"Well, too bad for him then, when you do."

"No, too bad for me. He's such a rogue, Flora. I can't believe I was ever attracted to him. Of course he didn't show his true colors prior to that fateful night. But he certainly showed them when I caught up to him on that ship that sailed before I could get off it. And I was *not* going to marry him and told him so."

"You sure stuck to your guns!"

"Don't try to inject humor into this deplorable situation. He threatened to ruin me publicly if I didn't accept his horrible temporary terms! And he's ordered me to go into hiding at home in Norford until he's satisfied enough time has passed to end this farce of a marriage."

"What happens when he finds out he can't end it amicably, but only with a scandalous divorce?"

"Once he sees that I wasn't lying, he won't end it a'tall, which is what I'm dreading. That was the only reason he married me, that slim bit of doubt he was having. He stated clearly that he will not let strangers raise *his* child. So I really hope I'm late in showing the proof he wants, so I can get out of this mess before he realizes there really is a baby."

"I don't think you've thought that through," Flora said hesitantly.

"There's no doubt in my mind that I despise him now," Rebecca insisted.

"I don't mean *that*. I mean you got what you needed, legitimacy for your child. If you quietly end the marriage so no one even hears about it, you'll be back where you started, but three or four months too late to do anything other than go away to have your baby in secret, then give the child up."

Rebecca paled. Why hadn't that occurred to her? Because she was too busy being furious with Rupert St. John to think beyond getting far away from him?

"I can see you got my point," Flora added with a satisfied nod.

"This is—intolerable. I can't bear the thought of being tied to him for—"

"Oh, stop it," Flora cut in sternly. "Do you really think he's going to continue being so despicable to you after he knows his silly conclusions are all wrong? He'll more likely go out of his way to be as charming as you could ever want, to make it up to you."

Rebecca snorted. "No, he'll just find some other reason to despise me. Don't forget, he claims I seduced him, that this is all my fault!"

"Did you?" Flora asked baldly. At Rebecca's glare, the maid amended in a conciliatory tone, "No, of course not. Can't imagine what I was thinking. But it makes you wonder how many times women have tried to trap him into marriage, for him to distrust the truth when it's right in front of him."

"Do *not* make excuses for him, Flora. And I've spent nearly four horrid days with the man, so I'd rather not talk about him anymore."

Flora nodded in agreement and picked up the book she had been reading. "How long has my mother been frantic over my disappearance?" Rebecca asked anxiously.

Flora's expression turned immediately sympathetic. "I waited as long as my nerves could bear to send word to her that you were missing. I kept praying you'd return at any moment. But after two days *and* nights and still no word from you, I couldn't wait any longer. And now another day has passed and the man John Keets found to deliver the message hasn't even returned yet. But I don't doubt he succeeded. I thought Lilly would be here last night, so I can't imagine what's delaying her. I expect her to arrive at any moment, though."

Rebecca sighed. She should be grateful that Lilly hadn't been worrying as long as she'd feared, but now she was worried about what was delaying her mother's arrival. And she didn't know whether she should stay at the palace and wait for her mother to arrive or try to find Lilly along the road on the way home. She might miss her in that case, since it was already getting dark. Besides, without her own coach and driver, she'd have to hire a hack, and it was doubtful she'd find one willing to drive her all the way to Norford at night.

"I suppose I will have to spend one more night here," Rebecca said. "But you can have my trunks brought up and I'll help you pack them so you can have time to pack up your flat before it gets too late tonight."

"We leave tomorrow?"

"Yes, first thing in the morning. If I could get us transportation tonight, I would."

"John can probably help with that if you want to leave now."

"But what if Mama arrives after we leave?"

"John can watch for her, too, and let her know you're safe and sound," Flora said. "That's going to be her main concern. She doesn't need to actually see you to be assured that you're fine."

"Poor Mr. Keets. We have quite taken advantage of his friendliness. I'll have to think of a way to compensate him for all his help."

"You don't need to do that," Flora said with a blush.

"Oh," Rebecca replied, understanding perfectly, and only a *little* uncomfortable with the subject of Flora's many lovers, now that she'd had her own fall from grace. "Hmm, well, I hope you're not going to miss him too terribly when we're back at home."

Flora grinned. "He promised to visit—often."

"Very well then, we can even send someone back for our belongings, I suppose, if he can find us a coach tonight. I will need to explain my absence these past few days to Lady Sarah, though, and let her know why I'm leaving my position as maid of honor. I'll go and do that now."

"You're going to tell her the truth then?" Flora asked in surprise.

"Goodness, no. That knowledge we will keep to ourselves.

But I have a ready excuse for Sarah. Her intrigues, can't bear to watch them anymore, et cetera. I'll even tell her that I went home these last few days to convince Mama of my desire to relinquish this post for good."

"You're going to do what?" Lilly Marshall said from the doorway.

Chapter Thirty-five

LILLY LOOKED WONDERFUL, BUT then she always did in the colder months when her cheeks retained a rosy glow from her daily rides. Rebecca, an excellent horsewoman, had learned from her mother and had always ridden with her early in the mornings before her classes began. She'd missed that in London. She'd missed her mother, too, terribly. Nearly two months without a visit!

"Don't tell me that I've bought a town house here in London for nothing," Lilly said as she entered the room and gave Rebecca a long, tight hug. "Though I suppose we can still make use of it with the winter Season soon upon us. How are you, darling? You look a little pallid. You haven't been sick, have you? Is that why you want to come home?"

Rebecca barely managed to keep her mouth from dropping open. Obviously, her mother didn't even know of her four-day absence. Which meant Lilly hadn't been anguished and worried, and Rebecca had agonized over that for nothing. And her mother as she walked in probably hadn't even heard more than the last few words Rebecca had been saying. That meant Rebecca could break the news to her gently. . . .

"She's married, she's having a baby, and she'll tell you all about it on the way home."

"Flora!" Rebecca exclaimed.

But Lilly admonished the maid with a stern look. "You've always had a rather tasteless sense of humor, Flora. But those aren't subjects to joke about."

Rebecca quickly tried to change the subject. "When did you decide to buy a house in town? You didn't mention it in your letters."

"I wanted to surprise you. I even came to London two days ago to finish the purchase, but there were some delays. Still wanting to make it a surprise, I resisted visiting you until the papers were signed, which didn't happen until about an hour ago. That was difficult, worse than being at home and missing you," Lilly added with a chuckle.

"I wasn't joking," Flora interjected with a mumble from across the room.

Both Marshall ladies glared at the maid now, then ignored her again. Rebecca reminded her mother, "But you said you weren't going to actually buy a house here."

"I know, I was determined not to. I had to cut the strings, as it were, since I knew that you'd probably never live at home again, at least not for any length of time. But I finally couldn't stand it any longer! So no matter where you end up living once you are married, we will not be so far away from each other again."

"I wasn't joking," the maid mumbled again.

"Flora, stop it, *please*," Rebecca said this time.

Unfortunately, a little too much angst was in her tone for

Lilly not to take notice. Her mother frowned in concern. "Is there something I should know about?" Lilly asked her directly.

Rebecca couldn't get the words out, could only stare at her mother. Her nervous stomach was back in spades.

"I'm only trying to keep you from getting all edgy about it again," Flora said as blithely as you please. "You don't need any more upset like that adding to your morning sickness. You've had far too much already."

Lilly wasn't stupid, and she was far too good with numbers not to add some up now and conclude in a hurt tone, "You got married the same week you arrived here? And didn't tell me or invite me to the wedding?"

Rebecca quickly assured her, "It wasn't like that, Mama. I just got married this morning out in the Channel as we were returning from France."

"France?!"

Rebecca winced. "You could say it was a wedding trip—of sorts."

But the rest was adding up now in Lilly's mind and she said, "Oh, good God, I need to sit down." But she didn't, she was still standing there in shock when she added, "Who is he?"

"Rupert St. John."

"Isn't he—oh, my, that handsome boy of Julie's? Well, *that* explains a bit, I suppose. He always did dazzle you whenever you saw him, didn't he?"

"Yes, until I got to know him," Rebecca replied, then wished she'd kept that grumble to herself.

Up went Lilly's brow. "Something else is wrong aside from the fact that you had to get married?"

"I suppose that the bride and groom hate each other could be considered a little something else," Flora said.

This time Lilly sat down. She started to say something, but changed her mind. She opened her mouth to start again, but again snapped it shut. Finally she burst out, "This sort of thing was never supposed to happen to you!" Then after giving herself a brief shake, she said, "Very well, as briefly as you can, please, so I can get beyond this sudden urge to go find a pistol."

Rebecca did keep it brief and tried not to leave anything out. She began at the beginning, explaining what Sarah Wheeler had tried to get her involved in and how that first meeting with Rupert had been somewhat amusing in retrospect, especially with them both making so many wrong assumptions. She admitted her fascination with him, despite his being such an obvious skirt-chaser. She even confessed that she'd agreed to help Mr. Jennings in his intrigues, and that's what had led her to seek out Rupert where she shouldn't have. But she spared nothing in the conclusion, repeating everything he had said and why.

Rebecca actually felt wonderful when she finished, as if a mountain of weight on her shoulders had just crumbled to dust. She should have remembered how Lilly dealt with the good and the bad that life offered. Her mother never pouted, never held grudges. She could get as angry over something as anyone else could, but she rarely ever stewed about it, preferring a quick burst of emotion to get it out of her system, then she'd be back to her normal cheerful self. Rebecca really wished she could be like that. And she wished she'd gone to Lilly first, instead of following Flora's advice—which had gotten her married.

Lilly stood up when Rebecca had finished and even smiled. It might not have been a wholehearted smile, but it was definitely a determined one.

"Very well," she said. "There is no need to rush home to Norford. I have a room for you at my hotel. I thought you might enjoy a break from the palace to go shopping with me to furnish the new house, but consider it a break from thinking about this sad situation instead. We'll have a nice reunion. We'll have some fun. And then you can decide what *you* want to do. So you can forget about your husband's silly dictates, which are quite irrelevant because they are based on his false analysis instead of the truth. So what do you say, darling? Shall we go have a nice dinner in London? And, well, *you* can't, but I feel like getting a little foxed while we're at it."

Chapter Thirty-six

Rebecca wasn't the least bit nervous when she arrived at Rupert's house this time. Lilly had offered to go with her, but Rebecca didn't want her mother to witness how sarcastic and insulting Rupert could be—or how she could stoop to the same level once he provoked her. She'd made the decision to go to Rupert herself. She might have made it in anger, but she was certain it was the right decision. It didn't matter how much she loathed the idea, or how much Rupert was bound to object. Their baby had to come first.

Besides, her mother had fully agreed with her and had even put the original idea in her head when she'd warned, "Don't let him get comfortable with this annulment idea when it isn't going to happen."

The same butler she'd dealt with before opened the door to her. Since her mother's driver was already lifting down one of her smaller trunks from the coach, the man should have displayed at least a little surprise or curiosity, but he masked his feelings well.

"I'm Rebecca St. John and I've come to stay," she explained. "So if you will send a footman out to help with my trunks, I would appreciate it. Please direct me to the marquis."

It took the butler a moment to reply. His eyes even flared briefly. He probably felt he should have been warned of her arrival and rightly so—but no one in the house knew about it.

"The marquis is unavailable," he replied inscrutably.

"Still sleeping at this hour?" she guessed.

"No, Lady Rebecca, he left quite early this morning. It was barely dawn. He took a small valise with him, so he may not return today. He did say as much."

She certainly wasn't expecting that news. She was ready for a blistering fight, and he wasn't there to have it. "May I speak with his mother?"

"Of course, follow me."

The butler didn't go far, stopping at the door to the dining room to announce loftily, "Lady St. John has arrived, madam."

Rebecca heard a testy tone, from inside the room. "Are you blind, Charles? I'm sitting right here."

"The *new* Lady St. John," he corrected.

Rebecca had a feeling Charles took some pleasure in being able to render the lady of the house speechless. But since he wouldn't be able to answer any questions Julie St. John might direct to him, Rebecca stepped around him and into the room.

"I am the new lady in question, previously Rebecca Marshall of the Norford Marshalls. As it happens, my family home is just down the road from your brother's estate, so you may know—"

"Lilly Marshall's girl?" Julie cut in.

"Yes, and presently—your daughter-in-law."

The older woman should have been bowled over, but Julie

St. John did no more than set down her fork to ask in a somewhat aggrieved tone, "Which one married you?"

"Your eldest. It was a brief ceremony performed at sea just last week."

A big smile formed on her mother-in-law's face, shocking Rebecca. "I must say, girl, you have succeeded where all others have failed. I commend you!"

"You aren't angry?"

"Good God, no, I'm delighted. I even knew both of your parents. They were the best of friends as I'm sure you've been told, so it was no surprise to anyone when they married. I'd already left home by then, but I heard the earl built that manor house just for Lilly, since it was close to her family home. Thought that was rather romantic of him when my brother mentioned it on one of my visits home. Damned inconvenient to live most of your life in an entailed house and to lose it when your husband passes on. At least that didn't happen to your mother."

Rebecca barely managed to steel her expression at the older woman's grumbling. She knew exactly what Julie was complaining about. She had assumed that Rupert was still living with his mother and had even mentioned it to Lilly this week.

"You have that backwards," Lilly had told her. "Julie still lives with him. He gained all of the marquis's properties along with the title when his father died."

Rebecca didn't miss that Julie had gone off on a different subject. Didn't the woman want to know why Rupert hadn't told her that he'd married?

Carefully Rebecca said, "I am pleased that you find me a suitable wife for your son, but I should warn you that he doesn't feel the same way. I am not here at his invitation, I am barging in, as it were."

"You two are fighting already?" Julie guessed. "Well *that* doesn't bode well, but it explains why he failed to mention this monumental event to me. I still find it incredible. I fully expected both of my younger boys to marry long before Rue got around to it."

"It's more than just a fight, Lady Julie. Rupert intends to have our marriage annulled."

The lady frowned. "I think I could have done without knowing *that* just yet. So I'm not going to get any grandchildren?"

"You are—at least one," Rebecca said with a shy smile.

Chapter Thirty-seven

IT DIDN'T TAKE LONG for Rupert to realize how much easier it was for him to think about Rebecca in a logical manner when she wasn't around to confound and provoke him. After returning her to Buckingham Palace and promptly going home himself, he barely had two days of respite before that speck of doubt Rebecca had planted in his mind began to grow and he had to acknowledge the life-changing consequences of her bearing his child.

How the deuce would they explain to people their decision to live apart in these early months if they had to stay married? But that would only be a problem if Rebecca really was enceinte, and that hadn't been proved yet.

It took another few days for Rupert to start thinking about the baby as real rather than a product of Rebecca's scheming. He even began to imagine what his baby would look like. That was a mistake. No sooner had he put a face to this child who probably didn't even exist than he was beset with a powerful emotion he couldn't quite describe, or shake off. Their child—no, it was his. Dammit, no, it really was *theirs*—if it was real.

He got good and foxed to try to stop thinking about the baby and Rebecca, but the notion that had got into his head didn't go away. He was going to have to fetch Rebecca back to London. After all, he couldn't trust her not to do something foolish. Did she even know what precautions to take? Did she realize that some things that were perfectly fine for her to do under normal circumstances could be a danger to an unborn baby?

Rupert simply packed a small valise in case he ran into bad weather along the way and rode straight to Norford to bring her home with him.

Their living in the same household wasn't an ideal situation by any means, but it would be the only way he could monitor her activities to keep them appropriate for an expectant mother. They could come up with a simple reason to be staying in the same household that had nothing to do with marriage. Their mothers came from the same neighborhood, after all, and with November coming to an end in just a few days, the long winter Season was already upon them. Julie could let it be known that she was sponsoring Rebecca for the Season. It was as simple as that.

He rode hard all the way to Norford, surprising even himself at how quickly the distance could be traversed when he wasn't making the journey with his mother in her slow, plodding coach. The anxiety he was experiencing about getting his unborn child under his protection in no way resembled any eagerness to see Rebecca again. At least he assured himself of that a half dozen times on that long ride. But the unexpected disappointment he felt when he didn't find her at home was partly responsible for the anger he felt as he rode back to London.

He had told her to go home. Did she really think she could

still do as she pleased? She had deliberately defied him. Since she wasn't really pregnant, she had obviously decided to keep her post at the palace. He'd be damned if he was going to go there to have it out with her, since that was an argument guaranteed to get loud and there were far too many eavesdroppers and gossips in the palace.

When he stepped through the front door of his house, he was too shocked at seeing her walk out of his parlor to react immediately. He stared at her hard. He was relieved that she was all right and no longer missing. But the anger he'd ridden home with hadn't dissipated, and soon he was scowling at her. She didn't exactly look cowed by his expression. Did her eyes reveal some anger of her own? Damn, she *did* look fetching in that lavender gown—her waist as thin as ever . . .

"Is there a *reason* why you are here?" he finally demanded.

With complete nonchalance she replied, "Well, I've brought my trunks. I do believe I'm moving in."

"The hell you are!"

"Nice of you to welcome me in your usual boorish manner" was all she said to that.

A muscle ticked in his jaw. It made not a jot of difference that he'd just gone to Norford and back this morning to bring her here himself. That had been his idea. *Her* coming here on her own was her idea, and it made him suspicious.

"Don't start your manipulations already," he warned her. "Answer my question."

"Why am I here? Shall we start with the obvious reason? Because I really am pregnant and once my pregnancy starts to show, I do not want to be in a position to have people ask me who my husband is and not believe me when I tell them that it's you."

"And the not-so-obvious answer?"

"Because you make me so furious that I spite myself to spite you!"

"You won't force my hand just by showing up here uninvited, I promise you won't. I admit to a small measure of doubt, but if you try to make this marriage a reality before the baby becomes a reality—"

"We *aren't* rehashing this again. Your mother knows, my mother knows, and *that*, if you aren't smart enough to figure it out, makes us married for real. I told you I didn't want to marry you, but if you'll recall, *you* insisted, so now *you* live with it. All I want is for my baby to be legitimate, and now it will be. So spread your lies that I took advantage of you if you must. How did you put it? That I seduced you? I don't care at this point."

With as much patience as he could muster where she was concerned, he asked, "Why are you doing this to me?"

"Because I'm not lying. I haven't lied to you since the night I told you I was looking for a scarf for Sarah."

Chapter Thirty-eight

REBECCA WONDERED IF HER emotions were always going to get so out of hand when she was around Rupert.

She walked away from him. There was just no talking to the man, and he made her so bloody furious she was once again saying things she'd rather not say. But it was his house! So walking away from him here meant he could follow her—and he did.

She didn't know where her trunks had been taken. Too angry to find the butler to ask him and too angry not to look for them herself, she began opening doors upstairs. Normally, she would never do anything that rude, but nothing about her current emotions was normal, and Rupert was dogging her steps.

When her hand reached to open the next-to-last door in the long corridor, Rupert warned, "That's . . . not . . ."

He didn't finish. Standing behind her once she'd opened the door, he could see that she'd found her trunks stacked in the large room. She didn't hesitate to enter.

Neither did he, and his tone was about as adamant as it could get when he said, "You are *not* staying in here."

It was a wonderful room. Dark blue and burgundy blended well in the plush carpet. Light blue and pale cream in the wallpaper made the large paintings with their dark wood frames stand out nicely. The thickly cushioned upholstery on the cherrywood sofa and reading chair was light cream, such a stark contrast with the dark carpet. The low table between them was a piece of art itself, the legs of it were so intricately carved.

The drapes at several windows were yet another shade of dark blue, embroidered with silver threads. An easel stood by the largest window, the painting that was apparently being worked on turned toward the light so she couldn't see what it was of. Several bookcases were so filled there wasn't room for even one more book. Twin bureaus, larger than any others she'd ever seen, sat side by side and were likely custom-made. A white marble fireplace wide enough to easily heat such a large room took up a good part of one wall.

Two other doors were on one wall, possibly leading to a water closet and a wardrobe, or connecting to another bedroom in the style of some master suites.

The entire room was grandly elegant, and the large bed, thrust oddly into one corner of the room, prompted her guess "Your room?" She tried to keep her voice neutral as she added, "I quite agree, I won't be staying in here. Charles must have presumed this was the logical place to put my trunks when I told him I am the new Lady St. John."

"On a first-name basis with my servants already?"

She turned around to find him walking across the room to stand in front of the easel like a guard dog. As if she cared that he painted or wanted to know what he'd find of interest to paint.

In reply to his question she said, "I merely heard your servant's name, but, fine, henceforth I will call him *your* butler, just as I will call this *your* house, just as I will call that"—she stabbed a finger toward the corner—"*your* bloody odd bed."

"What's wrong with my bed?"

"No one situates a bed so that one can only get in or out of it on one side unless it's a matter of not having enough room for it, which hasn't been the case for *your* beds. All three of them now that I've had the misfortune to view have been shoved into corners."

"You call that odd?"

Rebecca drew in her breath as he approached her. His expression had turned entirely too sensual, reminding her of the night they made love.

He must have been remembering the same thing, because he added, "I don't recall your being bothered by the bed in my room in the palace. In fact, you hardly seemed to notice it that night because you were paying so much attention to me. Don't you remember?"

How could she forget! But she wasn't going to admit that. Her blush, however, probably admitted it for her, so she quickly moved away from him.

"Did you ever think to ask why the beds are arranged that way instead of making snide assumptions?" he said, causing her burning cheeks to get even hotter. "There is nothing wrong with this arrangement—in fact, there is a good reason for it."

Now, thankfully, that he was no longer talking about their night of lovemaking, she was able to say, "Very well, I'll bite. What is the reason?"

"It's really none of your business, but since you've made an issue of it, I'm going to tell you. It's an appalling shortcoming of mine that I toss about so much in my sleep that I used to fall out of bed occasionally. Of course, it never happens when I have a soft bedmate beside me, which tends to lure me in the direction of warmth even while I'm asleep. But since that isn't usually the case here, to keep from waking the rest of the family when I hit the floor, I've found this a safer position for my bed."

She would never have imagined such an answer or that he'd admit it. And he'd made her feel that she ought to apologize.

So she was amazed at herself when she said quite scathingly, "What, the housemaids aren't pretty enough to tempt you?"

"Certainly, but mother frowns on that sort of cavorting in her house."

"I thought this was your house?"

He shrugged. "So it is, but since I share it with my family, I still respect her wishes on the matter."

Rebecca blushed again. Why couldn't she have just apologized as she should have? But she still couldn't bring herself to do so even now. She turned about to leave his room instead.

Without stopping, and in a completely dismissive tone, she said, "I'll find *your* butler and have my trunks moved immediately."

"Do you realize how far you have overstepped the bounds, Becca? I would suggest a more conciliatory attitude henceforth."

She paused. "Or?"

"I will put you in here."

She turned about to gauge the seriousness of that

statement. She caught a glint of mischief in his pale blue eyes, and something else. Was it desire—or anger? It had to be anger. And she wasn't supposed to be furious when he'd accused her of all sorts of bad behavior she was innocent of?

"You know, I told you that night I went to your room that I was assisting your friend Nigel, at his request," she reminded him. "You never bothered to confirm that, did you?"

"What's your point?"

"I *never* would have gone to your room if he hadn't assured me that you would act as a go-between for us."

"Yes, I did speak to Nigel and he confirmed that he told you to use me as a go-between. But, Becca, we both know you had other opportunities to deliver your information. Instead you broke all the rules by entering my room, late at night, fully expecting to find me abed at that hour, and *that's* what has put us in this intolerable situation. So there will be no blame-passing, Becca, when we both know exactly where the blame lies."

She shook her head in frustration. "I'm sure it will come as no surprise to you that I disagree. I might have been naive, but I didn't set out to seduce you! Please do us both a favor and don't pull a leaf from my book by spiting yourself to spite me. This will be a hands-off marriage just as you described it—for the duration."

"Actually, the way I described it was—a hands-off marriage *until* proof can be established. You don't really think I'll keep my hands off of you if we do end up having to remain married, do you? But don't try to tempt me in the meantime. If that is your current plan, to move in here to seduce me again so you really will get pregnant, I warn you—no, I *promise* you—you will regret it."

"And to think I used to liken you to an angel. I truly must have been out of my mind."

She mumbled that to herself on the way out the door, too low for him to hear. She'd let anger push her into coming here. She'd let anger widen the breach between them. But it wasn't anger filling her chest with pain just then. And it wasn't anger that brought tears to her eyes.

Chapter Thirty-nine

T HE WOMAN MADE HIM crazy! Rupert wondered how the deuce was he going to survive this close proximity to Rebecca. Bloody hell, he still wanted her badly, but he resented being manipulated into marriage by a scheming chit, no matter how desirable he found her. She'd be tempting him every time he turned around, all in supposed innocence. And it would work. There was no way it wouldn't work when she already tempted him—without even trying.

Rupert stayed in his room until Rebecca's trunks were removed, and a few minutes longer until he heard a door slam down the hall. She was going to chase him out of his own house. He could see no other solution.

He was halfway down the stairs when his step slowed to a halt. What was he doing? Since when did he choose the cowardly path? She really *was* making him crazy, to jump so quickly on such an easy out. He bloody well had more fortitude than that. And he knew her game plan! He just needed to ignore his immediate instinct for self-preservation long enough to come up with a plan to counter hers.

He was still standing on the stairs when the front door opened and his cousin Raphael Locke and his wife, Ophelia, stepped inside. The damn Season! He'd forgotten how many of his Locke relatives showed up in London at this time of the year. And they all visited his family, of course, some for weeks at a time. His cousin Amanda, Raphael's sister, was likely to arrive, too, since she was still on the marriage mart. She preferred to stay at his house where she had three likely escorts in him and his brothers, rather than with her own brother, who preferred to stay at home with his wife and young daughter.

Raphael and his wife's arrival cemented Rupert's decision. He'd have to stay. He knew how easily Rebecca would insinuate herself into the hearts of his family if he wasn't around to warn them of her duplicities. She was too adorable and amusing not to. While most men would be appalled to find a female in their family displaying an intelligence that equaled their own, the Lockes and St. Johns didn't fall into that group.

Still to this day, Rupert was dazzled by Ophelia Locke's incredible beauty every time he saw her. There was just no getting used to a face that unique. Ophelia and Rebecca would probably have a good deal in common, too—no, that was the old Ophelia he was thinking of. She used to excel at manipulating situations to suit herself, and resorting to lies to do it, just as Rebecca did. Ophelia was a raving beauty, unparalleled in that regard, yet she'd actually not been likable because of those bad qualities. But marriage to Rafe had turned her around completely. There was nothing *not* to like about the Ophelia who'd married his cousin.

"Didn't expect to find you here, old chap," Raphael said when he caught sight of Rupert.

Rupert grinned and traversed the remaining steps to join

the couple in the hall. "I try to limit myself to spending the night with only three women a week these days. You've caught me on one of my odd days."

"Was hoping not to catch you a'tall," Raphael shot back. "Came by to visit with Aunt Julie, anyway, so you can run along."

Oddly enough, Raphael Locke was only half-joking. He didn't experience much jealousy over his wife since he had no doubt about her love for him, but Rupert had provoked that jealousy one time too many. It had all been fun and games for Rupert when he'd flirted with Ophelia quite often in those first months of her marriage, but Rafe, who was well aware of his cousin's skirt-chasing reputation, hadn't found it the least bit amusing.

"What he meant was, we thought you might still be abed at this hour," Ophelia said, trying to make Rafe's dismissal sound a little more amiable.

"Don't worry, luv"—Rupert winked at Ophelia—"I'm used to his insecurities by now."

Raphael snorted and, as he marched to the parlor, shouted, "Where are you, Aunt Julie? You need to send that scamp of yours on an errand while I visit."

Ophelia scolded Rupert lightly, "I know you aren't serious, and at least you have stopped trying to seduce me at every turn as you used to do. But you really need to let him know you aren't serious."

"It was all fun and games, m'dear."

"Nonsense. You did it just to spark your mother's ire."

"That, too." Rupert grinned.

"And my husband's."

Rupert chuckled, "That, too."

"So it's time to stop provoking him, don't you think? I do like visiting your family, but it takes me days to convince Rafe to bring us to town—because of you."

"Good God," they heard Raphael exclaim in the other room. "When did that happen?"

Rupert sighed, prompting Ophelia to ask, "Is something wrong?"

"Yes, but then that's merely my opinion. My mother, on the other hand, probably thinks nothing could be more right with the world. But I'll let her tell you. She's probably busting at the seams."

He extended an arm toward the parlor. Ophelia gave him an annoyed look, then moved ahead of him.

But his mother didn't keep her in suspense. As soon as Ophelia appeared in the doorway, Julie announced, "Let me be the first to tell you about Rupert's marriage. He's found himself such a delightful girl, and they're already expecting an addition to the family."

Rupert leaned back against the doorframe and banged his head against the wood. Trust his mother to spill *all* of the beans at once.

Ophelia glanced back at him and, in a tone that was as close as she got to a pout these days, said, "I like weddings. Why weren't we invited?"

He closed his eyes. "Perhaps because *no* one was supposed to know about it yet."

"Yes, he wasn't even going to tell me," Julie added, though by her wide smile, she wasn't the least bit upset over that. "But I quite forgive him for it, now that I do know. You must know her, Rafe. She's a neighbor of yours. She even told me she might have gotten into the family sooner, that she had set her cap for you long ago."

"Oh?" Ophelia said, raising a brow at her husband.

Raphael blushed slightly. "I've no idea whom Aunt Julie is talking about, m'dear. She hasn't said *whom* he married yet."

Rupert's eyes were open wide now. It all came together in his mind—the reason for what Rebecca had set in motion. None of it had anything to do with palace intrigue, and everything to do with her own mercenary agenda. She had really been after marriage all along, one way or another—into the Locke family. He'd merely been her stepping-stone.

Chapter Forty

I'M THE BRIDE," REBECCA said from the doorway, bringing the room to momentary silence.

She managed not to blush while making such a bold statement. But there was no reason to beat around the bush, especially when she'd caught Raphael's remark as she approached the room. She should have just retreated when she heard so many voices in the parlor. But she didn't move into this house to hide. She was there to assure her place in Rupert's family—for her baby's sake, and this was a prime opportunity to do that.

Her remark brought every eye in the room to her, including Rupert's. "You forgot to say *lucky* bride, didn't you?" Rupert asked in a low voice as he stood beside her.

That was the usual response of a new bride, she supposed, but it definitely didn't apply to her. "No, I didn't," she whispered back with a false smile. "But I managed to withhold the 'unlucky' that was on the tip of my tongue. You can thank me later."

He snorted. She left his side to move farther into the room to join her mother-in-law on one of the brocade sofas. Julie was beaming at her. Raphael was smiling, too, probably having recognized her. Ophelia was the only one giving her a bemused look.

"You look familiar, though a name isn't coming to me. Haven't we met?" Ophelia asked finally.

"Yes, not long after you married. I was with my mother when we came to welcome you to the neighborhood."

"Yes, of course!" Ophelia exclaimed. "Lilly and Rebecca Marshall. I remember now—and that your mother said something that day that sparked my curiosity."

"Oh?"

"I don't think she meant for me to hear her. She mumbled rather low just after she was introduced to me, 'Well, that explains that.' Perhaps you recall and know what she was talking about? I had a feeling the remark was about me."

Rebecca burst out laughing, recalling the day they met Ophelia Locke for the first time. Rebecca had understood then how Raphael had succumbed to Ophelia so quickly. The woman was beyond beautiful. There were simply no words to describe it. Lilly had been of the same opinion and summed it up in those few simple words: "Well, that explains that."

"Indeed, it was about you," Rebecca said with a grin. "For several years my mother and I had been entertaining the idea that Raphael would make me a fine husband. So when he up and married you, out of the blue, without even a courtship making the rounds, we were quite curious to know why. But we merely had to meet you to understand why any man would have rushed you to the altar, once he gained your favor."

Ophelia was blushing now at the compliment, but her husband explained, "Oh, our courtship, as unusual as it was, made all the gossip mills in London. Phelia can tell you about it sometime. Word just hadn't reached Norford by the time I brought my wife home." Then he teased Rebecca, "I hope you weren't too disappointed?"

"Oh, I was devastated, to be sure—for about an hour," Rebecca teased back, making them laugh before she assured him, "You were merely an 'idea' for me, after all. Something not to take seriously, but to look forward to when I came of age. You just married before I got there!"

They all laughed—except Rupert. His scowl was so black he took it straight out of the room before anyone noticed. Rebecca caught it though before he so rudely left her alone with his family. She should have let it go. She should have taken that opportunity to explain things to the Lockes without Rupert giving them his deluded version. But she'd already told Julie the situation, and Julie could tell her relatives if she chose to. Rebecca excused herself and went after Rupert instead.

She didn't have to go far and followed him down the hall to the room he disappeared into, just catching the door before it closed in her face. She pushed it open. He swung around to pin her with his narrowed, pale blue eyes.

She closed the door behind her before she said, "How typical of you, to leave me to the wolves."

He snorted at such a ridiculous description of his family. "Save your melodramatics for a gullible audience. You had them in the palm of your hand."

"Does that excuse your rudeness?"

"My family expects no less of me. Besides, if you failed to notice, Rafe would have been delighted to see me go. Ever since I lusted after his wife, he's preferred I not be in the same room with her for very long."

Rebecca gasped. "You didn't."

He rolled his eyes. "Of course I did, I and every other man who has ever or will ever clap eyes on her. Most men contain their feelings discreetly. I was just more obvious about it than most."

Rebecca assumed he was just trying to provoke her. "So this is how it's going to be? You won't even stay in the same room with me when your family is visiting?"

He suddenly pressed her back against the wall. "Just how dumb do you think I am, Becca? As your mother would say, 'That explains that,' and it does, most clearly."

She couldn't say anything for a moment, couldn't even assimilate what he'd just said. She simply couldn't handle being this close to him. A wave of heat washed over her. Flutters tickled her belly. She couldn't get her eyes off the lips that were so close to hers.

"No ready excuse this time?" he continued with enough asperity to snap her eyes up to his.

She'd seen him angry so many times, yet this went quite a ways beyond that. A muscle was even ticking in his cheek. She could almost feel his fury, it was emanating from him so strongly. What the devil had he said? *Think!* She couldn't. She hadn't heard a single word since his body had moved in so close, and the wall at her back left her no avenue for escape.

"What are you insinuating now?"

"This isn't a good time to test my patience. When did you decide to do whatever it would take to get into my family? Before or after Rafe was removed from the top of your list? You picked a lousy second choice, Becca. I will *not* make you a faithful husband, if this farce must continue."

She sucked in her breath the moment she realized the conclusion he'd drawn. "Are you joking? Your cousin was one of the best catches in all of England, let alone in my neighborhood.

Every lady in Norford had her heart set on him, so why would I be the exception? And I was only thirteen when the idea that he could make me a wonderful husband occurred to my mother and me. But I'd only met him a few times, you know. He probably didn't remember either occasion. And if you must know, when he married Ophelia I was still only sixteen. I was disappointed, having thought of him as 'mine' for three years, but I certainly wasn't devastated or plotting on his replacement. In fact, I was looking forward to joining the rest of the debutantes for a Season of husband-hunting in London, at least until my mother obtained that appointment at the palace for me."

"I see you had an excuse ready," he replied caustically.

She knew immediately that no matter what she said now, he wouldn't believe her. He wouldn't even give her the benefit of a little doubt. She was guilty as charged, had used the oldest trick in the book to drag him to the altar. Never mind that he'd done the dragging, she'd apparently manipulated that, too. And he wasn't even allowing for his own incredible desirability! He thought she'd been after his family, so any member of it would have sufficed.

As usual, he managed to make her as furious as he was. And as had lately been happening, she didn't keep it to herself and retorted with the biggest thorn she could grasp.

"Nonsense," she replied, "why would I need an excuse prepared in advance? You've already implied that I'm smart enough to lie on the fly. Chew on that, Lord Know-it-all!"

She ducked under one of the arms he had planted on either side of her and rushed out of the room before he could stop her. She was going to cry again. She didn't even know why this time. It wasn't as if he hadn't already made it clear what he thought of her.

Chapter Forty-one

REBECCA WAITED UNTIL MIDAFTERNOON before she went downstairs again, for lunch. She had no appetite, but she couldn't only think of herself now, when it came to nourishment. She waited long enough to give the Lockes time to leave. She was in no mood to be sociable even if she was part of their family now. She was hoping to grab a plate in the kitchen and then disappear back to her new room again where she could mope in peace.

She was only able to execute half of that hurried plan. Plate in hand, she was mounting the stairs again when the front door opened behind her. She turned, hoping it was Flora arriving with the rest of their trunks. She'd forgotten to mention to Julie that her maid would need a room. But there in the foyer her old friend Amanda Locke was shrugging out of her coat.

Amanda noticed her immediately, exclaiming, "Becky?! What are *you* doing here? Is Aunt Julie sponsoring you for the Season—but wait, aren't you supposed to be at the palace? That's so exciting. I heard you got that post. Imagine, a real maid of honor! I was so thrilled for you! And maybe a little jealous." Amanda chuckled at herself. "Never even thought of doing something like that, but maybe I should have. Let the queen pick a husband for me, since I'm having no luck a'tall finding one for m'self. This is going to be my third Season! I could just cry."

Rebecca smiled slightly. Amanda certainly hadn't changed. They hadn't seen each other in years, but the beautiful child had grown into an even more beautiful woman that Rebecca would have recognized anywhere. And obviously her personality hadn't changed either over the years. She could still manage a hundred words a minute *and* juggle three or more subjects nearly in one breath!

They'd almost become the best of friends when they were children. Being such close neighbors, and only a few years apart in age with Amanda the senior, they'd enjoyed so many of the same things together—when they both still had only childish interests.

But then Amanda went away to the same private school that all her aunts had attended when they were young, and for a while, half the summers she didn't even come home to Norford, but visited at the homes of her new school friends. So they'd drifted apart, barely seeing each other anymore, and the age difference became even more pronounced as well, as Amanda's interests became more sophisticated and socially oriented.

Rebecca had often regretted that they never got around to renewing their friendship after Rebecca had also outgrown her childhood interests. Rebecca had never even had a chance to tell her old friend that she planned to marry her brother! That's how many years had passed since they'd spoken.

Rebecca came back down the stairs to try to explain her

presence in the St. John residence without revealing all the facts. "I've married. That's why I had to leave my post at the palace."

"Good God, *you've* married already?" Amanda gasped, then wailed, "Now I *am* going to cry!"

It didn't look as if Amanda was going to do any such thing, and she was brightly smiling when she gave Rebecca a tight hug of congratulations and said, "Finally, someone who can tell me all the wicked secrets about marriage that my father was too embarrassed to relate to me."

"You really don't know?"

"I was joking, course I do. I do have five aunts, after all, and each one of them took her turn at muddling through the delicate facts for me. But then you know how older women can be. They tell you something without *really* telling you anything, just alluding to this and that."

"So you really don't—"

"No, really, I do," Amanda cut in. "All my closest friends have married already—there, you see? I'm the *only* one who can't manage to find a husband!"

Rebecca couldn't imagine why. Amanda had the extraordinary good looks that so many of the Lockes had been blessed with—bright blond hair, pale blue eyes, and exquisite features. She was undoubtedly the prettiest debutante to come looking for a husband since her come-out—actually, come to think of it, two years ago would have been when Ophelia had had her debut, too, and no one, not even Amanda, could compare to *that* beauty. Still, that was two years ago. Amanda should have been snatched up by now.

"Is it your father's title? He is a duke, after all, and that might scare off—"

"No, no, there have been *so* many offers. I'm the one having the problem. I simply can't make up my mind, because I'm not feeling it here." Amanda pointed to her heart. "Did you feel it here? Yes, of course you did. Why marry otherwise?"

Rebecca started to explain that there were numerous other reasons to marry besides love, but she wasn't going to be the one to mention her particular reason when Amanda was still an innocent. If her family chose to tell her they could, but did Amanda really need to know that neither Rebecca nor Rupert had wanted the marriage? Not that it wouldn't become apparent if Amanda was there for a lengthy visit. But fortunately, for now, Amanda had answered her own question and Rebecca made no attempt to correct her.

"So, who is the lucky fellow?"

The question was asked with such curiosity that it occurred to Rebecca that Amanda hadn't even considered her three male cousins of this household. Of course, one of those cousins, Owen, was too young. Rebecca hadn't met Avery, the second son, yet, but if he was anything like Rupert, Amanda would likely have deemed them both *un*eligible bachelors.

"That would be me," Rupert replied as he came up the hall behind Rebecca. He stopped at her side and put his arm around her shoulder. She stiffened, but didn't shrug him off because Amanda's eyes were on them.

"You?" Amanda blinked at her cousin, then swung her eyes back to Rebecca with a delighted cry. "Oh, that's wonderful! We're finally going to become the best of friends, Becky! I can't believe I missed all the excitement. How did this happen before the Season has even begun? Did you meet at home, or here in London? When did this happen—wait a minute, why wasn't I invited to the wedding?"

"We were too impatient to wait for a normal wedding," Rupert said.

"You went all the way to Scotland to avoid posting the banns?" Amanda guessed. "How romantic!"

Rupert planted a kiss by Rebecca's ear, and as he did so, he whispered, "She doesn't need to know."

They were actually agreeing on something? Rebecca thought in amazement. What a surprise. As she turned to tell him so, her lips bumped right into his.

Chapter Forty-two

REBECCA KNEW VERY WELL that kiss was only for Amanda's benefit. That was the only reason she didn't immediately pull away. At least she assured herself of that before her senses got so confused that she simply forgot she wasn't supposed to enjoy it.

Shouldn't rogues taste as bad as they behaved? Yes, they should. That would be a clear warning right there. But her rogue didn't. Euphoria had overcome her every time she'd tasted him, and even now, when his promise to "never be faithful" was still so fresh in her mind, she couldn't prevent the bubbly giddiness that overcame her at his touch, at the way his hand was moving up and down her back.

It wasn't Amanda who broke Rebecca's trance. Amanda was just rocking on her heels and grinning that they were so much in love that they couldn't keep their feelings to themselves. At least Rebecca figured that was what Amanda was thinking when she caught sight of her when the plate Rebecca had been holding slid out of her fingers and shattered on the marble floor at their feet. That separated her and Rupert instantly.

Amanda began to giggle as Rebecca stared appalled at the mess she'd created. "Don't worry about that," Amanda said as she came forward to drag Rebecca toward the parlor. "One of the maids will clean it up. I want to hear all about this wonderful romance that has you two behaving so impulsively."

"That ought to be interesting," Raphael said from where he was lying on one of the sofas.

His sister stared at him. "I was wondering why you hadn't returned to your town house yet, but didn't expect you'd still be here visiting. Did you at least warn Aunt Julie that I would be staying here for a while?"

"Forgot to mention it, m'dear," Raphael said as he sat up. "But I'm sure she was expecting it, since you stayed here last Season and have decided to prolong everyone's agony by not marrying."

Amanda sputtered, "I'm doing no such thing!"

"You're done whining about it? Glad to hear it!"

She huffed over her brother's teasing. "Where's your wife? You've overstayed your welcome."

"Exactly what I was thinking," Rupert said as he joined them.

Raphael chuckled. "Might as well give it up, old boy. You've joined the ranks, as it were, which quite ends our little squabble. As for the ladies," Raphael added for his sister, "they went upstairs to find Rebecca so they can figure out which room can be turned into a nursery."

Amanda's eyes swung toward Rebecca. "Isn't that a bit premature?"

"Actually—no."

"My word, how long have you two been hiding this marriage?"

"Not long enough," Rupert said with a roll of his eyes.

Rebecca gave him an odd look. How easy he made it sound as if they'd merely wanted some time alone before they told the family the "good news." She would have preferred the truth, but then the truth was so unpleasant, and embarrassing, and . . . she had a feeling she was going to cry again.

"They must have missed me while I was in the kitchen. I'll go find them," she quickly said. "Excuse me."

For the second time that day she rushed out of the parlor. Rupert followed right behind her. Wanting to be alone, she stopped and asked, "What now?"

With a maid already cleaning up the mess in the hall, he took her arm and ushered her into his office again to speak in private. He still kept his voice low when he said, "We don't have to tell the whole family that this is a marriage made in hell."

He'd already mentioned that in regard to Amanda, but he also hadn't said anything to Ophelia and Raphael either to indicate all wasn't right with their marriage. But how were they supposed to conceal that when they couldn't be in the same room for long without snapping at each other?

"What are you suggesting?"

He seemed frustrated for a moment before replying, "You're good at acting. I'm suggesting we put a good face on this, at least for the rest of the family."

An insult and an olive branch in the same breath. No, he wasn't implying a truce, just a pretense. Something she was good at—in his opinion. She almost laughed.

"Why do you even want to try this, when you expect to end our marriage in several months?"

"Because you're in this house. Because you have already

announced the marriage, when I told you not to. You could have come here as a guest instead, you know. I even went to Norford to—never mind. But now that it's known, we need to put a good face on it."

"You haven't answered my question. Our having irreconcilable differences were your grounds for an annulment. What you are suggesting now puts an end to your easy out, doesn't it?"

"You already did that. You came here to force my hand. So be it, you've succeeded. There is always divorce instead, if it comes to that. But as to why? You said it yourself, Becca. For the baby."

She couldn't argue with that. She just hadn't expected him to think of the baby first—but then she should have. He'd married her for the baby's sake, after all.

She sighed. And made an effort to shake off all animosity—for the moment.

"Very well," she said. "But you realize your mother will probably say something to your relatives, if she hasn't already. I was honest with her."

"You gave her your version—or mine?"

She flushed with angry color. How short *that* truce was! He expected her to play the role of the happy bride when he couldn't keep his insults to himself?

"I gave her facts, not assumptions. And this isn't going to work if you're going to continue to deliberately provoke me at every turn!"

He raked an exasperated hand through his long hair. "I'm sorry, that was unintentional. I will make every effort to guard my tongue in mixed company."

She narrowed her eyes on him, guessing, "But not when we're alone?"

"The pretense is for others, not ourselves. Neither of us is delusional."

"Of course not, far be it for me to think there's any reality in this. But if you think I can portray genuine smiles and bubbly happiness while around others when I'm so furious that I'm plotting your demise, well, think again!"

He sighed now. "I see your point. I'm balancing on this thin thread of doubt, so bear with me, please. I will make some adjustments. As for my mother, it's *very* unlikely that she will mention anything untoward. She's so delighted with this turn of events, she will fight tooth and nail to assure nothing ruins our marriage."

"Then I guess the only thing left is for you to prove that you're up to the challenge. Give me a smile that isn't a sneer."

He wasn't expecting that, to go by his sudden surprise. But it was a reasonable request. She wasn't going to carry the entire charade on her shoulders alone. He had to do his share.

But *she* wasn't expecting one of those amazing smiles he'd dazzled her with before that fateful night she'd spent in his bed. She sucked in a sharp breath. Her heart started to thump loudly. Good God, how could he still do this to her?

"You don't need to be that convincing!" she snapped, and swung around to get her eyes off him. "Save your seductive smiles for your legion of conquests. I won't be one of those, so a decent smile will do, thank you."

He actually laughed. "That *was* a normal smile, Becca. If you don't believe me, turn around and I'll show you the difference."

"No! Seducing me isn't part of this bargain."

"Of course not. For now, this happy marriage is for show

only and I have already promised to keep my hands off you, haven't I?"

"Then henceforth keep your lips off me, too," she said on her way out the door. "There's to be no more accidental kisses."

She heard him laugh again before she closed the door behind her. Good Lord, what had she just agreed to? This was never going to work!

Chapter Forty-three

"B UT IT'S JUST A little ball! Were there so many at the palace that you've grown tired of them already?" Amanda asked.

While Rebecca sat with Amanda at the dining table, she remembered how stubborn her old friend could be once she got an idea in her head. When they were children, Amanda would ignore all answers unless they were the ones she was looking for.

Apparently, nothing had really changed in that regard over the years. At twenty years of age, Amanda still hadn't learned how to give in gracefully when she didn't get what she wanted. Rebecca, however, was no longer the easily manipulated younger friend who could be led astray and had developed her own brand of tenacity.

So she merely repeated for the second time, "It just doesn't feel right," then added, "I'm younger than you! That hardly makes me a proper chaperone."

"Nonsense, you just aren't used to being married yet. Your being a married woman makes you a perfectly acceptable chaperone for me. And I would so much rather go with you than with Avery, who hasn't come by for me to even ask him yet. Owen's too young. And Rue causes too much of a sensation with the ladies, which puts so many of the gentlemen present into such a huff that they stop dancing! At least at balls that's what tends to happen."

Rebecca kept from grinning even though she suspected Amanda was exaggerating just to make her point, not that Rupert couldn't cause a sensation, but that everyone stopped dancing because of it. Since she'd already been informed on the matter, she reminded Amanda, "You moved into this house for the Season because you have a number of ready chaperones, including your aunt. Suddenly they're all unacceptable?"

Amanda sighed and dropped her head onto the table. Fortunately, her dessert plate had already been pushed aside. They were the only two remaining in the dining room.

Julie had dragged Owen off for a weekly accounting of his studies. At sixteen, he was still somewhat bashful, but so polite! Rupert had also left the moment he was done eating, claiming an appointment. At night? She had no doubt he was really heading to whichever lady was currently on his seduction list. But she wasn't going to let it bother her. Really she wasn't.

"You're quite right," Amanda admitted, her forehead still forlornly on the table. "While I would prefer Avery, and he doesn't mind a'tall escorting me, he probably doesn't know I'm in town yet. Aunt Julie, though, got out of the habit of being sociable when she was raising her boys. She was fanatic about never leaving them alone, you know. While she'd agree to act as chaperone, she'll also spend the entire night grumbling, and believe me, there aren't very many men who don't quickly retreat after receiving one of her scowls."

"If they can be that easily intimidated, then they aren't for you."

Amanda's head snapped up. "Never thought of it like that! But that's so true. And thinking back, I must say some of those fellows she scared off, I was glad to see go. But still, you are completely missing my point. I would much, much rather go with you! It will be fun! And you seem to be quite levelheaded these days. Maybe *you* can help me narrow down my search for a husband. Do say yes. Please!"

Rebecca grinned, still a sucker after all for a prettily said *please* from her old friend. But then she'd also run out of excuses.

"Tomorrow night, you say?"

"Yes, and don't you dare tell me you have nothing to wear when you've just come from the palace!"

"Calm down, Mandy." Rebecca chuckled. "I'll go with you. I even have several ball gowns I haven't worn yet. While we'd been anticipating an endless stream of entertainments at Buckingham, and I had a wardrobe up to the task, my mother and I simply didn't take into account that the queen was nearing the end of her pregnancy when I got there. The palace was actually quite sedate during those last weeks."

Rebecca was beginning to feel an inkling of excitement. A real ball, not one filled to the brim with officials of the court, so many of them middle-aged or older. This would be mostly young men who came to town for the same reasons all the young ladies did, looking for a partner in matrimony. Endless dancing and no chaperone of her own! The brief fantasy ended right there. She almost laughed at herself, but it would probably have been a bitter laugh.

She could go, but it was questionable whether she could

have any fun. She was a married woman. There'd be no harmless flirtations for her, no excitement over gaining a dance with one of the more eligible bachelors. She'd have to decline dancing herself. It wouldn't be proper, at least not without her husband there to give his approval.

She almost changed her mind about going, but Amanda had launched into one of her endless streams of subjects, all pertaining to tomorrow night, and she was so obviously happy in her excitement that Rebecca didn't have the heart to back out on her. She'd go, and she'd probably end up stewing all night because her husband would be off pursuing one of his ladyloves instead of accompanying his wife to her very first Seasonal ball, dancing with her, causing a sensation, but this time because it would become known that he was no longer an eligible bachelor himself. He wouldn't like *that*. No indeed, look how hard he'd tried to keep their marriage a secret. Well, too bad for him. She'd be telling everyone she met, and see how his ladyloves liked that!

Chapter Forty-four

REBECCA STARED AND STARED at her waistline, unable to believe such an obvious difference was already taking place in her body. The ball gown Flora had just fastened her into fit her so snuggly now, it was almost uncomfortable. Seven weeks ago it had fit her perfectly! She couldn't be showing signs of the baby this soon!

Flora was patiently waiting for her to come over to the improvised vanity table they had put together for temporary use until she could go shopping for one. They had confiscated one of the satinwood console tables in the hall, and one of the upstairs maids had found an old mirror in the attic that only had a small crack in one corner. It would do, since Rebecca didn't really feel as if the room were hers yet.

Flora, watching her, began to laugh. "It's not what you're thinking, Becky. You've just gained some normal weight."

"I've done no such thing!"

"Of course you have, and it was to be expected when your usual activities were cut in half during your stay at the palace.

No daily rides with your mother, no up and down the stairs ten times a day, and far too many rich foods served at every meal, rather than what you were used to at home."

"But I haven't been able to keep down one of those meals since the morning sickness began."

"And you've compensated for that by eating too much at other meals, particularly at luncheons, when you're so famished from missing your breakfast."

Rebecca marched over to the vanity. She hated when Flora could prove her point so accurately like that, though in this case it was simply because Rebecca had too many other things on her mind lately to draw such an obvious conclusion herself. But before she got testy about it, which was another thing she deplored, but seemed unable to control anymore, Amanda walked in. As if they were still children who didn't require much privacy, she didn't even knock first.

Rebecca managed not to get snappy over that, too, but it took a concentrated effort. These drastic mood swings seemed to be getting worse. She hated them. But then she'd had no real peace of mind to counter them ever since she'd moved into Rupert's home. It had been particularly bad since last night when she'd sat at the window in her room that faced the street waiting to see when he'd come home and had finally fallen asleep in the chair before he did.

She'd only seen him once today, at luncheon, and he'd maintained his new everything-is-wonderful attitude, while she'd had to keep her mouth tightly shut and her gaze elsewhere just to not cause a scene. Amanda, of course, did enough talking for all of them, mostly about the ball tonight, so Rupert already knew she was going to accompany his cousin and had simply wished them a good time. Of course he didn't offer to join them, which would have been the husbandly thing to do. That would be taking the charade further than he cared to, Rebecca supposed.

Amanda was already fully dressed in an aqua gown with sparkling silver-thread embroidery along the edges. With a large teardrop pearl at her neck, more pearls at her wrists, fingers, and even in her hair, she looked exquisite. She made Rebecca feel positively dowdy in her bright lemon silk that was made appropriately pale with an overlay of ivory chiffon—*and her tight waist*. She was allowed darker, more vibrant colors now that she was married, she just didn't own any yet. And there was really no point in rushing out to have that corrected immediately, when she'd be outgrowing all of her clothes soon enough.

Draped over Amanda's arm was a fur-trimmed cloak, which she dropped on the bed before she remarked, "You're still using this room when there's a perfectly good bedroom attached to the master suite that you could be using instead for your dressing room?"

Rebecca kept her eyes on the mirror. She had lied yesterday when Amanda had found her in this room. Well, she hadn't actually lied, she just hadn't corrected the girl when Amanda assumed Rebecca wasn't actually sleeping in it, merely using it as an extra room to dress in.

"I believe we've decided the room off the master shall be the nursery, and your aunt Julie plans to furnish it within the month, so there was really no point—"

"Understood, and at least Rue's snoring hasn't driven you to separate rooms."

Rebecca choked back a hysterical laugh. "He snores?"

"Doesn't he? I thought most men did."

Trying not to blush, Rebecca said, "I'm a sound sleeper. I wouldn't notice."

"Then that works out well, doesn't it? It's something I've always worried about, m'self. I mean, I've heard how loudly my father snores. It rattles the windows! *How* do married women put up with that?" Then in the same breath: "Almost ready? The coach has been called."

"A few more minutes," Flora answered for Rebecca.

Amanda nodded and left to wait downstairs. Flora cocked a brow at Rebecca in the mirror the moment Amanda was gone. "She's very exuberant, isn't she?"

Rebecca had to grin. "You didn't know her as a child. She was even more excitable then."

"A personality like that can exhaust you. Don't let her tire you out in your condition."

Good advice, though Rebecca found Amanda's extreme chatter amusing for the most part, not exhausting—at least when the girl wasn't bringing up personal subjects.

Joining her friend downstairs, Rebecca actually expected Rupert to be present to see them off. And see how dowdy she looked—well, that wasn't really accurate. Her little mirror said she looked wonderful despite her tight waist; she merely *felt* dowdy. Just one more uncontrollable feeling to add to all the other unhappy feelings she'd been having.

This should be one of the most happy times of her life, instead of the most miserable. Other women had adoring husbands with whom they could share this miracle of birth. She had a faithless rogue who only wanted to *pretend* to be adoring.

The ride was short because this first early ball of the winter Season was taking place only a few blocks away. The excitement Rebecca had been feeling was completely gone now, replaced with something resembling panic when she realized she wasn't ready for this. She had wanted her marriage to be known. That was the whole point of barging in on Rupert. But she wasn't really prepared for it to become public knowledge yet. If she had to stomach well-wishing from perfect strangers, she would probably burst into tears. Her emotions were simply too raw to manage such a full-scale pretense of being the "happy bride."

They were stepping out of the coach in front of the Withers mansion when she abruptly whispered to Amanda, "Don't introduce me as the Marchioness of Rochwood."

"Why ever not?"

"Because I don't want to explain why Rupert isn't here with me."

"Oh, how silly! Men rarely come to these affairs if they don't have to. And you are—"

"Mandy, please, just say I'm your chaperone or just introduce me by my first name only. I don't know these people and they don't need to know me yet."

"Fine. As you wish. But I still think you're being silly."

For all of her aggrieved tone, Amanda was the one who got huffy with the butler when he stared at Rebecca for nearly a full minute, waiting for her to supply him with her title. "She's with me, and do *not* keep me standing here another moment. Announce me!"

Red-faced, the fellow did as told, and Amanda hooked her arm through Rebecca's to show that they were together as she led Rebecca into the large ballroom. Amanda didn't go far, and Rebecca couldn't miss her long, drawn-out sigh.

"Embarrassed for having been so sharp with the man?" Rebecca asked.

"Who? Oh, not a'tall. He was rude and deserved it. No, I've

just noticed none of my friends are here and probably won't be for any of the events this season. They're all married now or planning their weddings. A few even have children already. Emma Davis, who finished school when I did, is even expecting her second child!"

It wasn't just Amanda's forlorn expression but also the real melancholy of her tone that expressed how upset she was by this.

Rebecca put a consoling hand to Amanda's arm and said the only thing she could think of. "You'll be glad you waited when your man comes along. Imagine if you had married too soon the wrong fellow, and then the right one shows up."

Amanda blinked, then the most brilliant smile appeared. "That would be horrible, wouldn't it?"

"Dreadful." Rebecca grinned.

Having just shared something so personal with Amanda, Rebecca was actually feeling a little better herself. Misery really does love company, she supposed. And Amanda forgot all about her own doldrums the moment a group of young men who'd noticed her entrance converged on her. Many of them already knew her from previous Seasons, and all of them were eager to get a promise of a dance from her. With a shake of her head, Rebecca stepped back when some of them turned toward her as well. Dancing meant conversation, and she'd already decided to avoid that.

"You caused quite a stir leaving your post at the palace like you did, without a good reason."

Rebecca groaned inwardly. She recognized Elizabeth Marly's voice behind her. Watching Amanda laugh now as one of the young men led her onto the dance floor, with the rest of the gentlemen dispersing, Rebecca turned to her old nemesis, steeling herself to withstand an unpleasant conversation. She almost laughed, though, at Elizabeth's ensemble, a gaudy orange gown with sleeves that were far too plump. The girl still had no sense of taste or style.

"I had a good reason," Rebecca replied. "I conveyed it to Lady Sarah. If she chose not to share it—"

"Sarah has been dismissed," Elizabeth said in an annoyed tone. "Constance, that selfish twit, complained one time too many about the minor tasks she'd been asked to do, and it reached the ears of the duchess."

"So the queen's mother really didn't know about Sarah's intrigues?"

"Intrigues?" Elizabeth scoffed derisively. "Sarah just tried to keep abreast of things is all. So she went about it a bit oddly," Elizabeth added with a shrug. "No one was ever hurt by it."

Incredulous over such an indifferent attitude, Rebecca replied, "How do you know that? You were just her willing lackey. You have no idea what she did with the information she gathered or whom she hurt with it."

"Does it matter now?" Elizabeth said peevishly. "The duchess was furious and sent her away immediately, despite their long association. She won't tolerate any scandal whatsoever linked with her personal entourage that might reflect poorly on the queen."

"There was a scandal?"

"You aren't listening! It was nipped in the bud. But the position is *so* boring now, with Sarah gone."

"Is that why you're here?"

"Of course. The heir apparent isn't even a month old yet. Other than the celebrations over his birth, Drina still isn't making appearances or ordering entertainments yet. So what was your excuse for leaving?"

Rebecca should have just pointed out bluntly that it was no

business of Elizabeth's, since they hadn't even been civil acquaintances, much less friends. She couldn't imagine what devil had got into her to make her say, "I married Rupert."

Elizabeth's face twisted with rage. "You did no such thing!"

"Ask him."

The girl stared with such venom, it was amazing how she got it under control long enough to feign an indifferent shrug. "It doesn't matter. It wasn't marriage I wanted from him anyway, when it was so obvious that he won't make a good husband. What a pity you didn't realize that sooner. A brief affair with him is highly desirable though. I should thank you. You've given me something else to gloat over—when I have him in my bed again."

Rebecca saw red. The urge she had to fly at Elizabeth with her nails bared was too compelling. She couldn't resist it. That Elizabeth immediately stomped off wasn't going to stop her. She was going to cause the worst scandal London had seen in decades, and she didn't care!

Chapter Forty-five

I ACTUALLY EXPECTED TO FIND you alone, just not out here in the middle of the room standing out like the proverbial sore thumb."

Rebecca swung around. Her surprise was so great on finding her husband grinning at her over his teasing remark that her brief burst of fury dissipated. He looked so handsome in his formal black coat and breeches, his black hair orderly, but still caressing his wide shoulders. All that black was such a contrast to those beautiful pale eyes of his.

She had to make a concerted effort to tamp down that old bedazzlement he could still make her feel. "What are *you* doing here?"

"You two left the house before I finished dressing," Rupert scolded in an offhand manner.

Her eyes flared. "You intended to join us? Then why didn't you say so?"

"I was going to make it a surprise, but I should have known that my cousin would be out the door the very moment you were both ready."

Her mind still a little hazy from the anger Elizabeth had provoked, Rebecca couldn't begin to guess at Rupert's motive. "But why come a'tall? Amanda only needed one chaperone."

"Because I thought you might appreciate a little company. Having escorted Mandy before m'self to these affairs, I know that the young bucks don't give her a moment of peace. She doesn't mind, of course, but that leaves her chaperones alone to twiddle their thumbs."

Being nice? Rescuing her? Did he really think she'd believe that?

"It didn't occur to you that I might spend the evening dancing as well?" she said.

"You're married now, so, no, that didn't occur to me a'tall."

She choked back a laugh. Marriage was supposed to be no fun in his eyes? Now why didn't that surprise her?

But he hadn't finished and added, "I pictured you bored to tears, stuck in the back of the room with the matrons and mamas. But since you've mentioned dancing, I recall that you're rather good at it."

He didn't ask if she wanted to. With him. As he finished that remark, he was already twirling her onto the dance floor. By dint of will, Rebecca held herself stiffly. Why was he really doing this? God, it would be so easy to relax into him . . . no!

"How could you make love to Elizabeth?!"

"Who?"

She'd no sooner blurted out that accusation than she was appalled and filled to the brim with embarrassment and regret that she couldn't keep her mouth shut. But his "who" sent her back over the edge of fury. "What do you mean, who? You just saw me talking to her!"

"If anyone was with you when I arrived, I'm afraid I didn't notice. My eyes were only on you."

She blushed. She didn't believe a word of it, yet she still blushed! "Elizabeth Marly," she reminded him.

"Good God, yes, how could I forget her? Such an obnoxious little chit. And that's quite a far-fetched conclusion you've drawn, m'dear."

"No conclusion a'tall, the words came from her own mouth just moments ago."

He cocked a brow at her. "Well, if that's true, it certainly wouldn't be the first time that's happened. Fascinating how some women will tarnish their own reputation just to claim an intimacy with me. Out of jealousy or just for bragging rights." He shrugged. "I've never quite understood motives like that. But it isn't necessary to consummate what is implied, you know. I learned that long ago."

"What is that supposed to mean?"

"That with Beth it was nothing more than flirting and implying that I wanted to bed her, then avoiding actually doing so."

"So she wasn't a target on your conquest list, you merely let her think she was? Does that amuse you?"

"Now you're taking offense on her behalf when you don't like her any more than I do?" He chuckled over that. "There was a good reason at the time. It's no longer important. But you know you're sounding like a jealous wife? Are you jealous, luv? I find that rather amusing, all things considered."

"Don't start laughing too soon, because I'm nothing of the sort."

"No?"

He was still grinning, prompting her to snap, "Your

unexpected presence here smacks of jealousy as well, as in checking up on your wife, but you don't hear me accusing you of it."

"I believe you just did."

His amusement was irritating her. When it was at her expense, it usually did. Yet her anger was gone. It wasn't that she wanted to believe him, it was that she knew Elizabeth was adept at lying. If her emotions weren't so tumultuous, Rebecca would never have believed her old antagonist to begin with. And why the deuce did she even care?

He twirled her around a few more times before he said offhandedly, "Aren't you tired of fighting yet? I'm beginning to find it quite tedious m'self. I've even given you the benefit of the doubt—"

"Don't do me any favor."

He cocked his head to the side because she'd turned away to mumble that. "Are you challenging me to make you sweet and lovable again? I believe you are!"

Her eyes flew back to his, but she couldn't do anything more than sputter over that absurdity. His pale eyes were twinkling, holding back laughter no doubt. What the devil was he doing! He couldn't be serious. Yet he rubbed his cheek against hers right there on the dance floor!

"What—?"

She should never have turned in toward that unexpected caress. Was she destined to bump lips with him by accident? She drew back instantly while she had the presence of mind to do so. But he didn't. In fact, he moved in closer, his mouth actually pursuing hers until there was nothing accidental about it! She stumbled as her senses whirled. That just encouraged him to hold her closer and kiss her more deeply. She was fast approaching the point of not caring!

Desperately, she tore her mouth away to gasp out, "You're going to cause a scandal!"

"I do believe it would be worth it," he said softly by her ear. "But it's only a minor infraction and quite overlooked, since everyone here knows we're married."

"No, they don't. I didn't have it announced."

He stopped abruptly. Several other couples even bumped into them. "Why not?"

She looked away from his frown, which made her feel distinctly uneasy. How to explain her earlier hesitancy without him seeing it for what it was, a full-blown panic? But he didn't wait for her answer.

Suddenly he was leading her off the dance floor. He began a social circuit around the room, missing no one who wasn't currently dancing. From group to group he stopped to introduce Rebecca as his wife, the Marchioness of Rochwood. He did it curtly, as if he were completing a task assigned to him, which gave her the odd feeling that he was punishing her. She was mortified. Most of those people thought he was joking! They knew him. They knew his reputation. And he wasn't behaving the least bit normally.

He even had an excuse to offer for why no one had heard even a hint about their marriage until now. "We've been secretly married for quite some time. We tried to hide it from her mum, who wanted better for her than me. But there's no point in keeping it under wraps any longer, now she's found us out."

Rebecca could have played along, injected a bit of humor about her mother to support his story, but she was too shocked to get a single word out. When she actually ended up on the dance floor again with his hands more tightly clamped to her waist and hand, she stared up at him, bewildered.

"How could you do that?"

"You will not deny who I am, Becca. I have developed the most profound protectiveness for my child whom I acknowledge you might be carrying. So for now we're married and I'd appreciate if you bloody well acted like it."

She was getting even more confused by his behavior. "For the sake of appearances?"

He looked so deeply into her eyes she ended up holding her breath in suspense. Then he glanced away and told her what she wanted to hear: "Yes, for appearances."

At least she thought that's what she wanted to hear. However, perversely, her reaction was the exact opposite of what it should have been.

"But your habits undergo no change in this pretense? Or do you think anyone was fooled yesterday by your so-called 'appointment' last night? That is what you told your mother, correct? That you had an appointment?"

His eyes came back to hers. "Are we showing signs of jealousy again?"

"I'm asking a pertinent question," she said stiffly. "If you think this pretense is going to only be one-sided, then it ends now."

Incredibly, his humor returned abruptly, his grin quite wide. "Before you start turning green, I suppose I must admit that *appointment* wasn't a good word for it, since it wasn't a scheduled meeting. I merely went to see my solicitor, and, no, he doesn't wear skirts."

She ignored that ridiculous attempt at a joke. "At night?" she scoffed.

He sighed. "As a last resort, yes. I'd already gone to his office at normal hours. He tried to fob me off until next week, but my patience is at an all-time low. However, with five other clients there waiting for him, I decided to call on him later at his home at an hour I knew he would be there, to get my business taken care of."

"What was so important—"

"Haven't you reached the limit on your questions yet?"

Teasing at the moment was so inappropriate, her mouth dropped open incredulously. But that *had* just been teasing and he went on, "I was having my will changed to include my unborn child. It took longer than I expected because he tried to convince me to wait until the child was born, and I in turn convinced him why that wasn't a good idea."

"Why not?"

"In case something should happen to me in the interim."

Fortunately, Amanda caught his attention just then as she danced by and waved, so he didn't see Rebecca blanch. He might have felt the sudden moisture in her palm though, as she also broke out in a cold sweat. He'd given such a logical answer, yet hearing it she was overcome with fear—of losing him? Was she out of her mind?

Chapter Forty-six

IT COULD HAVE BEEN called the scam of the century, their pretense of a happy marriage, yet as several weeks passed and it continued with such perfection, Rebecca had to pinch herself to keep from believing it herself.

The *Angel* was being too good. From the night of the Withers' ball, he had been attentive to her in the extreme. To make up for his behavior?

Rebecca couldn't really guess and certainly wasn't going to ask. But he danced with her again and again that night. He stayed by her side when she needed to rest. He even took them on the circuit again, but this time he left everyone laughing, herself included.

His good behavior continued at home, too, even when it was just the two of them in the company of Julie, who knew the real situation, or with Owen and Amanda, who didn't.

But it was more than that. Even when they found themselves alone enough to exchange personal remarks, he didn't reveal any of his earlier anger that had kept sparking her own.

She began to think he'd actually been serious about not want-ing to fight anymore. But for however long it was going to last, she took advantage of the peace and did nothing to roil the calm waters.

They were at dinner one night when Avery, Julie's middle son, finally made an appearance. Rebecca noted that although the three brothers didn't actually look alike other than having the same dark hair and blue eyes, they still had a distinct family resemblance.

"Sorry for such a long absence, Mother," Avery said on his way to a chair, pausing only to drop a kiss of greeting on the top of Amanda's head as he passed her. "I was at a house party in the country that lasted longer than I had anticipated. At the Millards' estate, the one they have outside York. I believe you know them."

"Indeed," Julie replied with a raised brow. "Don't they have a pretty young daughter not quite old enough yet for a come-out?"

Avery grinned bashfully. "She'll be old enough by next sum-mer." His pale blue eyes then fell on Rebecca and stayed on her, though he was still speaking to his mother. "And who's your beautiful guest? I do believe I should have rushed home sooner, after all."

"Not on this account," Julie said in a gruff scold that abruptly turned to a proud smile as she added, "Rebecca St. John, meet my second son, Avery."

"St. John?" Avery said with some confusion. "A long-lost relative?"

"A *new* relative and a most delightful addition to the family. She married your brother."

Avery's eyes went incredulously to Owen, who started to blush. But Rupert was quick to say, "Not him, me, you ass."

Which made Avery burst out laughing. "Nice try, old man, but I know a whopper when I hear it. The only way *you* will ever marry is if you get pushed through the trapdoor. You've said as much."

Julie immediately threw a spoon at him. "What?" he gasped in surprise.

But Rupert had also left his chair to slap his younger brother on the back of his head, and that prompted an even louder "*What?* I was joking, but then *you* were joking, too. What the deuce is going on here?"

"Did it sound like *I* was joking?" Julie demanded with a quelling look.

"Well . . . no, you wouldn't, would you," Avery admitted, beginning to look a little queasy.

"Exactly," Julie humphed.

Cringing and standing back up, Avery said, "Excuse me while I go dig this foot out of my mouth."

"Sit down," Rupert said on his way back to the head of the table, then to his mother, "You *did* send him word, right? He merely wasn't in London to receive it?"

"Actually, I thought you would want that pleasure, so, no, I was able to resist doing so. Wasn't easy though. I have been bursting at the seams, as it were."

And Amanda, sitting beside Rebecca, said, "Don't blush, Becky. The St. Johns are always like this. You'll get used to it."

Rebecca was only a little embarrassed, but she *was* amazed that Rupert had reacted so strongly to the word *trap*, since it was his opinion of marriage as well. But even in the face of a tasteless joke, he was behaving protectively, as a husband should.

"Well, let's not make this mistake again," Rupert said to

Julie. "Make an announcement in the papers already, Mama. I know you've been bursting at those seams, too."

Julie chuckled with a nod, but Amanda interjected. "Not really necessary at this point."

"Course it is," Julie disagreed.

To which Amanda persisted, "I'm guessing he didn't tell you that he personally introduced Becky to every single person at the Withers' ball the other night—as his wife? Believe me, Aunt Julie, their marriage is definitely making the rounds on the gossip mills."

"In a good light, I hope?"

Amanda blinked. "Well, of course, why wouldn't it be?" Then she said, guessing, "Oh, because they're already expecting?"

"They are?" Avery choked out.

"Well, they didn't *just* get married, you know," Amanda replied to her cousin, then corrected herself, "No, you didn't know, did you? Sorry. But they were hiding it from her mama," Amanda explained, then laughed. "At least that's what I heard at the ball. But the 'expecting' part wasn't mentioned during the introductions. No reason to tell people what isn't any of their business, after all."

Julie was frowning at Rupert. Rupert failed to notice since he was giving his cousin a fond look. Rebecca was wishing she could crawl under the table, still not used to having her pregnancy discussed so openly.

Avery, glancing around the table at the wide range of expressions, sighed. "I think I'll stay home the next time I get invited to the country. All the excitement seems to happen when I'm not around to enjoy it."

Chapter Forty-seven

ORNING CALLERS BEGAN TO show up at Rupert's home the week following the ball, with the pretense of visiting his mother. Julie wasn't really in the habit of receiving this number of callers, yet Rupert had never seen his mother so accommodating. Her gruff, manly role had been shelved! She was now the doting mother-in-law and soon-to-be-doting grandmother, though she didn't share that with her unexpected guests. She obviously wanted to, but she was waiting for his permission to do so, and he certainly wasn't ready to give it.

Rebecca had no clue, thankfully, that at least half of the women who showed up at Rupert's door that week were his former lovers. His mother had no clue, either. But the ladies simply refused to believe that he'd married, despite the gossip attesting that the confirmation had come from him. They knew him, so it was logical to doubt a rumor like this. They wanted to see it firsthand and hear it from his mother.

Rupert had never been so glad that he'd finished with those women on good terms, was even friends with a few of them.

Not one of them came by to stir up trouble. Oddly, the women he'd spent some time flirting with but hadn't gotten around to pursuing any further were the ones who felt slighted. Some of them had proved vindictive. They weren't young girls, though. Elizabeth Marly had been the only exception, but then she'd been business rather than pleasure.

Rebecca handled the company well. She was exceptionally good with people, articulate and amusing and not the least bit shy. His own family had taken to her well. He wasn't sure that was a good thing, though he supposed it was better than their all condemning her for the trap she'd led him into and treating her like a pariah.

His anger was still present, he'd merely locked it up so tightly he tended to forget it was there. He'd locked it up for a good reason. He was protecting his baby. He didn't want his anger to invite her own, which might affect the baby adversely.

His truce with her, though, was having unexpected results that put him in a different sort of quandary. She hadn't been in his house for long, yet he seemed to be getting used to the idea that she was there to stay. It had snuck up on him and now wouldn't go away. And he didn't mind it! Which made no sense a'tall. She *would* be leaving, just as soon as her biggest lie came to light. But what if she didn't? What if he kept her instead?

He couldn't deny that if he *had* been looking for a wife, she would have made a prime candidate. She was delightfully pretty, exceptionally intelligent, and too witty by half. She could make him laugh even when he was furious with her! If he was going to be brutally honest, he admired too bloody many things about her. Even his attraction to her went a little too far. He shouldn't still want a woman who'd brought about his downfall. Yet he did.

Being pulled in completely opposite directions was quite unsettling. Look at his ridiculous reaction at that ball to her wanting to keep their marriage under wraps. Where in the bloody hell did that anger and jealousy come from? It would be too easy for Rebecca to conclude from his own actions that he was getting proprietary over her. And by keeping his anger in hand for the most part, and telling her he was tired of fighting, regardless if it was true or not, he could well have given her the impression that she'd won the war. Which wasn't the case a'tall.

So he was rather glad when the missive arrived from Nigel requesting a meeting. Rupert was ready to sink his teeth into anything that would get him out of the house and away from Rebecca's constant presence.

He arrived at the palace at the appointed hour. Nigel only kept him waiting a few minutes.

"Has Pearson been apprehended?" Rupert asked.

"It wasn't necessary," Nigel said on his way to his liquor cabinet. "Brandy?"

Rupert had stiffened. "No, and why wasn't it necessary? The evidence I sent you wasn't conclusive enough?"

His own brandy in hand and wearing his usual inscrutable expression, Nigel took the chair next to him. "On the contrary, the evidence would have gotten him hung, but your bullet saved us the trouble. The wound you gave him was severe enough that he died a few days after you returned to England."

"What the hell, my aim is better than that and I wasn't trying to kill him."

Nigel shrugged, unperturbed. "By your own account, you were being bounced about in a fleeing coach. Perfectly understandable to have your aim fly off the mark in such a case. So, we are satisfied that justice has been served. A job well done, dear boy."

Rupert didn't care for unexpected endings like that. Annoyed, he broached his summons. "I hope you're not sending me out of the country again. I'd prefer to remain close to home just now."

"Someone ill?"

"No."

When Rupert didn't elaborate, Nigel made a face and got directly to the business at hand. "Sarah is finally out of the palace for good."

"By choice?"

"No."

When Nigel didn't elaborate, Rupert almost laughed. Touché. But he knew Nigel wouldn't leave it at that, and he didn't.

"By all accounts she has retired from intrigue as well, since she no longer has a horde of lackeys to do her bidding. She's getting married, though, which is what leads me to believe she's retired from intrigue."

Now that was a surprise. "Sarah married? But who would have her?"

"Lord Alberton. Not a bad catch, though the young debutantes might not think so, him being in his late forties. But he's titled, rich, and easy on the eye."

"While Sarah is exactly the opposite on all accounts. What'd she do, blackmail him into it?"

Nigel shrugged. "He was one of her targets last year, so that would be my guess."

"Over the attempt on the queen?"

"No, I have given up trying to associate Alberton with that foul deed. Mere coincidence is all that turned out to be, that he happened to be seen upbraiding the boy who shot at her. But during that investigation I did turn up another bit of sordid business where he risked a brief affair with a young married duchess."

"And you think that's what Sarah has on him?"

"That's my guess. In fact, I'm almost inclined to believe that most of her scandal gathering was in the interest of her buying herself a husband. She may have lined her pockets a little along the way, but I have a feeling she'd prefer a prime catch over money."

"He's not exactly a prime catch at his age."

"For a woman *her* age, he is. And those in the ton tend to put a great deal of stock in the criteria that Lord Alberton fills."

Rupert raised a brow. "Bragging rights?"

"If you want to call it that."

"But if that's the case, why did she wait so long?"

"Shopping?" Nigel rolled his eyes over his own catty remark. "Who can ascertain the mind of a woman? But she could have merely wanted a decent-sized list of titles to choose from. Regardless, I'd just like to be absolutely sure that she's done with ferreting out information that she had no business knowing about."

This was to be Rupert's job? He couldn't help groaning, "Not her again."

"You're still friends with her, aren't you?"

"I've let that peter out, so she might not see it that way."

"Well, now that she's out of the palace, it might not hurt to simply be honest with her—and ask her directly. They are having a party tonight at Alberton's house to announce their engagement. I've obtained an invitation for you and a companion."

Rupert sighed and accepted the folded invitation Nigel

handed him. "I suppose my wife can be considered a companion."

"That isn't funny."

"What part of it do you consider a joke?"

"*You've* married?"

"Too busy digging deep to notice what's floating on the surface in plain sight? It's the current on-dit making the rounds."

Nigel didn't merely look shocked, he looked devastated. And it certainly wasn't because he was the last to know. But for once, Rupert didn't fly off the handle over this obvious reminder of how Nigel felt about him. He even understood a little better, now that he was having feelings of his own that were quite out of his control.

Nigel recovered somewhat after draining his brandy. At least he managed to get his expression under control.

His voice, however, was still shaky when he said, "I . . . suppose congratulations are in order."

Rupert kept his own voice toneless. "Not really. It may just be a temporary arrangement. We won't know for a few more months."

"So it's like that? But I thought you stayed away from young virgins."

"I do—did. But having one show up in my room at the palace late at night was a bit more'n I could resist. The very audacity of that suggested she wasn't virginal, but she was." Rupert sighed.

"Who is she?"

"Our last maid of honor, Rebecca Marshall, who is no longer a maid."

Nigel looked appalled now. "Good God, I hope this wasn't *my* fault!"

Rupert's eyes narrowed slightly as he said, "Rest easy. You merely supplied her with an excuse to enact her own agenda, which was to get into my family one way or another."

Did he *really* believe that now? Doubts. There were too many where she was concerned. Yet to find her innocent on all counts was to admit that he'd gone beyond the pale himself. With any other supposed innocent showing up in his room looking and sounding so sexy, he would have been leaping out the bloody window in a panic to escape such an obvious trap. So the truth was, he hadn't *wanted* to resist Rebecca.

Nigel broke into his thoughts, observing, "She didn't strike me as mercenary."

Rupert choked back a laugh as he stood up to leave. "It's a fallacy of ours to think most women are empty-headed and in need of our guidance because of it. It's only what they want you to think, you know."

"They aren't all as intelligent as this girl."

"Of course not, no more than all men are created equal. But you'd be surprised just how many are smarter than they let on."

Rupert made his way to the door. Behind him, Nigel remarked, "I find myself surprised to say, she's well suited to you."

Rupert stopped and swung around angrily. "You are *not* going to try to enlist her again."

"No, wouldn't dream of it. I *was* sorry when she decided not to work for me. They may not all be empty-headed chits, as you say, but it's still quite rare to find a girl that young with the intelligence to improvise as needed. I merely recalled that you'd found her to be a challenge, even remarked on it. I think in a wife, with anything less than that sort of challenge, you'd find yourself bored very quickly. At least she'll keep you on your toes."

That didn't deserve a reply. Challenge indeed. The woman was nothing *but* a challenge. He didn't want to stand that bloody high on his toes!

Chapter Forty-eight

THEY HAD ATTENDED SEVERAL more parties as chaperones for Amanda, but this was the first time Rupert was taking Rebecca to a party himself. He hadn't told her much about it, merely what time to be ready, and to wear something fetchingly wifely, whatever the deuce that meant. She couldn't say exactly what got her so excited about it.

Amanda was pouting upstairs because Julie had scolded her for trying to intrude on a private affair when Amanda had asked to join them. That could be what had triggered Rebecca's excitement. It sounded so personal, "private affair." And with so little information volunteered, this evening's party had the feel of a surprise to it.

So she took special care with her appearance that night and ignored that her pink and violet, laced evening gown was yet another dress from her wardrobe that was fitting her far too snugly now. An amethyst pendant was attached to the velvet choker around her neck; thin, wispy golden curls dangled at her temples; an actual spark of blue was in her dark eyes, so rarely seen. Because the excitement was building to an uncontainable level?

She fairly flew downstairs the moment Flora pronounced her ready. Of course Rupert wasn't anywhere to be seen yet. So with a sigh she joined Julie and Owen in the parlor. They paused in their card game to chat with her and remark on how fetching she looked.

Though Julie did whisper in an aside to her, "It's time for you to get a new wardrobe, gel, that gives you a little room to breath. I'll take you shopping next week."

Rebecca was still blushing a little over that when Rupert walked in and Julie said in complete disgruntlement, "Rebecca, *why* haven't you burned his wardrobe yet?"

Rebecca turned to see what had provoked that question, then just stared. Her husband was wearing one of those horribly bright satin coats better suited to a costume ball, this one in a ghastly orange, with excessive lace at the wrists and the throat. With his long black hair and his soft cheeks so smoothly shaved, it made him look somewhat effeminate when she knew he was anything but.

But he actually looked to be trying not to laugh when he said to his mother, "She'll do nothing of the sort. She likes my taste in clothes. It reminds her of when we first met."

Rebecca continued to just stare, her mind in a whirl. It sounded as if he was just teasing, but she couldn't be sure. To imply that she had fond memories of their first meeting wasn't even remotely amusing. She had nothing of the sort.

"You can't seriously intend to take your wife out wearing something like that?" Julie continued.

"What's wrong with what she's wearing?"

"Not her, you fool. You! You're married now. Your old taste in clothes—"

"Marriage has nothing to do with taste, Mother," Rupert cut in. "Well, perhaps a little, at least in women, but nothing a'tall to do with one's wardrobe. Shall we go, m'dear?"

The last was added for Rebecca as he put an arm around her to lead her out of the room. His hand on her hip was all she could think about.

But his mother refused to be dismissed so easily. Julie actually shouted after him, "Find a new tailor! You're mortifying your wife!"

Rebecca refrained from glancing at him to see how he took that remark. Perhaps this was a costume ball they were headed to and he hadn't mentioned it because he didn't want to risk his wife's showing up in a man's garb again. He could just have said so. She did have a number of costumes now that didn't include breeches.

His crested coach was waiting outside for them, Matthew on the driver's box. Once they were inside it with the door closed, seated on opposite benches, she watched incredulously as Rupert performed an immediate transformation.

He shrugged out of his bright satin coat first and laid it on the seat beside him. The long stream of lace at his cuffs wasn't actually a part of his white lawn shirt after all, was merely tied to his wrists to make it seem so, and he untied those now and tossed them on top of the coat. The flowing cravat came off next, to reveal a thin, fashionable one beneath it. Finally he stood up—well, not really, he was too tall for that, but he got off his seat so he could lift it up to put the discarded items away and take out another coat that had been stashed there, a quite tasteful one in dark navy blue with a thin trim of black satin on the lapels.

She understood now, or thought she did. His apparel had been a ruse to tease his mother with? Julie was the only one who made a fuss about it. But why go to such extremes? Yet she'd seen it quite often during the week, how gruff and mulish Julie got when he said something she disapproved of, and he did it so often! All in jest? Julie didn't seem to take it that way.

He finally looked over at her and asked pointedly, "*Were you mortified?*"

Confused was what she'd been, but she wasn't going to say so. "Um, not really, though I confess I suspected we were going to a costume ball and you simply forgot to mention it. Why do you tease your mother so mercilessly?"

"Out of the goodness of my heart." That made not a jot of sense to her until he added, "It gives her purpose, to think she still needs to whip me into shape. Although I suppose I could tone it down for a while. It's getting quite hard to get a spark out of her while she's so bloody delighted with me."

He seemed exasperated and annoyed at the last part of his remark and got back to making sure he now looked presentable, smoothing out his sleeves, jerking down his lapels to make sure they were straight. She finally understood Amanda's remark to her earlier in the week, when she'd tried to explain her aunt's bullish demeanor wasn't natural at all.

"It's a trait she's developed," Amanda had told Rebecca. "She felt she had to make the sacrifice, to give up her softer side so she could take on the role of both parents for her sons while they were so young. An extreme transformation that mostly amused the family after she couldn't be talked out of it. Stubbornness runs in our family, you know."

Amused now, and feeling an odd sort of tenderness for the eldest son who was still trying to make sure his mother didn't feel she'd wasted the effort, Rebecca said, "At least you didn't need to change your breeches."

He glanced up again instantly, pinning her eyes with his, his own suddenly gone lambent. "Now why didn't I think of that? Would it inspire you to ravish me?"

She wasn't going to answer that! Yet an image was now branded in her mind of him sitting there with no breeches. Her blush was acute.

He took pity on her though and took his overly sensual gaze off her to say, "You needn't worry in that regard—at least until spring. I draw the line at freezing my arse during the winter months."

He wouldn't have been cold. The weather was quite chilly, but certainly not that extreme yet so early in December. And besides, a brazier was heating the enclosed space nicely so they didn't need to bundle up in coats just to go from coach to party and back. But she appreciated his attempt to diffuse her discomfort over her thoughtless humor.

She managed to keep her eyes off him for the remainder of that short ride. No matter what he wore, the man was still far too handsome not to affect her in unwanted ways. Still thinking about him with no pants on, she got so uncomfortably hot by the time they reached their destination, she wished she'd brought a fan with her. In the winter.

But all heat left her when she recognized the house they alighted in front of. Lord Alberton's residence on Wigmore Street.

Good God, she'd been set up, was her first thought. Did Rupert want some kind of closure on what she'd told him so long ago? Was he trying to *prove* her excuse for showing up in his room in the palace that night had been a lie?

Chapter Forty-nine

Tight-lipped and growing angrier by the minute, Rebecca made no remark as Rupert escorted her to the door Flora had knocked on for Constance so many weeks ago. It was opened as they approached by the butler, stationed there, who ushered them inside quickly to make sure as little cold as possible got into the house.

The sound of many people talking and laughing drew them to the parlor. Rebecca began to relax slightly. It really was a party, though why Rupert would want to come to one at this particular house she still found suspicious. He could at least have warned her. That he hadn't done so was why she wasn't letting down her guard completely.

Before they were greeted by anyone, she asked him, "Why are we here?"

"It's an engagement party I couldn't decline."

"Anyone I know?"

"Yes" was all he said before their host arrived to welcome them.

Rebecca hadn't really got a good look at Lord Alberton that day she'd helped Constance. She hadn't been interested enough to try. He was quite a handsome man, though, probably in his late forties, jet-black hair, clear green eyes, an athletic physique that would have done a younger man proud. He had an odd air about him, however, that she couldn't quite place until his expression changed as he moved away from them to speak with someone else.

"Is he the groom?" she asked. At Rupert's nod she added, "He doesn't seem too happy."

She immediately wished she had kept that observation to herself. It was a distinct reminder of how Rupert had come to the altar, not that they'd had an altar. A brisk wind, a gloomy sky, a rocking ship, their brief ceremony wasn't worth remembering. And Lord Alberton had that same sort of mood that Rupert had had. Still, Lord Alberton had been gracious in welcoming them, though he seemed not to know Rupert other than by name, which was not surprising as there was probably a twenty-year age difference between them.

Rupert led her farther into the room to a couple he was acquainted with. After a few moments of conversation that she was easily able to participate in, he left her there to fetch them refreshments, obviously thinking he was leaving her in good hands.

Despite being relaxed with the couple, Rebecca still kept an eye on Rupert and saw that he'd been detained by an older woman. Nothing really to take note of, but then he was detained again. Well, that was typical of a party, she supposed. Unless a controversial subject arose that could gather a crowd into hot debate, guests more often circulated, hoping to hear the latest gossip.

Another couple joined her group, which distracted her for a while longer, then the first couple moved on. But the second couple didn't stay long, and suddenly she was standing there alone, amused to see that Rupert still hadn't reached the refreshments. She walked over to join him, but she didn't get far.

"Who invited *you?*"

She knew that voice, so her expression was composed when she turned around. "Hello, Sarah. How—unexpected, to see you here."

"Very amusing," Sarah said in a disagreeable tone, though oddly, she didn't look annoyed.

Rebecca wasn't really surprised to find Sarah Wheeler at the party. The lady obviously knew Lord Alberton since they had corresponded. But she was surprised by the older woman's appearance.

She was wearing a pretty rose-colored gown that actually revealed she had some curves after all. Her hair had also been arranged in a soft, lovely coiffure that was quite a change from the severe arrangement she'd previously worn. The combination was exactly what Rebecca had predicted. Sarah didn't look nearly as plain as she had at the palace. Her surly, impatient mood seemed to have changed, too, but something else improved her looks even more dramatically. She still wasn't pretty, but you almost didn't notice that. A spark of gaiety? A glow of excitement?

Rebecca discounted those guesses when Sarah said, "You were directly responsible for my downfall."

"What downfall?"

"The duchess dismissed me from her employ."

"I wasn't even there. How can you possibly blame me for that?"

"But it began with you giving my girls the courage to defy me and think for themselves. Even Evelyn refused to do as she was told if it didn't involve the duchess."

"Which was as it should be," Rebecca pointed out. "You never had a right to involve those young women in your sordid intrigues."

Sarah waved that aside. "I should seek retribution. I can, you know. What do you think the ton would say if they knew you cavorted with St. John in the palace?"

Rebecca almost smiled. "I think they will conclude that I should have left my post sooner than I did, since I was already secretly married to him."

"Were you? I think not," Sarah scoffed. "But I've no desire to involve you in a scandal. My dismissal has led to other things that I'm not entirely displeased with. In fact, I prevaricated so long, I went beyond the point of realizing I didn't need to any longer. Quite the waste of time, that. So I could almost say I'm grateful for your interference. If you weren't so annoying, I would say it."

Rebecca choked back a laugh that Sarah had said it anyway. "What other things are you talking about?"

"Don't pretend to be ignorant. You know very well this party is in my honor. I'm soon to be a blushing bride."

Sarah flounced off with a smirk, leaving Rebecca standing there dumbfounded. Sarah getting married, and to such a handsome man as Alberton? Well, there was no accounting for taste, she supposed. Or was the groom not so happy at this turn of events? Yet another member of the ton forced to the altar?

She'd be a hypocrite to feel bad for Lord Alberton when she'd done the same thing to Rupert, more or less. Actually, she'd done nothing of the sort. She had refused to marry him, he had done the insisting. She'd merely insisted on making it known to his family.

An elderly lady joined her before she could continue on her way to Rupert. They had met at the Withers' ball, though Rebecca couldn't remember her name. Unfortunately, the woman was a gossipmonger. Not wanting to be rude, Rebecca was forced to listen to all the latest on-dits about people she didn't know and, to go by what she was hearing, didn't want to know. Until the woman mentioned Amanda's name. Apparently, Amanda's having three Seasons without landing a husband had become a source of speculation that was now making the rounds. Rebecca hoped her old friend wasn't aware of it. Amanda got upset over the silliest things, but this wasn't the least bit silly.

Rebecca knew her husband wasn't going to rescue her, not this time. He might need rescuing himself, though, because she saw that the latest person to have detained him was the bride-to-be.

Chapter Fifty

T<small>HIS IS QUITE A</small> delightful surprise, m'dear," Rupert told
Sarah as he casually led her off to the side of the room, away
from any eavesdroppers.

"It is, isn't it?" Sarah beamed at him. "I was in love with
Alberton years ago, when I was a young chit. He wasn't ready
for marriage back then, though."

And still wasn't, Rupert was sure. Nearing fifty and never
wed was as accurate a description as there was for a confirmed
bachelor. He wondered if Alberton was going to put a good
face on the marriage or stick Sarah somewhere in the country
where he could ignore her, and she'd have little to say about it.
Her ace in the hole wouldn't be as useful after the marriage,
when leaking whatever she had on Alberton would embroil her
in the same scandal. Did she realize that?

If it was true that she used to love him, she might be setting
herself up for some heartache, too. But Rupert had a feeling
Sarah's profession of love for Alberton was merely an excuse to
explain why she appeared so happy about the marriage. It was

more likely that all she wanted was Alberton's title and wealth, and to at long last be removed from the list of old maids.

Nigel wanted Rupert to be brutally direct with Sarah to find out if she was done with her intrigues, but as usual, he preferred to use his own methods of interrogation.

So he said, "Nigel Jennings approached me recently. He was aware that we were quite chummy for a while and tasked me with an odd request. He claims you trafficked in information that the queen wouldn't want to come to light."

Sarah didn't turn defensive; she actually laughed. "Nigel is such a silly chap. He got it into his head early on that I had some sort of authority in the duchess's chambers, when that wasn't the case a'tall."

Rupert raised a brow. "That's an assumption most everyone made, Sarah."

"Yes, I know." She grinned. "And I encouraged it and took advantage of it. But the truth is, the duchess grudgingly accepted the maids as part of her entourage because she understands ceremony well enough. She didn't ask for them. She couldn't even talk to them! So she pretty much just ignored them and devoted herself to her own interests, which were her daughter and granddaughter. She merely asked me to make sure the maids didn't get into any mischief while they were associated with her."

Incredulous, Rupert asked, "Were you trying to make sure they did?"

"Not at all. I used them for harmless errands that kept them busy so they *wouldn't* get into mischief."

"Nigel knows what you dabbled in. Not exactly harmless, by the sound of it."

"Harmless enough for the maids," Sarah replied with a

careless shrug. "But it was nothing that would have disturbed the court."

"What was it then?"

"An old grudge I'd been nursing that resurfaced when the duchess moved us into the palace. I had never thought to be that close to them again, right in London, but—"

"Close to whom?"

"The men who scorned me when I was young. They were all on my list of acceptable husbands back when I had my useless come-out," Sarah said with some bitterness. "I put myself forward to each of them. They weren't even kind in fobbing me off. One even laughed at me. So I developed a desire for revenge, but I had no way of obtaining it until I was back in London and had the means to spy on them and ferret out damaging tidbits that weren't common knowledge."

"So you were going to bring them down?"

"It was a thought, a nice thought. I really, really enjoyed knowing that I could ruin them. I savored it. It absolutely delighted me. But then it lost its luster. I became bored with it."

"You didn't really plan to ruin any of them, did you?" he guessed.

"Of course not. Knowing that I could, *their* knowing that I could, was all that mattered. And then Nigel Jennings completely distracted me with his silly assumptions and I began to encourage his erroneous conclusions. I quite enjoyed that cat-and-mouse game with him. It was highly entertaining. I think he did, too. But that's all it was. A nice distraction."

"Including sending my wife to break into his room? Just part of your entertainment?"

She choked back a laugh. "She wasn't supposed to be caught! How alarming that was! But whoever it was who discovered her there must not have mentioned it to Nigel. Perhaps another thief? How amusing, two thieves in the same room at the same time! But I'm surprised she told you about that. She was quite angry about it and flatly refused to do another thing for me, even had the nerve to threaten me. Uppity wench, but then I'm sure you know that by now."

Rupert groaned inwardly. From the horse's mouth, as it were. All true, everything Rebecca had told him. She should have just shot him. There was no way she'd ever forgive him. He might as well just shoot himself.

"I've surprised you," Sarah said, breaking into his thoughts. "You can admit it."

Sarah's antics hadn't put the dumbfounded look on his face, but she was deluding herself if she really thought she hadn't put the innocent maids in danger of scandal. She had escaped lightly over taking that risk, with the duchess merely giving her the boot.

But as to her observation, he allowed, "I think the only thing I'm really surprised at is that you considered Alberton acceptable as a husband all those years ago. He was and has always been a rake. Some might even say he's progressed to a state of degeneracy."

Her eyes gleamed with obvious titillation over that prediction. Good God, was she hoping so?

But then she actually giggled. "I didn't have him on my list. He is more'n ten years my senior, after all, and was deep into debauchery before I came of age. But he was still fascinating by all accounts, at least I found him to be. In the same way you were, come to think of it—before you married. How long *have* you been married?"

Immediately on guard, he countered, "What did my wife tell you?"

She chuckled. "Touché. Forgive me, but old habits are hard to break, and it was an enjoyable pastime. Ferreting out secrets can be likened to digging for treasure, you never know what you will find."

"If Lord Alberton wasn't on your original list, how is it that you've managed to rope in such a confirmed bachelor—without using blackmail?"

"Such a nasty word, that," she said with a tsk. "And not something I've ever actually done. But if you must know, when my misuse of the maids reached the duchess's ears and she sent me away, I chewed over a little tidbit that I stumbled upon concerning him and presented it to him. I wasn't expecting his offer of marriage. I'm not sure what I was expecting, perhaps no more than an association with him of the sort I had with you. I would have settled for friendship with someone as exciting as he is. But I'll allow that he may have *thought* I was blackmailing him, and I was too pleased by his proposal to disabuse him of that."

"And what happens when the luster wears off your marriage, too? You don't think you'll be tempted to return to your cat-and-mouse games with Nigel?"

"Nigel again? Come now, Nigel is old hat. I'm quite done with him and the business of gathering secrets." Then she nodded toward her future husband. "But look there. Do you really think I can get bored with him? Ever?"

Rupert wanted to wince on the groom's behalf. She made him sound like a toy, not a man. But if the thought of bordello-style sex with him excited her, she wasn't likely to think so after she became a part of it. Then again, maybe she would. They could, in fact, be ideally suited to each other, a match made of bliss, as it were. He suddenly wished he could say the same about his own marriage.

He glanced over at *his* wife—when did he start thinking of her as his? She was giving an old dame her rapt attention when she was probably bored to tears. She was polite that way. Courteous, charming, with a delightful sense of humor. Good God, she really was everything he could ask for in a wife, *and* the mother of his children. She only grew thorns when he picked her petals.

What had he been resisting, to put up such a fight? A loss of variety? Hell, who needed variety when one single woman could fulfill every one of his needs and offered more variety in moods than he'd ever come across.

There was no need to remain at the party. He had what Nigel had sent him for. He was certain Sarah was telling the truth, too. The only woman who'd ever fooled him had been Rebecca, and now he knew she hadn't fooled him. He'd been a fool because he'd misconstrued her actions. But he did have a spark of sympathy for Lord Alberton, even though they were nothing alike, which is why he wanted to have a word with him before leaving the party.

Rupert wasn't sure he was going to warn him that no blackmail was involved in his marriage. He should. But—Sarah seemed so bloody happy! Even if he'd never liked the woman, how could he ruin that for her?

But the matter was decided for him with just one question. "Shouldn't you look a little more happy at your own engagement party?" Rupert asked Lord Alberton.

The man laughed, though not a bit of humor was in it. "If you knew me, you'd know this is as happy as I get. A word of advice, m'boy. Never live your fantasies. Keep them up here"—Alberton tapped his head—"always out of reach. But I'm not displeased with this match, far from it. I get the odd sense that Sarah *knows* me and still likes me. You can't imagine how refreshing that will be."

Rupert could imagine. If the dissolute lord sensed even a little of the excitement Sarah had displayed tonight while discussing him and his unusual proclivities, yes, Alberton might just think he'd found his ideal match.

In the same vein, Rupert knew that *he'd* found his own ideal match, too. He just couldn't imagine how he was going to convince her of it.

But that wasn't what he was thinking about on the ride home. Unable to take his eyes off of his wife, he said, "There's something about riding in a coach with you that drives me crazy."

Rebecca's dark blue eyes flared, but she didn't protest when he moved across to her seat and gathered her into his arms. Catching his wife off guard did have its advantages, which was fortunate, because she really did inflame his passions without even trying. One heady taste of her and most of his control was gone.

"Could it be because we nearly made love in this coach before?" he said against her lips. "Or could it be because I suspect you were sitting here earlier tonight thinking of me with my breeches off?"

Rebecca gasped but he just thrust his tongue deeply inside her until she no longer seemed to feel like upbraiding him for that teasing remark. He loved teasing her. It was too bad she was rarely in a mood for it.

Unfortunately, she didn't let his last remark go unanswered, though they were nearly home before she pulled away from his arms to say breathlessly, "I was doing nothing of the sort."

Her cheeks were flushed. Her lips were lushly swollen from his kisses. It was one of the hardest things he'd ever done, keeping himself from reaching for her again. But they were home, and she'd found refuge in her indignation again.

Chapter Fifty-one

REBECCA WOKE UP IN an odd, hurtful mood that she couldn't quite grasp the reason for, and it wouldn't go away. The previous evening had turned out to be more exciting than she had anticipated. Not the party, that had been quite boring, but in the coach . . .

Rupert's risqué remark and the look he'd given her on the way to the party still made her blush when she thought about it. But she felt he would have made the remark to any female companion, rogue that he was, so it hadn't really been for her in particular. Even if he did mention it again on the way home! His other remarks on the way home reinforced that feeling. He'd just been being himself, an outrageous rake trying to seduce whichever woman was near at hand.

Her own feelings, though, had gone over the edge for a rogue. That was the problem. She'd fallen in love with a man who obviously desired her, and whom she desired, but a man who would never be able to tell her he loved her or be faithful to her. That was what was upsetting her and making her so dangerously emotional.

She almost stayed in her room because of it. But as soon as the morning sickness passed, she was famished as usual. So she went downstairs to have breakfast and simply hoped everyone else had finished, so she wouldn't have to pretend she was the happy bride today, when she was anything but happy.

At least the late hour afforded her an empty breakfast room to eat in. And trying not to think about anything that would make her mood even worse, she paid a little more attention to what she was eating and stared aghast as she caught herself reaching for yet another sausage when she was already quite full! So she had thoughtlessly been eating more than she should. Well, that at least was a relief. She had begun to think she was going to give birth to an abnormally large baby because her pregnancy was showing so soon.

That didn't improve her mood, though. Now she also felt disgusted with herself. So it certainly wasn't a good time for Rupert to catch her as she was leaving the breakfast room and to put his hands on her waist. It was obvious that he was actually measuring her girth, which mortified her.

"Damn," he said. "Have you been stuffing yourself with desserts just to prolong the suspense?"

She failed to note the humor in his tone. All she gathered from his remark was that he still didn't believe she was pregnant.

"You've found me out at last," she snapped. "I'm merely going to give birth to a pastry."

"That's not funny, Becca."

"Neither was your absurd remark. Do you really think I like that my body is going to be disfigured? I hate it, but not as much as I hate you!"

She burst into tears before she managed to run up the stairs and out of his sight, because she didn't mean what she'd said about her body. That was an acceptable change to accommodate the baby she already loved wholeheartedly. She didn't mean it about him, either. She'd never hated him. He'd made her more angry than she'd ever been in her life, yet it hadn't brought her to the point of hating him.

He followed her upstairs and knocked on her door for a while. She didn't answer, and he didn't try the handle to see that it wasn't locked. When he finally went away, she cried herself to sleep, but after only a brief nap she was awake again by noon—and famished again! Good grief, it was starting to be amusing. At least it lightened her mood quite a bit and allowed her to get back into the "happy" pretense when she joined the family for lunch.

Rupert refrained from saying a single word to her at this meal. After her earlier outburst, she wasn't surprised by his reticence. His eyes kept returning to her, though, and while he kept his look perfectly inscrutable unless he was baiting his mother, she sensed his—concern? No, probably just curiosity over why she'd reacted so strongly to what had been a jest. A jest in poor taste, but still, she didn't think he'd been serious.

He disappeared after the meal, so she was able to relax for a while with his mother in the parlor. She liked Julie. It was hard not to when the woman was so obviously pleased with her. And Rebecca seemed to be having a good influence on her. Each day, Julie's tone got a little less gruff, almost as if the female was slowly emerging from the cocoon again. At least it seemed so until Rupert would begin his teasing again.

As was Rebecca's habit, she went upstairs to change for dinner. Most households of the gentry treated the last meal of the day more formally than the others, even without guests to impress. She left her room at the very moment Rupert was entering his. He stopped. She thought about ducking back inside hers.

"A moment, Becca," he said, and moved quickly toward her, as if he'd read her mind.

She immediately went on guard, her defenses firmly in place. She didn't want to answer any questions about her silly behavior that morning, which is what she guessed he wanted to discuss.

She was already forming an excuse when he said, "I'll be gone most of the day tomorrow on business. I mention it because I'll be leaving so early in the morning, I probably won't see you."

Hardly what she was expecting to hear, but with her defenses so tightly in place, her tone sounded a bit too stiff even to her ears when she replied, "You don't need to give me your agenda when I'm merely—"

She didn't get to finish. He was suddenly kissing her into silence. She didn't know if he was preventing her from saying *wife* or *guest*. She wasn't even sure what she had been going to say. A moment later as her arms slipped about his neck, she didn't care.

God, how could he still do this to her, inflame her instantly like this? Famished again, this time for the taste of him! All of the doubts, the angers, the insecurities, and the strange moods gone with the simple touch of his mouth and the knowledge that he *wanted* to kiss her. Wanted it! Of course he wouldn't be doing it if he didn't want to! Would he?

Her hold tightened on him. Something like happiness began to rise, mixed in with such powerful yearnings she was overwhelmed by it. She heard his groan. She didn't guess it had nothing to do with passion until he abruptly set her back from him.

"Stop looking so bloody fetching," he said.

He might as well have knocked her over, she was that surprised. He felt he'd been enticed into kissing her because of the way she looked?! What sort of nonsense was that?

Hurt, and more than a little frustrated to have such a pleasant kiss end that way, she snapped back, "Excuse me while I go smear mud on my face," and pushed him out of her way to stomp down the corridor.

"You'll find some in the backyard!" he called after her in what now sounded suspiciously like *amusement.*

"Thank you!" she shouted back, not the least bit amused herself.

She continued downstairs, though she didn't want to now. She didn't want to see him again tonight, for the next week, actually forever! So she intended to tell her mother-in-law that she was going to take her meal in her room and retire early, but she wasn't expecting to see the guest sitting beside Julie on the sofa.

"Mother!"

Lilly beamed at her and stood up for a quick hug. "I resisted coming as long as I could." She laughed at herself. "This should be getting easier, but it's not—yet, anyway. But I refuse to appear like the meddling mother checking up on you every few days."

"Don't be silly," Rebecca replied, and joined them on the sofa. "Tell her she'll be welcome anytime, Julie."

"Already did, gel."

So easily, Rebecca's mood took a complete turn with her mother's visit. Lilly represented comfort, security, love, the things Rebecca had been missing the most. She wasn't so young to think anymore her mother could fix everything, but her mere presence helped tremendously.

They had a nice, if not private, reunion before Rupert joined them. He didn't exactly ruin it, but if he insisted on enacting their pretense tonight, even for her mother, it surely would. Unfortunately, he entered the room wearing a horribly bright lime-green dinner jacket that had his mother immediately scowling at him. So even after that kiss upstairs, he'd decided on an evening of humorously baiting his mother again. Bad timing, with her own mother there, or maybe not. At least it kept Rebecca's own mood light for the moment, since she knew why he did it.

Nor did Julie hold her tongue, remarking in disgust, "I see your taste is still beyond flamboyant. You're a bloody peacock, Rue."

He actually looked behind him as he replied, "I thought I had my feathers tucked away nicely."

Rebecca had to put a hand to her mouth to stifle a laugh. Julie merely glowered at him. Lilly didn't know what to think, of course. But this being the first time she was officially meeting him, he couldn't have picked a worse time to tease his mother with his clothes.

And he *was* going to enact the pretense! Before Rupert greeted Lilly in the most gracious manner, he leaned down to give Rebecca a husbandly peck on the cheek that lasted a little longer than it should have. Then he bent over Lilly's hand to kiss it.

"I must thank you, Lilly, for raising such a remarkable daughter," he said.

Rebecca suspected that her mother had just been won over by that simple statement! Lilly was beaming with pride and cast Rebecca a loving look before she replied to Rupert, "She is, isn't she? And I hope you've been taking good care of my daughter?"

"Not as often as I'd like to!"

All three women blushed over that risqué reply. So typical of him! But his roguish wink for Lilly confirmed he was only teasing, and Lilly took it in that light.

Rebecca could have wished he'd just stuck to being charming for this first meeting of theirs with her mother, but she was still able to grin when Lilly whispered at her side a few minutes later, "He has atrocious taste, doesn't he? I'm so sorry, m'dear. That's going to be quite embarrassing for you."

"It won't be. He just likes to tease his mother by letting her think he does."

On the way to the dining room, Lilly even found a private moment to tell her, "The suspense was killing me. I know this was pretty much my suggestion, but I didn't expect it to turn out this well."

Rebecca groaned inwardly. If her mother would leave right then, she wouldn't have to know. But Lilly wasn't leaving. She stayed for dinner, and unfortunately Rupert took the seat beside Rebecca before her mother could. Her guard went back up, and not a moment too soon.

She'd barely sat down when he reminded her of that kiss: "Couldn't find any mud?" He said it so casually, she couldn't tell if he was teasing.

"Behave," she hissed at him.

"Never." He grinned at her.

That brought on a slight blush, which in turn brought back her earlier frustration. "If you're trying to punish me by making me want you, I won't fall for that again," she warned him.

"*Do* you want me?"

What a ridiculous question. How could she not want him? But she wasn't telling him that. For him to even ask proved his intent was wicked in some form.

"Be at ease, Becca." Then he completely ruined that by

adding, "I'm not going to ravish you here at the table, though I confess, I'll probably be thinking about nothing else."

She could have melted off the chair right to the floor, and not just from the scalding blush that flew up her cheeks. She was seeing him in her mind making love to her on the table! She couldn't look down at the table without seeing it now! Oh, God . . .

She had no idea how she got through that meal. She barely heard a word around her. Why was he doing this to her? It was mean, and petty. Was it revenge for putting the ball and chain on him?

Of course he went on as if he hadn't put her into another turmoil, keeping the dinner conversation flowing, even making her mother laugh quite often. And her mother didn't leave after dinner. She wanted a private reunion and asked Rebecca if they could go somewhere to have it. There was no point in hiding it. Rebecca took her upstairs to her room, the room she didn't share with a husband.

Chapter Fifty-two

Rebecca stared out her window at a coach plodding down the street out front. A few flakes of early snow were flickering around its double-lit lamps. It wasn't cold enough yet for the snow to do anything but melt as soon as it hit the ground, but obviously the weather was beginning to turn more wintery. Like her thoughts the last few days.

"I almost thought you were fine," Lilly was saying behind her as she paced the floor. "You were certainly putting on a good show—at first. But I know you too well to be fooled for long. So what was all that pretense about downstairs? Are you two having a fight?"

"When haven't we been?" Rebecca said with a sigh as she turned around.

"I don't understand. The gossip is that *he* announced your marriage at some ball a few weeks ago. Usually if a man does that, he intends to make a go of it. So the gossip isn't true a'tall?"

"It is, but that was just a silly reaction he had that night because I hadn't announced it when I got there. We called a truce for appearances, even for his family. It was his idea. But two weeks of him being so nice made me realize . . . I love him!"

Rebecca burst into tears immediately. Lilly, appalled, rushed over to gather her into her arms.

"What part of that *wasn't* a happy statement?" Lilly asked carefully after the worst of the sobs died down.

Rebecca stood back to wipe her eyes with her sleeve. "What's happy about a pretense? And now he's not being so nice anymore. His roguish tendencies are showing up again. I'm surprised he kept them under wraps this long."

Taking immediate offense on her behalf, Lilly demanded, "He's being unfaithful already?"

"You expected it, too?"

"Well, he wasn't exactly in the market for a wife, so it was a distinct possibility, considering his reputation." Lilly sighed.

"I know, you prepared me well enough for the foibles of the male—"

"Only if they aren't madly in love!" Lilly corrected her.

"Which he isn't. But that wasn't what I was referring to. I meant with me."

"*You've* been unfaithful?" Lilly said, aghast.

Rebecca blinked, then couldn't help the mild chuckle. "No, of course not. I was referring to Rue being roguish with me when he swore he wouldn't touch me prior to seeing proof of my pregnancy."

Lilly didn't even blush and said matter-of-factly, "You're living in the same house. You're his wife. You should have expected him to behave that way, even if you aren't sharing the same room with him."

Rebecca blushed. "I didn't mean that, either. He's just being entirely too risqué in his remarks again, and kissing me when he doesn't even want to!"

"Well, he must want—"

"Really, he doesn't want to. He even gets angry about it, when it happens, as if he really can't help himself. It's like I said, he's reverting to form, his natural tendency to chase any skirt around—even his wife's."

"I see. And this is making you even more unhappy?" Lilly guessed.

"He doesn't even like me, Mama!"

Lilly winced at the pain Rebecca had been unable to keep out of her tone. She put an arm around Rebecca and led her to the edge of the bed, where they sat.

After a few caught breaths from the earlier sobbing, Rebecca added, "My emotions are out of control, too. There have been such wild swings in my moods, some so inexplicable I'm not even sure it has anything to do with him."

"They're due to the baby. I couldn't have been happier when I was pregnant with you, and yet I still snapped at your father occasionally for absolutely no reason. But coupled with this other—" Lilly paused to sigh. "This should be a quiet, happy time for you—well, at least reasonably peaceful. That it's not is unacceptable. I never thought I'd say it's a bad thing for you to be in love. I feel responsible now for suggesting you come here. Would you like to leave? Distance might help you to look at this sad situation more clearly."

"But the baby?"

"It's already been protected by the public announcement of your marriage. You accomplished what you came here for—unless you came here for more than that?"

"No! That was climbing over the wall of his fury to force

him to accept the facts. It's still there, that fury. I'm sure it is. Anger like that can't just disappear. And he'll never believe that I didn't trap him into this marriage. I came here for the baby's sake and no more."

"Then you're going to stay for the same reason?"

"I didn't love him then." Rebecca stared at the floor, fighting against tears. "It's harder, now that I do."

Lilly knitted her brows. "Have you been crying a lot over this?"

"Not too much."

"Becky," her mother said in a warning tone.

"Only since I stopped denying what I feel for him."

"Have you thought about telling him?"

Rebecca was appalled. "I can't do that! He's only putting a good face on it for appearances. We were fighting terribly those first few days and having trouble keeping it private. So he offered this temporary trace. I think it was easier being furious with him. It really was."

"That settles it," Lilly said in one of her more adamant tones. "I'm taking you out of here. This sort of emotional turmoil can't be good for the baby. So pack your bags tonight. I'll come for you in the morning. And I'll deal with your husband if he tries to stop us."

"Stop us? He'd probably hold the door open."

Rebecca caught that note of bitterness. So did Lilly, raising a brow at her. Was her love going to turn to hate because it was unrequited? She could hope . . .

"As it happens, he won't be home in the morning," Rebecca remarked. "He mentioned that earlier today. Fateful, d'you think?"

"Perhaps."

Chapter Fifty-three

Rupert returned home late from his business trip, two days late. He'd sent notes to both his mother and Rebecca, letting them know of the unexpected delay. His wife hadn't been there to receive hers. She hadn't left him one either. Her mother did, though, and in no uncertain terms warned him to leave her daughter alone.

Finding out that Rebecca had returned to Norford with her mother, and not just for a visit but for good, left him floundering in a sea of emotions. He was angry, shocked, and not just a little hurt. Pretty damn good reasons to go out and get foxed, which was exactly what he did. But not before he sent a man to make sure she was still in Norford and to make sure she stayed there until he could decide what to do.

No decisions had been made last night, well, some had, but he was smart enough not to act on them when he was drunk, and they made no sense come morning. Actually it was afternoon by the time he crawled out of bed. He still wasn't clearheaded enough to decide what to do—or to be confronted by his mother.

But Julie was waiting for him—and quite angry, by the look of it. The moment he came downstairs, she pushed him into the parlor and stood there blocking the exit with her stout, bristling body.

"I actually thought you'd come to your senses when you disappeared last night," she said furiously. "But my spies tell me you didn't leave for Norford to fetch your wife home."

"You're having me followed?"

"No, I'm having Rebecca watched. She's the caretaker of my grandchild. I'm not going to be the last to know if anything out of the ordinary should happen."

He wondered if her spy had stumbled upon his last night. When did he start thinking like his mother?

He took a seat on the sofa, where afternoon tea had been served. She came over and poured them each a cup. Neither of them drank it.

"You never should have got your heart set on a grandchild that may not be real," he said. "You know as well as I that traps of this sort are rather common."

No matter how many times he said it, thought it, it still sounded trite even to him, but Julie scoffed with a loud snort, "Rubbish. I know very well that you believe the baby is as real as I do, so don't feed me that drivel. What are you waiting for? You should have gone after Rebecca yesterday as soon as you found out she was gone."

"I had a blistering note from her mother warning me that she'd geld me if I didn't allow Becca some peace during these early months of her pregnancy."

"You could have assured her of some peace right here. She didn't have to hie off to the country for it. So what *really* sent you off drinking instead of fetching her back? And do *not* try to tell me you're afraid of her mother."

He sighed. "Of course not. But I need to consider Rebecca's feelings in all of this. She obviously wasn't happy here."

"And you weren't happy because of it?" Julie guessed. "Rue, what's got into you? You've never been this wishy-washy before."

"I've never been in love before. Nor have I ever said so many really stupid things in anger that will likely never be forgiven. I've dug m'self into a hole and don't have a bloody ladder for getting out of it."

She actually smiled at him. Of course, he wasn't in the habit of making such bald confessions to his mother, so for the moment she was rather pleased with him for doing so and offered her advice.

"What's wrong with the truth? It tends to be a wonderful foundation to build on."

Those words struck such a keen note, he stood up abruptly. He didn't quite get to the door, though. It was suddenly blocked by his uncle, whom the butler had just let in. The Duke of Norford was standing there scowling at him.

"So you *are* here?" Preston Locke said. "Then what's your wife doing in my neighborhood while you're in this one?"

"Good to see you, Uncle. You don't come to London often. I hope this isn't why you've come this time."

"Actually, since my sister and her son didn't see fit to inform me personally about this marriage, and it already appears to be in a shambles, yes, I believe that's exactly why I've come."

Rupert flushed guiltily. He had intended to visit his uncle with Rebecca when he went to fetch her the first time. But having not found her in Norford then, he'd rushed back to London without giving his uncle another thought.

"It's a long story," Rupert began, "and I was just—"

"Sit down," Preston said in a tone that brooked no refusal.

Rupert's uncle was a big man. Raphael took after him. Both men were of the same height and had the same coloring. Preston's blond hair might be getting a little gray at the temples, but he was still a strapping man, and when he used that authoritative tone, no one in the family dared disobey. Rupert was no exception. He sat down.

Julie tried to ease the sudden tension by saying, "Just in time for tea, Preston. I believe I can explain—"

"I'd rather hear it from Rue. Why did Lilly Marshall, whom I came across this morning while she was having her morning ride, warn me that the problems in your marriage could well lead to divorce?"

"The hell they will," Rupert stated unequivocally.

"Exactly what I wanted to say to Lilly, but without the facts, my tongue was tied. I don't *like* having my tongue tied, Rue. I don't *like* hearing about marriages in my family secondhand. And I definitely don't like hearing that a scandal in *my* family might be imminent. Now since you did marry the girl, why do mother and daughter think that there is no recourse other than a divorce?"

"I've done and said some stupid things," Rupert admitted.

"Good God, don't tell me you've already been unfaithful and she found out?"

Rupert actually grinned. "No, it's nothing like that."

"Good to hear, because marriage is the time to put away your libertine ways and behave responsibly. Is that your intention?"

"Certainly."

"Then what is the problem?"

Rupert sighed. "I wasn't ready to get leg-shackled. I didn't just feel trapped into it, I was sure I was being trapped into it."

"She claimed to be pregnant?" At Rupert's nod, Preston added, "Lilly forgot to mention that tidbit. Not that it matters at this point. What does matter is that you married her. I know the Marshalls. Rebecca is a lovely girl. Why wouldn't you want her for your wife?"

"I do. But I'm not so sure she'll forgive me for doubting her."

"Well, she's certainly not going to forgive you while you're sitting on your arse here, is she?"

Rupert chuckled and stood up to leave.

Julie sputtered, "Your uncle tells you to go and you go? Didn't I—"

"I was already going because of what you pointed out to me, that truth is a wonderful foundation to build on. Bloody hell, Mother! What would I do if I didn't have you to kick some sense into me?"

Chapter Fifty-four

I THOUGHT HE WAS IN the coach with you, but he wasn't. Where is he? When is he coming?!"

Staring down the barrel of the pistol pointed just inches from her face, Rebecca didn't think she'd get a word out, was sure of it. She'd even stopped breathing. The woman was enraged. It was written all over her twisted expression, and pouring out of her eyes. That rage predicted imminent death.

Rebecca was afraid to even look down to see if her mother was all right where she was sprawled on the floor at their feet. Lilly had escorted the woman into the room. Having been told by the woman that she was Rebecca's friend, Lilly had probably thought the visit might cheer Rebecca up. Lilly had no way of knowing she'd let a viper into the house instead. But then Mary Pearson, nearing the end of her pregnancy, looked as innocent as a lamb—until her face became twisted with hatred.

Rebecca had leaped forward as Mary struck her mother on the head with her pistol, only to be stopped when Mary thrust the pistol in her face. Now Lilly wasn't getting up or making a sound.

Rebecca had no doubt that Mary had been referring to Rupert, but she couldn't think of that yet and finally managed to say, "Please, let me see to her. She's my mother. You would want one of your own children to make sure you were all right if you were hurt, wouldn't you?"

Mary immediately nodded consent. Rebecca realized in that moment that she might have found the key to dealing with Mary—the woman's natural motherly instincts. Rebecca dropped to one knee next to Lilly and carefully examined her head. There was no blood. And her mother was breathing, looked quite peaceful in fact. At least a bit of Rebecca's fear was removed.

"A pillow. Please," she asked without glancing up.

Mary actually left her side to remove a thin cushion from the sofa and came back and handed it to her. Rebecca slipped it under her mother's head, then pressed her luck, adding, "Her doctor should be—"

"No," Mary cut in. "She'll be fine—you may not be. Now answer me. Where is your husband?"

Rebecca stood up. The pistol returned to its previous position, too close to her for her to think of much else. She wondered if it would fire instantly if she tried to knock it aside.

She was gathering the courage to try when Mary continued, "I want to finish this so I can go home to my children!"

"Finish what?"

"Killing your husband."

Rebecca sucked in a breath. "No!"

"I have to. Samuel told me to. He recognized the crest on your coach from his younger days in London and told—"

"Impossible!"

"He did," Mary insisted. "He told me to find St. John in

London and kill him to avenge his death, avenge our children's loss of their beloved father! It's the only way my Samuel will rest in peace!"

Incredulous, Rebecca said, "Your husband died?"

The cold metal of the pistol stabbed against her cheek as Mary screeched, "Don't pretend ignorance! You were there when it happened! You might even have fired the shot!"

Recalling that horrible afternoon in France and the race away from flying bullets, Rebecca said, "I was sprawled on the floor of the coach, hiding from all the shots being fired at us. I didn't know anyone was hit. I was protecting my baby from being shot!"

Mary blanched, but then glanced down at Rebecca's waist and frowned. "You aren't showing, even a little. I don't believe you're pregnant."

Rebecca almost laughed hysterically. She'd only *just* gotten rid of her thickened waist. It had taken a few days for the bloating to go away, but with Rupert no longer present and distracting her so much that she didn't even notice what she was doing, she'd stopped stuffing herself with food.

Without that evidence, she was forced to say, "Neither does my husband. That's why we're estranged. He thinks I trapped him into this marriage, and the evidence that I didn't is taking too long to show up! And the longer it takes, the more I hate him for doubting me." That wasn't true, but Mary appeared too interested for her to stop now. "I entered his life with a bang, but I left it with a whisper. He didn't even try to stop me. But I thought he was in London. If he's not there, I don't know where he is. And I don't care."

Rebecca had to force the last words out. Tears nearly came to her eyes, but this was no time to get emotional!

"Then maybe I will kill him for both of us," Mary declared.

Rebecca didn't want Mary's sympathy, she wanted her to see reason!

"He's a rogue," Rebecca said, "but he doesn't deserve to die for it. I don't understand how you can want revenge for your husband when he was in the wrong. He was supplying the weapons that were killing our own men in India. He would have been hung for treason, Mary."

"No! That was war. There will always be casualties in war. Samuel did nothing wrong, yet those fools lied and got him kicked out of the army. They ruined us!"

Rebecca held her tongue as she realized that Mary hadn't been ignorant of what her husband had done, after all. That left her only one possible way to reason with Mary—reminding the woman of her large brood of children.

"I'm sorry for your loss, Mary. I'm even more sorry for your children. No matter Samuel's crimes, he was a wonderful father, wasn't he?"

"There could never be a better father," Mary agreed as tears filled her eyes.

"That was so very obvious. It's terrible to lose a parent, but I can't imagine how horrible it will be for your children to lose both of their parents. Who will raise them and give them the love that you won't be there to give them?"

"Stop it! They aren't going to lose me!"

"They will if you continue down this path. Too many people will know. Will you kill us all?"

"If I must!" Mary snarled.

"I *really* wish she hadn't said that," Lilly complained as she kicked Mary's legs out from under her.

The pistol fired as Mary fell, but thankfully the ball only

lodged in the wall. Though the pistol probably only had the one shot, Lilly still grappled with the woman to get it out of her hand. But Rebecca wasn't watching her mother's amazing display of derring-do. She was staring at Rupert, who had appeared in the doorway and was now charging across the room toward the struggling women.

He had come! Rebecca had been so sure he wouldn't, but he was there and . . . what if he had come a minute sooner? She paled at the thought that if he'd entered the room when Mary had still been standing there with the pistol in her hand, he might now be dead.

But in seconds he had taken the weapon safely away from Mary and was helping both women to their feet. Mary was crying hysterically. Some of the servants had shown up because of the pistol's report, and Rupert directed a footman to take Mary to another room and guard her there until the magistrate arrived.

Lilly, dusting her skirts, said drily, "A bit tardy, weren't you, St. John?"

Rupert grinned at her. "It would appear you had everything quite under control. Very impressive, Lilly. And to think I actually thought that note you left for me was a bluff. Now I'm not so sure!"

Lilly blushed despite his teasing tone. Rebecca raised a brow at her mother. "What note?"

"I merely warned him of some unpleasant consequences if you weren't allowed some peace."

Rebecca blushed as well, knowing how frank her mother could be. She'd probably been quite threatening. "But you came anyway?"

"Did you really think I wouldn't?"

Since that was exactly what she'd thought, she clamped her mouth shut.

Rupert said, "This was my fault. I think now that I am a man of family, I will have to retire from assisting our mutual friend anymore. Repercussions of this sort can no longer be tolerated. It didn't even help that I had a man watching the house. I suppose he can be forgiven for not thinking Mary Pearson could be a threat."

"I knew about him," Rebecca replied. "I found him hiding in the garden this morning. I took him some cookies."

Rupert laughed. "Did you? How embarrassing for him, but that was probably my mother's spy. Mine would have been better hidden!"

Chapter Fifty-five

I T WAS EVENING BY the time they had answered all the magistrate's questions and Mary Pearson was taken away. Lilly had held her tongue until then, but she finally asked Rupert, "Are you ready to discuss what you're doing here?"

"Certainly—with your daughter." He suddenly swept Rebecca into his arms and carried her out of the room.

"Now just a minute!" Lilly protested behind them.

Rupert didn't stop, in fact, he was nearly running up the stairs to the second floor. Incredulous, Rebecca pointed out, "She might follow us."

"She won't," he replied with typical male confidence. "I suppose I'll have to try each of these doors to find out which one is yours, just as you did at my house."

He was doing just that, but she said, "Or you could ask."

He glanced down at her. "And you'd tell me?"

"Why don't you try that one." She nodded toward the door he'd been about to open.

He entered her bedroom. Flora had been in to turn the bed

down and leave a lamp burning low. He took one look at the bed, centered on one wall, set her down, and marched over to shove it into the corner. Rebecca began to laugh. Why didn't that surprise her?

But then he was back and picked her up again and actually tossed her lightly onto the bed before he followed her down onto it and stole her breath with a fervent kiss. She wrapped her arms around his neck. Her toes curled. If he actually had anything to discuss, she didn't care at that point. But that's always how it had been with him. She could be furious, and her anger would instantly be gone once he put his mouth to hers.

He kissed her a little longer, deeply, lovingly, then he leaned back to say, "Will you please forgive me?"

"For what?"

"For being such a bloody ass. For doubting you. For—"

"Wait." She leaned up on her elbow. "Are you saying you believe I'm pregnant now? And look at me before you answer that, because there's not a jot of proof yet to support it." She ran a hand over her flat stomach to draw his eyes there.

"Taking you at your word? Absolutely."

"Why?"

"Because I love you."

She drew in her breath. She searched his pale blue eyes. She saw the so tender look on his face and tears welled in her eyes.

"You do, don't you?" she said in wonder.

"I resisted that, you know. Loving you is going to be a whole new way of life for me. I honestly didn't think I was ready for such a drastic change. And therein was my problem. I was thinking too much and making excuses, and ignoring the fact that it was too late. You had already dug deeply into my heart."

"So you thought driving me away would fix that?"

"I wasn't trying to drive you off, Becca. I'm not even sure why you left."

"You were playing the rogue again, tempting me when you had no intention of . . . oh, I see." She blushed furiously. "You were serious!"

He chuckled and hugged her close. "You are the most delightfully exasperating woman I've ever known, but I love you for that, too. Yes, I was trying to show you how much I wanted you in a typically roguish way without saying the words that scared me. But the only thing I'm scared of now is losing you. So I'm going to show you right now how much I want you."

He touched her tenderly on her check as he began to kiss her again. That kiss wasn't just filled with desire, it was filled with so much more. Then he kissed her belly. He gently laid his head on it. Tears of tenderness came to her eyes. She loved him so much.

He was showing her, in so many ways, the depth of his feelings, the care he took with undressing her, his gaze that kept returning to hers, sensually hot and yet conveying so much emotion. He was being careful with her because of her condition. She could have told him that wasn't necessary yet, but she was enjoying the leisurely pace of his lovemaking while it lasted, and she knew it wouldn't last long. There was simply too much desire in his expression. His restraint amazed her! She knew it was only for her sake because as he slowly removed her clothes, he was practically ripping off his own.

After her last piece of clothing was tossed to the floor, she stretched in sensual bliss under his hands as he caressed her from head to toe and back again. Hands spread wide, he was reaching every part of her body in that long caress. He even dipped his thumbs between her legs for a brief teasing moment before he went on to cup her breasts in his hands. He was leaning over her and planting kisses along the way. His silken hair trailed across her already sensitized skin in a highly erotic way.

"So I *was* tempting you?" he said before his mouth closed over one breast and, with a groan, she arched up toward him of her own accord.

Was. Still was. Always would! But when she managed to open her eyes to find his on hers even as he suckled at her breast, she realized he was serious. He wasn't sure.

"You can't imagine how much," she murmured.

"Then you have too much willpower, luv. I really thought I was losing my touch."

"I don't think that's possible," she gasped out and gripped his hair to pull his mouth up to hers.

The kiss that followed was passionate in the extreme and well met. Rebecca was done with leisurely. She wanted him now! But he wasn't finished inflaming her senses. He slid one of his long fingers inside her. Waves of pleasure immediately began building in her core and would have put her over the edge had she let it.

But she practiced some of that willpower he'd just mentioned and whispered against his lips, "No."

"Yes."

"No, I want *you* inside me."

He groaned and was so quick to accommodate her, she barely had time to wrap her arms tightly around him before he slid smoothly inside her. Oh, God, the heat of him, the fullness, the amazing length that went so deep. There was no stopping it that time, she was utterly consumed by that incredibly sweet pleasure that went on and on and was still throbbing around him when he reached his own orgasm.

She held him dearly to her, her rogue, her husband, her love. "Anytime, anywhere, ask, and I am yours," she thought she heard him say, and she smiled dreamily, but she was still blissfully savoring the aftermath of their pleasure too much to respond more than that. He'd moved half to the side of her to get the bulk of his weight off her, leaving his other half draped over her, a leg over her hips, his arm tight across her chest, his lips by her neck, brushing her skin with feather-soft kisses.

"So it's not my imagination? You do love me, too?" he asked.

Rebecca had to get her head out of the clouds for that question. She moved her head back so she could see his face. Had he been dying to ask her that? Because he looked so positive, she feigned a stern look. "Really, you don't deserve to hear that."

"You're right," he agreed, though he wasn't agreeing at all, he was exuding far too much confidence.

So she added, "Should I try to convince you it's just your beautiful face I'm in love with? Yes, I think I should."

"Good God, don't do that!" he exclaimed, then sighed. "Very well, *that* I deserved. And you're the only woman who can get away with saying that, you know, but, please, let that be the last time. I'm *not* beautiful, Becca. Only women are."

"On the contrary." She gave him a most tender look. "Angels are, too."

He groaned and rolled her under him again. "I'm not an angel, either. Angels don't have carnal thoughts like these." He kissed her deeply.

She certainly didn't give it another thought. Instead she

found out what it was like making love with this man without controversy between them, when emotions weren't frayed, when love guided their hands, their thoughts, their hearts, filling them with the most profound happiness.

When she came up for breath a while later, she said, "Oh my. I never thought I'd say I'm so very glad you're a rogue instead of an angel. But I suppose it's all right as long as you're *my* rogue."